CLAIRE ASKEW

A Matter of Time

HODDER

First published in Great Britain in 2022 by Hodder & Stoughton
An Hachette UK company

This paperback edition published in 2022

1

A CIP catalogue record for this title is available from the British Library

Paperback ISBN 978 1 529 32744 1

Typeset in Plantin Light by Hewer Text UK Ltd, Edinburgh
Printed and bound in Great Britain by Clays Ltd, Elcograf S.p.A.

Hodder & Stoughton policy is to use papers that are natural, renewable
and recyclable products and made from wood grown in sustainable
forests. The logging and manufacturing processes are expected to
conform to the environmental regulations of the country of origin.

Hodder & Stoughton Ltd
Carmelite House
50 Victoria Embankment
London EC4Y 0DZ

www.hodder.co.uk

Praise for *A Matter of Time*:

'Claire Askew is proving to be a master of
the suspenseful police procedural'
Sunday Times Crime Club

'A breathless, real-time, *24*-style thriller that combines
nail-biting tension with boundless compassion'
Erin Kelly

'Tell Jack Bauer he's been supplanted . . . taut'
The i newspaper

'An engrossing and thought provoking read'
Belfast Telegraph

'The tension builds to genuinely frightening peaks . . .
enjoy the breathtaking thrill of the ride'
The Scotsman

'This nail-biter keeps up a rollicking pace – this is
one you're likely to devour in one sitting'
My Weekly

'Breathtaking'
On Magazine

'This 24-style thriller is filled with nail-biting tension'
The Scots Magazine

'Tension-packed'
Carlisle Living

'Nail-biting'
Crime Monthly

'Very tense, sad and tragic, a thought provoking read'
NB Books

'Phew, the electric tension in this nail-biting, clock-ticking, thriller
almost blew my fuses! Tension reaches screaming point . . . unmissable!'
Peterborough Telegraph

Also by Claire Askew

All the Hidden Truths
What You Pay For
Cover Your Tracks

For my parents

Cleaning the shotgun was a ritual he'd always loved. As a boy, he used to stand in the doorway of the barn and watch his father do it, never allowed closer than the threshold because his mother feared guns and wanted him to fear them, too. But the shotgun – its barrel a pillar of trapped light by the time his father was done with it – held no fear, only fascination. When he was fifteen, his mother gave in, and although he'd already held it many times without her knowing – sneaking the key to the gun cupboard whenever he could – he was allowed to work and shoot and clean the shotgun for himself. His father once remarked that he'd a skill with it, and in his teens he'd basked for as long as he could in the compliment's rare, awkward glow.

Every week he cleaned the gun, normally on a Saturday morning. In winter he'd sit under the kitchen light, clapping a little heat into his hands before he could start. But now it was June, the early sun already warming the scabbed tabletop, the hawthorn stand outside a riot of dawn chorus. It was only Friday, but he couldn't wait another day. This thing had to be done.

The cleaning kit had also been his father's, and each time he undid the leather roll and spread the tools out, he caught a snatch of the old barn's smell. These were the same rods, worn smooth at the ends by his father's hands, though the jags and brushes and mops he'd mostly replaced. The brass jag threw sparks of sunlight as he set up the rod, arranged the oils and lubricants, then opened up the gun. The sting of cold metal on his fingertips. His father had left him this beautiful object, and though that was years ago, he still couldn't quite think of it as only *his*. He'd be sixty himself, soon, and no one to pass it on to – this gun as much a piece of him as his own right arm.

Yes, it had to be done. A gun was a tool; it practically *asked* to be used. He sprayed cleaner through each barrel, then waited, let it do its work. He'd been abandoned, he thought – and made a fool of, too. He put in the brush and worked it, felt it prickling away the smears of leaden dirt. The bristles came out sooty-looking: good. This clean needed to be thorough. *He* had no power left to get what he wanted, but that wasn't an impediment. Few people dared to argue with a shotgun. This gun could open doors, extract apologies, where he could not. A shotgun demanded the utmost respect.

He mopped each barrel slowly, then cleaned the ejectors, dotting their motions with grease. The fore-end was pristine but he polished and greased it anyway, his pulse flicking up as he thought about what he must do. Not long now before he'd need to put on his boots, shoulder the gun, and walk out into the June morning.

The last thing was oil. Oil on the barrel and a rag to bring out its lethal shine. By the time he'd finished, his wrist ached with the rubbing down, and he could see his face reflected in the muzzle, glassy and dark. He reached for the cartridges automatically, then paused. The package made a smattering sound in his shaking hand. He always loaded the gun once it had been cleaned, always. Force of habit, he thought.

Now he looked down at the little vials of shot, their gold tops gleaming. This wasn't what he wanted, was it? The shotgun was coming with him, but only as a threat: doors opened. Apologies extracted. Respect demanded. He wasn't going to fire it. It wasn't like that.

And yet. He thought again of his father, a man who never had to ask for anything more than once. Would this plan still be effective, with an unloaded gun? Would he still be able to say what he wanted, knowing the chambers were empty, and any threats he made were empty, too? His own hesitation made his cheeks burn, picturing his old man. What if his bluff was called? What if they didn't do what he was asking? What if they *laughed*?

He fingered two cartridges up out of the box, and rolled them on his open palm. He almost laughed himself: what did it matter, after all? He wasn't going to fire the gun. He wasn't. That wasn't in the plan.

He knew every inch of this shotgun by heart. Without looking – without witnessing himself – he checked the action, opened the chamber, and pushed the ammunition in.

07:00

HOUR ONE

To DI Helen Birch, there was little better in the world than a hot shower. She'd never been a bath person – she didn't have time to be still for that long – but she thought of hot showers as an essential human right, up there with clean water and freedom of expression. Today, the skylight in the bathroom's sloping ceiling was a square of bright aquamarine, and sent a hot, dusty pillar of sunlight down into the room. Birch hummed as she rinsed conditioner out of her hair. Today was going to be a good day: it was Friday, the sun was shining, and she had the morning off.

Outside, commuter traffic was beginning to pick up: when she switched off the water, Birch could hear the distant chug of a 26 bus making its way along Joppa Road towards the city. But when she padded back through to her bedroom at the front of the house, her head wrapped in a towel, the sound of the road faded and she could hear the soft, nearby breath of the sea. It was still one of her favourite things about living in this house on the Portobello promenade: its proximity to the waves. The surf had been creeping closer each morning, and in a couple of hours, there'd be a high tide.

Birch glanced in her dressing table mirror, and grinned at herself. The way she'd twisted the towel around her hair, she looked like a cupcake piled high with white frosting. Her phone was on the vanity in front of her, and as she looked down at it, it lit up with a text message notification, as if commanded.

Listened to that podcast episode last night! Actually not bad. I don't think you have anything to worry about.

Birch closed her eyes, and pulled in a long breath. It's going to be a good day, remember? she told herself. I will *not* get anxious about this. She opened her eyes again. A second text had appeared below the first: *it's pretty good in fact*, and a smiley face emoji. The texts were from DC Amy Kato, Birch's friend, colleague, and – apparently, this morning – personal cheerleader.

I'll take your word for it, Birch texted back. *Not listening to it myself until McLeod makes me.*

She added a tongue-out, winking emoji to prevent the reply from sounding too crabbit. With her free hand, she knocked on the chipboard top of the dressing table once, twice. It wasn't quite wood, but it was close enough. Let's hope DCI McLeod has forgotten all about it, she thought.

But Birch couldn't forget about it herself – not now Amy had prodded it to the forefront of her mind. As she got dressed, she found herself mentally running back over the whole sorry business. January, it must have been – an email had come in from the Police Scotland national news desk, forwarding on a media inquiry. The subject line read 'Scot Free fortnightly true crime podcast' and below the news desk's brief explanatory note, there was a breathless, chirpy sort of email addressed *Dear Helen*.

Dear Helen,

We are Mac and Stuart, aka Scot Free, a fortnightly true crime podcast examining interesting Scottish crimes, both contemporary and historical. We're currently researching and scripting an episode on the Three Rivers case of two years ago. Here's the episode blurb we're working with at the moment:

'It was a fine, sunny morning in May when 20-year-old Ryan Summers walked into the Tweed campus of Edinburgh's Three Rivers College and began to shoot at his classmates. Within thirty minutes, thirteen young women were dead, and Summers had turned the gun on himself. The tragedy left our country reeling and the local community struggling to cope. In the weeks that followed, questions were raised in the press and by the victims' families over the official police response to an incident which represented the greatest loss of life from gun violence in Scotland since the Dunblane massacre in 1996. In this episode, we'll retell the full story of that fateful day, and revisit those questions, with input from eyewitnesses, from individuals close to the victims, and from Police Scotland. This promises to be our most challenging and in-depth episode yet.'

We're writing to you because we'd love for you to be involved in the episode. We know you were among the first responders on the scene at Three Rivers, and you played a significant role in the subsequent investigation. If you're willing to be featured, we'll happily meet you at a time and place that's convenient for you, to record an interview. We're hoping that members of the victims' families will also be involved.

If you have any questions, just let us know. We're really hoping you'd like to join us.

All best wishes,

Mac and Stuart, Scot Free

That was nearly six months ago, but Birch remembered quite clearly that she'd wrinkled her nose, said 'you must be bloody joking' out loud into the silence of her office, and hit *delete*.

Now, she shook herself. She'd never get out of the house if she kept up this daydreaming. She decided to risk it and wear her new charcoal jeans. Yes, they were jeans, but they were smart jeans, and she could pair them with a blouse. They'd do for the office later – it was Friday, after all. Birch gnawed at the little plastic tab with her front teeth until it broke, and the tags came away. It'd be nice to have pockets for once – she owned probably a dozen pairs of black poly-mix trousers, and not a single pair had pockets.

As it turned out, DCI McLeod had also received an email from the podcasters, asking if he'd be willing to appear on the episode.

'I don't know what's more absurd,' he'd said, having stalked into Birch's office to confirm that she, too, had been contacted. 'The request, or the fact that the news desk deemed it worthy of forwarding on!'

'Maybe they thought it was a good idea,' Birch had said, hoping McLeod hadn't already called the news desk to tear a strip off someone. 'Positive publicity, or something.'

McLeod had looked down his nose at her.

'You *want* to do this?'

She had to be honest.

'I really don't, sir,' she'd said. 'To tell you the truth, I deleted the email as soon as I'd read it.'

McLeod huffed air out through his nose.

'Then that settles it. Think on it no more, Helen. I'll let them know in no uncertain terms that *no one* from Police Scotland will be taking part.'

Birch puttered downstairs, still in bare feet, goosebumps rising on her arms. The blouse she'd picked was thin: the weather app told her it would be another hot June day, but it was still early. Yesterday's shoes were beside the back door: plain black ballet pumps. They were flimsy slip-ons, but they'd do. Today was going to be a light day, Birch was determined. When she got into the office later, she'd use the afternoon to blast through her to-do list: her inbox needed serious attention. She'd be sitting down all day: driving to HMP Low Moss to see her brother, Charlie, driving back into Edinburgh, and then sitting at her desk. Birch opened the fridge door to retrieve milk, and found the fridge empty but for its red-topped carton, half a bar of Galaxy, and a bag of sodden-looking salad. Okay, and Aldi on the way home, she thought. She couldn't really justify another takeaway this week.

She had forgotten about the whole thing with the podcasters, until a blustery day about a fortnight ago when Amy had walked into her office without knocking. Normally it wouldn't have mattered, but Birch had decided to devote that particular afternoon to organising the paper files on a particularly gnarly case. She'd spread the various pages out on the floor, and was sorting them into chronological piles, when Amy walked in. The opening door created a draught – Birch had watched from her cross-legged position on the carpet as the last half-hour of good work was undone in a small hurricane of paper.

'Shit,' Amy said. 'I'm so sorry.'

Birch levered herself up off the floor.

'It's okay,' she said. 'It's not the greatest filing system in the world, this. I deserve it.'

Amy was still cringing.

'Really,' Birch said, 'it's fine. What can I do you for?'

Amy had waved her phone at Birch. The screen was lit, but Birch didn't recognise what was on it.

'I'm just back from my lunch break,' Amy said. 'I've been listening to that podcast. You know the one – Scot Free. They emailed you and McLeod a while back?'

The memory of that day in January had fallen into Birch's head.

'Yes, I remember them.'

'Okay,' Amy continued, 'so, they've made the episode, and it's going to air in the next slot, two weeks from now. I've just listened to their teaser for it at the end of the current episode. And, I'm just wondering, marm – is it possible that either you or DCI McLeod . . .'

'That we *what*?'

Amy squirmed.

'What I'm trying to ask is . . . were either of you a little short with them when you turned down their invitation?'

Birch frowned.

'I don't think I *did* turn down their invitation,' she said. 'I just deleted the email. McLeod said he was going to respond.'

Amy bit her lip.

'Well,' she said, 'I think he might have pissed them off a bit.'

Behind her on the kitchen worktop, her phone began to ring. It set the plate and knife she'd taken down from the cupboard vibrating, the sound like a trilling porcelain bell. Birch squinted at the caller ID before swiping to answer: *Anjan*.

'Hey, honeyface,' she said. The half-second of silence before Anjan replied confirmed he was still adjusting to her pet names.

'Morning, Helen,' he said.

Okay, it's no *honeyface*, Birch thought, but at least he sounds chirpy.

'Sorry it's early – I know you have the morning off today,' Anjan went on. 'I'm just getting to the office and I wanted to catch you before you head out. I am right in remembering you're going to see my client, yes?'

'You are.' Birch smiled. They'd been an item – on and off – for almost eighteen months, and Anjan still couldn't help talking to her like a lawyer. 'I'm heading over there in a bit. Just having toast.'

'Well,' Anjan said, 'I thought you might like to give Charlie a little good news while you're there.'

Occasionally, Birch had moments like this one: moments where she felt as though she were looking down on her own life from above, as if it were a giant and very strange game of *The Sims*. I am a police officer, she thought, whose wee brother is doing time for a whole bunch of nefarious crimes, and just to complicate things that little bit further, I'm dating his defence lawyer. She shivered, balling her toes in her shoes. If it weren't for how boring everything else is, she thought, my life could be a soap opera.

'Helen?'

'Yes, sorry. Good news?'

She thought she could sense Anjan smiling on the other end of the phone. She imagined him sitting in the warm, plush interior of his car, waiting to get out and go into the office. In the background, she heard the chug and suck of a street-cleaning truck doing its morning rounds.

'You might have done the maths yourself,' Anjan said, 'but today marks six months to the day since Charlie's sentence was extended. As of this moment, he's out of the doghouse. I'd like you to tell him for me.'

Birch felt a pang of guilt. She *hadn't* done the maths, and now she felt like she should have.

'I'd like you to tell him, also,' Anjan said, 'that I hope he's learned from this experience. We don't want a repetition of the sort of behaviour that led to this extension. He doesn't want to appear before an inquiry panel again, mark my words. Six extra months was a lucky break. They won't be so lenient if there's a next time, so tell him: there must not *be* a next time.'

Birch grinned.

'I'll pass on that scolding,' she said, 'but I'm pretty sure he's aware. You know I've henpecked him plenty myself since the decision was handed down.'

Now she knew Anjan was smiling.

'That's my girl,' he said. 'Kindly tell him that I hope I never again have the pleasure of working with him.'

'Got it,' Birch said. 'If he gets into any more prison fights, he's on his own.'

'Tell him he *shouldn't*—'

Birch laughed.

'Anjan,' she said, 'I'm kidding. Don't worry, I'm sure he'd be delighted if he never saw you again, either.'

'You know,' Anjan said, putting on a mock-wounded voice, 'I get that a lot.'

'Me too.'

'I can't imagine anyone not wanting to see *you* ever again.'

Birch blushed. One of the upsides of their two busy jobs – of only seeing one another sporadically, in between caseloads and paperwork and meetings – was the fact that they hadn't got comfy, hadn't got too accustomed to one another. Anjan could still give her butterflies.

'Speaking of seeing each other,' she said, 'are you free for a drink tonight?'

She waited for a beat, while Anjan checked the calendar he somehow managed to accurately keep and update in his mind. Birch's own calendar was a mess of double-bookings and scribblings-out on the wall beside the kitchen door.

'You know,' he said, slowly, 'I think I can go one better. Dinner?'

Birch grinned again, warmed now by the conversation's turn, her toes uncurling.

'Lovely,' she said. 'Anywhere you particularly fancy?'

'Somewhere near my place. The Outsider? I'll get Jennie to call and book.'

'Sounds great,' Birch said. Not for the first time, she felt a pang of jealousy about Jennie. Not because she was another woman in Anjan's life – Jennie was happily married and soon to become a grandmother – but because Birch wished that she, too, had a secretary she could pass her life admin on to. 'Say hi to her for me, would you?'

'I will. Shall we say seven thirty? I might not be able to get away before then.'

'Not a problem.' It was Friday, Birch reminded herself. If she didn't have a hot date of her own, Amy Kato might be persuaded to come out for a glass of wine or two after work – then Birch could go on afterwards to the Outsider. She resolved to text Amy as soon as she finished the call. It was too long since the two of them had caught up outside work.

'Well, my day is better already,' Anjan said. 'I'm looking forward to it.'

It wasn't until Birch flicked back to her text app and saw Amy's earlier messages that she remembered about the podcast, and the squirm of anxiety returned. Amy had played the preview clip to Birch that day two weeks ago, standing amid the scattered papers on her office floor.

'We'll be taking a deep dive into the Police Scotland response to Three Rivers,' one of them said – in the recording, they sounded identical, their Edinburgh-inflected voices nearly impossible to tell apart. 'In the months that followed the tragedy, questions were asked about the investigation, and many failings were brought to light. We'll examine those failings one by one, and ask: was the aftermath of the shooting mismanaged? Do Police Scotland have blood on their hands?'

'As we'll discuss next time' – okay, that was the other one speaking, now – 'Police Scotland declined to comment, and refused to be part of our Three Rivers episode in any way. We'll be looking at why that might be: what's being hidden by those officers we approached in good faith?'

Amy had cut off the sound.

'That's about it,' she said. 'Subtle, it is not.'

Birch had realised she'd been shaking her head erratically, and forced herself to stop.

'But what do they have?' she asked, knowing even as she formed the words that Amy could have no real idea. 'What information can they possibly have?'

Amy winced.

'It sounds like they might have talked to Grant Lockley.'

Birch had shuddered, then, thinking back to all the damage Grant Lockley and his snide tabloid column had done. His endless attempts to sabotage the Three Rivers investigation with negative press; his callous door-stepping of the victims' families. Grant Lockley phoning at all hours of the day and night. Grant Lockley going through bins, quite literally digging for dirt. He lived in a twelve-by-eight-foot box now, just like Charlie. And yet, here he was again: finding a platform for his odious views.

Amy's texts this morning had done very little to reassure Birch: *it's pretty good in fact,* smiley face. How could anything that involved Grant Lockley be anything approaching *pretty good*?

*   *   *

Walking down the promenade to her car, Birch could see the long, flat gleam of the Firth of Forth as it stretched out under a cloudless sky, all the way to Fife. Sunlight glinted in pinpricks off the distant buildings of Burntisland and Kinghorn. In the shipping lane, a freighter shimmered, heat already pulsing down on to the water. No, Birch thought, I won't give this headspace. It's my morning off. I'm going to have a quiet day, and then a lovely dinner with Anjan. Today is going to be *a good day*.

'It *is*, damn it,' she said, opening the car door and shoving all thoughts of Grant Lockley out of her head. As she turned the key in the ignition, Radio Forth 1 started up, playing some clubby track she'd never heard before, but which immediately made her pulse quicken.

'It's going to be *a good day*.' As she nosed her CID Mondeo out of its space, Birch said the words aloud, hoping she could make them come true.

HOUR TWO

Gerald Hodgson

1hr ▼ Public

If you're reading this, then I've already set off. Perhaps you're reading this later, and I've already done it. Perhaps there are people saying bad things about me – they might even be spreading lies. So if you've come to this page looking for what really happened, here's some truth for you.

If you're friends with me on here, then you know what I did back in 2001. You know that I went to jail for it, and you know that I served five years. I still maintain I was jailed for doing the right thing, for being a good person, for trying to help.

You should all know that I went quietly. I pled guilty and I showed remorse even though I didn't necessarily feel it at the time, because my solicitor told me to and said things would be better for me if I did. It didn't seem to work: five years was a long sentence, and the press said I was made an example of.

I had thought 2001 was the worst year of my life: the things I had to see and do were things no human being should ever experience. But then I realised I was wrong: prison was even worse. The lack of privacy, the beatings, the boredom, the flashbacks, the nightmares, the four walls. But more fool me, I was wrong again. The years since my release have been worse still.

Can you imagine being labelled the way I have been? They called me a saboteur, they said I ruined lives, they said I jeopardised a large-scale emergency response operation, they called me a traitor. When I got out I thought I could start again, but my face had been on the front of all the tabloids and people shouted that word at me in the street. Traitor. No one would speak to me. I came out to find I had no friends left, no family. Everyone disowned me.

Imagine spending five years in prison wondering if anyone will ever visit. Wondering if there'll ever be a letter. Wondering if anyone will ever pick up the phone when you call. No one did. I had a fiancée when I went inside. I came out and she'd cut all ties. It took me a long time to find out she'd moved away and shacked up with someone else. Plenty of you knew, and no one would tell me.

But I found her, partly thanks to this site, thanks to some of you being careless with pictures of her. For years I've kept an eye out, not doing anything because it would arouse suspicion, or because someone might call the police and I'd have to go back to prison. I will not go back to prison. I didn't deserve to be there all those years and I don't deserve to be there now.

But I can't carry on like I have been, either, just surviving, going day to day just trying to keep breathing, trying to stay numb. I have to do something, because I can't do this any more. This isn't any kind of a life.

HOUR THREE

The prison's visitor car park was practically empty, though Birch was running late. She'd seen it before: on days when the weather was fine, fewer family members turned up. She understood. The whole visiting process was depressing: feeding coins into lockers in order to surrender your worldly possessions, walking through the metal detector, having an ugly, pixelated photo of your face taken by webcam. Then the doors and doors and doors, the screw on duty peering through the narrow window in each one before pressing a fob to the electronic lock pad and letting everyone through. The inmates already in the Visit Room, each one always seated at the same table. Birch was sure they'd chosen the far corner for Charlie on purpose, knowing she'd have to walk the length and breadth of the room to reach him. Don't look at anyone, don't engage, just keep your eyes on Charlie's face until you're sitting down – this was her mantra, every week. That said, she'd been coming here for over a year, and her peripheral vision had sharpened. There were three perps in that Visit Room that she'd personally collared, and several others whose cases she'd worked. She knew exactly which tables were theirs, and knew by sight who each of their visitors were. She noticed whenever a table was empty, no matter where it was in the room, and made a mental note when one of the usual inmates had been replaced by somebody new. Usually the new man wore a green sweatshirt, which meant he was on remand. If he was lucky, he'd be there for a few weeks, and then his table would be empty again. If he wasn't, she'd know soon enough: his sweatshirt would change from green to black, which meant he'd been found guilty and was there to stay.

Yes, it was incredibly tempting to turn the car around and drive right back out the way she'd come: back to the M9, past the shining Kelpies rearing up on the roadside, glimpsing the clean white struts of the Queensferry Crossing and the heat haze off the sea below. She shook herself. Nope, she thought, not me, not even today. She'd visited her brother every single week since he went inside, and she wasn't about to break the pattern now.

As she killed the Mondeo's engine, Birch glanced at the dashboard clock: 8.59. The radio news jingle was playing. She'd stay five minutes to hear the headlines and listen to the weather. This is Scotland, she thought, grinning to herself. It could be snowing by lunchtime.

'A breaking story,' the newsreader said, cutting in over the end of the jingle. 'Police in the Scottish Borders have received multiple reports of a shooting just outside the town of Kelso, where hundreds of visitors are currently headed for the annual Border Union Show. We're hearing that shots have been fired at the showground in Springwood Park, and an evacuation is currently under way. Local residents are being told to stay in their homes as the gunman is still at large. Police Scotland are describing the situation as a developing incident – that's all we know for now, but we'll have more for you in the next hour.'

Birch's phone was in her hand before she really knew who she wanted to call. McLeod's mobile rang out. She swore, and dialled his desk extension. She counted six rings and was ready to hang up and try the switchboard, when suddenly, he answered.

'This is McLeod.'

'Sir, it's Helen Birch here. I'm just hearing about Kelso—'

'Helen,' McLeod said. 'Where are you?'

'I'm in the car park at Low Moss. I took the morning off.' Like an idiot, she wanted to say. Of all the days for something like this to happen . . .

'Yes,' McLeod said, his tone sharp: he'd forgotten she wouldn't be in. 'Okay. How are you hearing about this?'

'It's on the radio,' she said. 'Forth 1.'

There was a pause. McLeod hated the press, and liked to make it known that social media and twenty-four-hour news had, in his opinion, ruined policework for ever.

'What do we know, sir?'

She heard McLeod pull in a breath.

'Hopefully more than Forth 1,' he said, 'though not much. Only one gunman, thank goodness – nothing's confirmed, but witnesses on social media are saying he's armed with a shotgun, and fired from a vehicle as he moved through the showground. No word on casualties yet – we're all just hoping he was a bad shot. Theory is it's some farmer gone loopy. But it's going to be a nightmare – our first responders are reporting queues of farm vehicles on every road into the town, headed for that bloody showground. They're trying to evacuate, but it's gridlock.'

Birch hesitated. She realised the radio was still chattering away to itself in the background, the newsreader having moved on to other stories. She flicked the stereo off.

'Have they got him?' she asked. In the background, she could hear voices: other people waiting for McLeod's attention.

'Have they—?'

'The suspect,' Birch said, 'have they apprehended him?'

'God, I didn't say that? No, Birch, that's the worst part. He's still at large, and our Borders colleagues are stuck in a cattle-truck traffic jam.'

Birch grimaced. She was trying to do the maths on casualties, on just how bad things might be. The shotgun part was a relief, assuming it was licensed. Legal shotguns could carry a maximum of three rounds at a time, and reloading inside a vehicle would be tricky.

'Are we mobilising to go down there? Do you need me to come in?'

'No.' McLeod practically barked at her. 'We're sitting tight for now – we don't know what this is yet. You're due in when?'

'Lunchtime,' Birch said. 'But I can—'

'No, Helen, you carry on as you are. If I need you, I'll phone. Right now we're just waiting for more information. There are officers on the scene from Hawick and Galashiels as well as smaller local stations. If they need us there too, they'll let us know.'

'I'm just visiting Charlie; it's no big deal to come back.'

McLeod made a sound that registered only as a crackle in Birch's receiver.

'For goodness' sake, Birch, listen to me. It may well turn out that our shooter couldn't hit a barn door – if you'll excuse the agricultural reference. It may well be that he's sitting in a layby having his rights read as we speak. The approach right now is, let's hope this is a minor incident, and behave accordingly. If I hear anything at all, I'll phone.'

'Well,' Birch said, 'if you do, you'll get my voicemail. I have to leave my phone—'

'Just one second, Birch.'

There were voices in the background once again, but they sounded more distant – McLeod was holding the phone at arm's length, so she couldn't hear. She caught the words *Low Moss*, and then flinched as McLeod repeated them, louder, in her ear.

'You're at Low Moss, you said?'

'Yes.'

'Interesting.' There was a pause, and then McLeod went on. 'I can tell you that we do have a possible ID on the suspected gunman. Like I said, nothing's confirmed, so I want you to be discreet. But if he is who we think he is . . .'

'He's a former inmate here?'

'One Gerald Hodgson, goes by Gerry. He served five years, 2002 to 2007.'

'On what charge?' Birch glanced out of her passenger-side window at the glass doors of the prison lobby. Sunlight was bouncing off them, turning them into mirrors for the blue sky, the dark tarmac. She couldn't see inside.

'Perverting the course of justice,' McLeod said. 'I don't have any details yet, just that.'

'You want me to speak to someone here? See if the prison officers know anything?'

McLeod was quiet again: Birch could sense him mulling it over.

'Probably best not,' he said. 'Like I say, it's all still developing, and we don't have confirmation that it's definitely him. But as you're going in anyway, maybe just . . . pay attention. See if there's an atmosphere in the place.'

Birch almost laughed: there could be few places on earth with less atmosphere than a prison Visit Room. They were designed that way.

'But Birch,' McLeod added, 'bear in mind this could be nothing. Not a single piece of the information I've given you is fully confirmed, you understand?'

'I do, sir.'

'Good.' Birch could hear chatter in the background again – it sounded more urgent this time. 'Check your phone once you get out. We're bound to have more information soon.'

When Birch hung up, she realised her hands were shaking. The words *this could be nothing* echoed in her ears. *Just hoping he was a bad shot.* Reluctantly, she switched the phone to silent, took the keys from the ignition and grabbed her handbag from the passenger seat. What farmer is a bad shot? she thought, as she strode towards the prison's doors. And for that matter, how many farmers do a five-year stretch for perverting the course of justice?

Full body hugs weren't really allowed in the Visit Room, though a peck on the cheek was considered acceptable, according to the guidelines. Birch saw Charlie's eyes widen in shock as she barrelled up to the table too fast, mistiming the greeting and almost headbutting him.

'Wow, Nella,' he said. 'Nice to see you, too.'

His stubble scraped her skin as she adjusted her course and landed an awkward kiss on his cheekbone, his carbolic soap smell catching in her throat.

'Sorry. I was in my own little world.'

She scraped the plastic chair out from under the table, and sat.

'There's a major incident,' she said. 'It's happening right now.'

Charlie manoeuvred himself into his seat more slowly than she had done: he could never resist an opportunity to wind her up.

'Happening now? Funny, Nella, I don't see your crystal ball anywhere.'

She rolled her eyes.

'I just got off a call with McLeod,' she said. 'We've got a guy at large with a shotgun at the Border Union Show.'

Charlie let out a low whistle.

'Well,' he said, 'I know it's a bit spit and sawdust down in the Borders, but I didn't realise they still shot at each other.'

Birch felt a pang of affection in spite of her mounting annoyance: *a bit spit and sawdust* was one of their mother's expressions.

'Be serious, would you? I only just heard.'

She waited as Charlie rearranged his face into a sombre expression. It took him a moment or two: annoying his big sister was one of his few sources of entertainment.

'Wouldn't you be better getting out of here, then? Going to help?'

Birch leaned forward over the table, waving his question away. She shouldn't be talking about this with anyone, least of all her hardened criminal of a brother. But she'd started now.

'We have a suspect,' she said, keeping her voice close to a whisper. 'He used to be . . .'

She let the sentence tail off, but glanced across the Visit Room.

'Ah.' She saw a light come on behind Charlie's eyes. 'He's an alumnus of this fine institution. I see.'

Birch nodded.

'Anyone I know?'

'Not unless you know him from your previous life,' Birch said. This was how she referred to the fourteen years Charlie had spent working as a lowlife-for-hire in Solomon Carradice's crew. It was the euphemism she was most comfortable with: it placed Charlie's bad behaviour firmly in the past. 'He was released in 2007.'

Charlie leaned forward too, now.

'What's his name?'

'Gerald Hodgson. Goes by Gerry. He did five years for perverting the course of justice.'

Charlie snorted.

'Pretty lame charge.'

'Are you serious? It's not a competition. And even if it were, it'd be the worst competition ever.'

He shrugged.

'I guess we can't all go down for GBH.' Birch could see the corners of his mouth twitching: she mustn't rise to his bait.

'And the rest,' she spat. 'It's not big and it's not clever, Charles.'

'Mind you,' Charlie said, raising an eyebrow at her, 'five years isn't just a shit and a shower. He must have done something fairly major.'

'Sorry to ruin your jail Top Trumps, honey, but I don't have any details. That's all I know for now.'

Charlie sat back in his chair.

'Gerald Hodgson,' he said.

'Or Gerry.'

'Perverting the course of justice,' Charlie said, musing now, 'and now he's shooting up an agricultural show? Weird trajectory.'

Birch nodded.

'It might not be him, of course,' she said, remembering McLeod's various disclaimers. 'It's not confirmed, and you *have* to keep it to yourself. But . . . I assume you've never heard of him?'

Charlie shook his head. Birch allowed herself another quick glance around the room: she'd been ordered to check for an atmosphere. There was nothing out of the ordinary, she didn't think: no undercurrent of excitement, no communal buzz. There was just the usual low hubbub of muttered conversation.

'And you haven't heard about anything maybe going down today?'

Charlie shook his head.

'You think this is something big?'

Birch sat back in her chair, too, mimicking her brother's pose.

'Probably not,' she said. 'I don't know. I think I'm just jumpy about the word *shooting* these days, after what happened with Three Rivers.'

'Yeah,' Charlie said, 'I can see how it would get you thinking about that. I'm sorry, Nella, I shouldn't have taken the piss. You okay?'

'I'm okay, yes. To be honest, I was already thinking about Three Rivers this morning, before I heard— but hey, that doesn't matter. I shouldn't have said anything about this, I'm sorry. Just keep it to yourself, okay? Forget I mentioned it.'

Charlie gave her a look that she decided to ignore. Instead, she looked over her shoulder, hoping no one else in the room had overheard anything she'd said in the last sixty seconds. Her thoughts were jangling – she needed to change the subject.

'So . . . Anjan wanted me to tell you,' she said, 'your extra six months is up. Your extended sentence has all been served. As of today, you're back to regular programming.'

Charlie's face fell.

'Great,' he said. 'Six months down, twelve years to go.'

Birch clenched her teeth. Charlie's sentence actually wasn't bad, in light of . . . well, everything.

'I know it sucks,' she said, 'but you know, the deal you got in the end was—'

Her brother held up a hand. They'd had this conversation many times.

'I know, I know,' he said. 'Let's not get into all that. I'm here and it's my own bastard fault, the end. What else does Anjan say?'

Birch recalled the conversation earlier that morning, and managed to smile.

'Obviously,' she said, 'the message comes with his usual scolding. Don't ever do it again, you had your one chance and you won't get another. They let you off lightly but next time you'll be in real trouble. Etcetera.'

'Oh yes,' Charlie said, 'I hope you told him I know it all chapter and verse already, thanks to you.'

Birch's smile widened.

'I mentioned that,' she said.

Charlie fixed her with a serious look, though he was still half smiling.

'I know it, too,' he said. 'I do know it, I promise. Now they've moved that kid out of here, there'll be no more trouble, I swear. It was . . . teething problems. Call it that.'

'Oh yes? You're telling me that if some other jumped-up little scrote comes along, you'll—'

'I'll do absolutely nothing, Nella,' Charlie said. 'I swear. I've learned my lesson. Turn the other cheek.'

'You're quoting the Bible? Are you going to turn into that sort of prisoner?'

Charlie laughed.

'Unlikely,' he said, 'though Maw would have loved that, wouldn't she?'

Birch snorted.

'She'd be livid, more like. All those Sundays when we were teenagers, her trying to bribe us out of bed to go to church with her, remember? If she were to find out you'd become an ardent Protestant after she'd died, after all that—'

Charlie was still laughing.

'Nae danger,' he said. 'I have got into yoga, though.'

'You're having me on.'

'I'm not,' Charlie said, 'honest. We get yoga on Thursday mornings, and I've started going. Three weeks now, and I've decided I like it.' He pressed his hands together in front of his chest, and closed his eyes. 'It's very serene.'

'Well,' Birch said, 'you're clearly a reformed character. I'll tell Anjan.'

Charlie made a *pfft* sound, opening his eyes again.

'He won't believe it,' he said, 'but it's kind of true. I actually do like it.'

For a moment they sat quietly, smiling at each other, while the low chatter from the other tables ebbed and flowed around them. Birch tried not to think about Kelso, or McLeod, or shotguns.

'How's Dad?' Charlie asked.

She shrugged.

'I dunno,' she said. 'He came round to Anjan's last week for a coffee, and then we had a walk round the Meadows. It was okay, I guess – he didn't piss me off too much.'

'Nella.'

Birch sighed.

'I'm – look, I'm trying, okay? But it's hard, seeing him. I'm still so angry with him, and I can't just turn that off.'

Charlie nodded.

'He's been here a couple of times, lately,' he said. 'He comes on Saturdays. We never have much to talk about. Occasionally he'll remember something he and I did together, and he'll be like, *mind that time, Charlie?* But I almost never do. I was so little when he left. I think he forgets that.'

'Yeah,' Birch said. 'I remember some stuff, but not all of it's good. And I'm not sure I want to remember what he was like then.'

Charlie was nodding.

'Is he really off the drink? It's hard to tell, when I don't see him often.'

'He really seems to be,' Birch said. 'You know I am *so* ready to call bullshit on him, so I've been eagle-eyed looking for signs. But he really does seem to be staying sober. He tells me about his meetings. I mean, he obviously hates the whole process, but it seems to be working.'

They were quiet again, and then Charlie said, 'It's a hell of a thing.'

'What is?'

'That he's done that. That he's got clean. I mean, don't get me wrong, Nella, he's a dreadful old soak who's done a lot of shitty things in his life and I'm not in any way forgetting about that, but – he's really making an effort now. For us. For the first time in his fucking life, he's actually putting his kids first.'

Birch didn't speak, but she realised she was nodding, slowly.

'I'm almost sad,' Charlie went on, 'that Mum didn't live to see it. Jamieson Birch, finally getting clean and taking care of business.'

'Yeah – decades too late.'

Charlie waited until she met his eye.

'Come on, Nella,' he said, 'you have to admit, it's something. The old man's trying.'

Now Birch could feel a smile flickering on her own face.

'You're right,' she said, letting it widen into a grin. 'He's very trying.'

HOUR FOUR

Gerald Hodgson
31 May 02:47 ▼ Public

I'm not going to lie, money is tight these days. I'm living alone with only one income, and livestock haulage isn't exactly where you go to work if you want to become a millionaire.

I remember the very first job I earned money from. It was the spring I turned thirteen, and I started working as a lamber. Mostly I mucked out the birthing pens and filled up the water butts, but I also got to move the flock, which was my favourite thing about the job. I couldn't drive, obviously, but I would walk the length and breadth of that farm, sometimes several times in a day, moving parts of the flock to where they needed to be. I liked shepherding the new mothers and their lambs out on to the pastures once they were ready, and bringing the ewes who hadn't lambed yet down to the nearer fields to go into the sheds when the time came. I learned how to work with the dogs, what commands to give them, and I'd walk acres and acres with those dogs in all weathers. I loved it. It's strange to miss being up in some pasture soaked to the skin with sideways rain and a dog that can't hear you calling because the wind's so high, but I miss it now.

Driving a livestock lorry was a good job for a while, especially when I still had Sophie and our household had two incomes. When foot-and-mouth came it got much harder, and local people were all suspicious of us drivers. Where had we been, what had we picked up, where were we going? Where might we carry it? We were persona non grata. And me especially, with what happened.

When I got out of prison I spent a few years out of work, as some of you will remember. Everyone in Dumfries and Galloway remembered my face from the papers. That was why I had to move. I did some odd jobs for cash in hand but in the end I had to go back to the driving. It was hard because it brought back so many bad memories of what went on in 2001. It's still hard now. I'm glad I have a steady job now and it's a job I know how to do and I'm good at it. But I still get flashbacks. And like I say, money is tight. I can't lie, I'm struggling with the rent some months. I'm struggling to know what else I can do when I don't have any other skills, and of course, I have the criminal record.

I can see why people come out of prison and become career criminals. I can see why for some people, that's an easier option than this. I find myself wishing I could go back to being thirteen and out in the big weather with the dogs. I feel like if I could go back in time, I could change everything. Or maybe I'd just freeze time and stay there for ever, working for peanuts and a hot meal at the end of the day. It was a crap manual job really, but when I was out there I felt like the king of those fields. I felt like I didn't have a care in the world.

HOUR FIVE

By the end of her visit with Charlie, Birch had all but forgotten about Kelso and the shooting, until she made it back to the prison lobby. As soon as she'd glimpsed her phone in the locker's dim alcove, the recollection hit her. But there were no voicemails, no messages, and only a blanket email from McLeod telling all Fettes Avenue personnel to hold on and wait for further news before taking any action. She prickled with anger at the lack of update, but then checked herself. No news is good news, Helen, she thought. Perhaps it's all blown over by now.

She'd missed the 10 a.m. bulletin but drove back towards Edinburgh with the radio on anyway, just in case a special broadcast interrupted Forth 1's programming. All the resolve she'd had when she set out that morning had disappeared: Birch drove on autopilot, stray thoughts igniting then disappearing like distress flares. It had got properly warm, as the weather forecast had promised, and she felt a pang of sadness imagining Charlie trudging back to his cell, unable to see the beautiful day outside. But a moment later she found herself thinking about Anjan, wondering what he was doing, and then she was thinking of the Kelso shooter again. Was he Gerald Hodgson, known as Gerry? Or was that report wrong, and he was actually someone else entirely? Was he in custody? Where had he been taken? Birch couldn't answer any of her own questions, or even ponder them for long. She realised she'd begun thinking about her father, and what Charlie had said about him finally making an effort for them.

'Too little, too late,' she hissed. But even her annoyance didn't last.

When she arrived at Fettes Avenue station, she could hear that things were different to usual before she reached the bullpen. Climbing the stairs, she could hear far more talk than she'd expected, even for coffee time: a low hum of voices that sounded not unlike the Visit Room she'd left behind at Low Moss. Pushing open the swing door and stepping into the space, Birch could see that most people were distracted. Officers stood together in knots of three or four, talking, glancing up often at one of the wall-mounted TVs on which the red-and-white tickers of twenty-four-hour news were rolling. Several of her colleagues were on the phone. Many faces around the room were creased into a similar frown: a frown of frustration, of waiting for news that couldn't come quickly enough. That means he's still at large, she thought.

'Marm.' Amy Kato was walking across the room towards Birch. 'You're back early.'

Birch jerked her head towards the nearest TV.

'I wanted to be around for this,' she said. 'Seemed wrong to take a long lunch, you know?'

Amy nodded.

'Catch me up,' Birch said, 'I'm a couple of hours behind everyone else.'

Amy stepped backward, and Birch followed, moving further into the bullpen and closer to the TVs. The sound was muted, but subtitles were on, and the tickers relayed over and over the same words: BORDER UNION SHOW GUNMAN STILL

AT LARGE, LOCALS TOLD BY POLICE TO STAY INSIDE.

'Okay,' Amy said. 'There are five people at Borders General Hospital being treated for gunshot wounds. Two are critical, we don't know yet about the others. Some folk were also treated at the scene for minor injuries. Witness statements suggest he was firing quite indiscriminately – only one man there knew who he was.'

'This is the witness who gave the name Gerald Hodgson?' Birch asked.

'It is. This guy is a farmer: he says he thinks Hodgson shot at him deliberately. They'd had an altercation, apparently, years ago, and he reckons it was revenge. But he's the only person to suggest that the shooting was anything other than a sort of random spree.'

'Can we trust the ID?' Birch asked. 'If they were enemies, I mean.'

'It still hasn't been confirmed,' Amy said, 'but we're hearing that Hodgson didn't turn up for work this morning, and can't be found at his address. It fits.'

'They're at large – both our gunman and Hodgson.'

'Yes. But there's more. We've been looking at status updates from Hodgson's Facebook page, and early this morning he posted something that's ringing alarm bells. Something like, *if you're reading this, then I've already done it.* He doesn't say what, but it definitely reads as a threat.'

'It was premeditated then. Maybe he did have targets in mind.' Birch remembered her earlier conversation with McLeod. 'He might just have been a bad shot.'

Amy nodded.

'It's certainly possible. We're also concerned about a couple of quite rambling posts he made last week. Both times, he talks about an ex-girlfriend. We're trying to track her down just now.'

Birch felt her brain catch up with her ears.

'We? McLeod said there was no involvement beyond the Borders yet.'

'There isn't, on the ground,' Amy said. 'But we've taken on some behind the scenes stuff, following up on his social media and so on. Borders are dealing with a full-scale manhunt. They genuinely seem to have no idea where he is. I've listened in on some of the calls, and I'll be honest, there's a lot of panic.'

Birch frowned.

'How far can he have got?'

Amy made a face.

'The issue seems to be his vehicle. Witnesses say he was driving a green, short-wheelbase Land Rover Defender. You can guess at how many people attending the Border Union Show were also driving the exact same vehicle, or something very close to it. Hodgson got out of the showfield before our guys could get in. At that hour, everyone was arriving, and the roads were *full* of Land Rovers. Plus, it's the Borders. You've been to the Borders, right? It's pretty remote.'

Birch nodded.

'I have,' she said. 'It's pretty damn rural down there.'

'I've been looking at Kelso on the map,' Amy said, 'and Hodgson could very quickly have got off any sort of main road. No one down there is going to look twice at a Land Rover. Plus, it's an off-road vehicle. He could have driven up the side of Cheviot for all we know.'

'I take your point,' Birch said.

'It's been over two hours,' Amy continued, 'since the last confirmed sighting of the vehicle. You should know that if they don't find him soon, I think we'll be called down there to support. Or some of us. Uniforms, at least.'

Birch rolled her eyes, and dropped her voice to a whisper.

'I tried to tell McLeod,' she said, 'when we spoke on the phone, earlier. I mean, I didn't get chance, but I tried to. He was determined it wouldn't be a big deal.'

Amy tipped her head to one side.

'To be fair,' she said, 'two hours ago, it could still have been a local thing. The Borders guys are doing their best.'

Birch looked up at the nearest TV. Shaky camera-phone footage showed two uniformed officers waving down cars.

'They've set up roadblocks?'

'On the major routes,' Amy said. 'But if he's a local, he's unlikely to use the major routes. We've sent helicopters out at the request of the Borders team, and Mountain Rescue have scrambled a couple as well. They're out over some of the higher ground, looking for him. But the Land Rover really is a kicker. There must be thousands of Land Rovers down there.'

Birch screwed up her face. She tried to think of everything she knew about the Scottish Borders. It was just down the road, really, a very pretty and unspoiled area right on the doorstep – the sort of place she always felt she should visit more often, but rarely did. She and Anjan had done a romantic weekend down there a few months ago, staying in the rather posh town of Melrose. They hadn't done much beyond wandering around the crumbling abbey and eating cream teas – Anjan had brought cases to work on, and Birch hadn't slept well in the chilly bed-and-breakfast room. But just driving down there, she had been struck by the land, the remoteness of it – Amy was right, *remote* was the exact word. Big skies that stretched on for ever. Huge fields ploughed in neat rows that repeated for miles like a giant candlewick throw. Old grey beech trees on the roadside, signs for obscure-sounding places like Lilliesleaf and Smailholm. Glimpses of wet, single track roads shining on the sides of hills. She shivered. The Borders was a perfect place to get lost.

Amy rattled a piece of paper, shaking Birch back into the here and now.

'We may have traced the gun,' Amy said. Birch glanced down at the print-out in her colleague's hand. 'Gerald Hodgson owns a shotgun. He's had a shotgun certificate ever since 1978, and has no gun-related priors. Because he served a custodial sentence back in the early 2000s, the shotgun licence became null and void and he should have surrendered the weapon, but it seems he got out of doing it by moving to Scotland. He's registered in Cumbria, where he's originally from, though lived for a time in Dumfries and Galloway after he got out of Low Moss. Now he's a Borders resident. It looks like he just ran away from the paper trail, and it never caught up with him.'

'Great,' Birch said, 'the press will love that.'

'We'll have some explaining to do, marm, yes.'

'McLeod will be thrilled.'

They exchanged looks. Amy nodded.

'Where in the Borders does Hodgson live?'

Amy looked back down at the piece of paper.

'Just outside Kelso,' she said, 'a place called Cessford.'

Birch shook her head.

'Never heard of it.'

Amy laughed.

'I'm not surprised,' she said, 'it looks tiny. It's basically one farm and a few farm labourers' cottages, though it has an old castle, too. Hodgson's given address is one of the cottages – we're trying to trace the landlord.'

'He works on the farm?' Birch asked.

'Kind of,' Amy said. 'He's a cattle-truck driver. He works for a livestock haulage firm with a few yards in the area. Hodgson usually works out of one in the next village over.' Amy paused to squint at the paper again.

'Morebattle, the place is called,' she said.

Birch tried to laugh, but couldn't seem to. She couldn't take her eyes off the TV.

'They love a weird place name, the Borderers,' she said. On the screen, footage of a grounded Mountain Rescue helicopter, its blades rotating slowly. The ticker scrolled endlessly below it: POLICE URGE LOCAL RESIDENTS: STAY INDOORS. A thought struck her.

'He's just running, now, right?' she said. She could hear a spike of panic in her own voice. 'We think he's just running – he's not going off to target anyone? Another gathering?'

Amy shrugged.

'Honestly, marm,' she said. 'We don't know much.'

Birch closed her eyes. This, she thought, was supposed to be a good day.

'Only that he's armed,' she said, opening her eyes again, 'and – well, something. Crazy, angry, vengeful. Maybe all three.'

'Yep,' Amy said, her voice grim. 'And we have absolutely no idea where he is.'

HOUR SIX

Gerald Hodgson

2 June 03:16 ▼ Public

I want you to imagine what it was like for me in 2001, if you can. Sophie and I were engaged, and when it all went down she said she'd support me. She said to my face that she believed what I did was right, that she'd always defend me, and she sat in court throughout my trial. As they announced the verdict, and the judge passed sentence, I looked at her face. She cried. She had said she'd be on my side.

Every week I waited for her to come and visit me. At first I assumed there was some kind of mix-up, some administrative reason why she couldn't come, or they wouldn't let her in. I thought maybe a new prisoner wasn't allowed visitors at first. But after a while I realised she wasn't coming for some other reason, one I didn't know.

I wrote to her, two letters a week for the first year of my sentence. One hundred and four letters. I never received a reply. The letters weren't returned, so I assume she received them. I don't know if she read them. I started writing the same letter out twice, and sending one copy to her address and another copy to her parents, in case she'd moved. Her parents never replied either. I spent some time in a state of terror: had something happened to Sophie? Had she been in a car accident or got sick? Surely someone would have told me? But eventually it sank in. Sophie didn't mean it when she said she supported me – or she only meant it up until the verdict was announced.

I couldn't find her at first, when I got out. I went to her old house in Longtown and found she'd moved. The new people said they had no forwarding address. Her parents had gone, too. Their house had a Sold sign outside. The first couple of months, I used to drive up and down the main street, looking into the windows of the pubs, waiting across the road from the petrol station. Sophie used to go in there to get bits and pieces in the evenings – if we ran out of milk or fancied a few beers. I never saw her. I realised she must have moved away, but I didn't know where.

Then I joined Facebook. Without knowing it, some of you helped me to find her. You tagged her in photos, or mentioned her. That was how I found out she'd met someone else. She'd got married.

I want you to imagine that, though I suspect you can't. We were engaged. We were supposed to spend the rest of our lives together. She said she supported me. She lied. She left me to rot in jail, alone. She ignored every attempt I made to contact her. She must have pretended I never existed. By the time I got out, she was married to someone else. She threw me away.

I found out she was living in the Borders. Then I found out it was Kelso. I had this plan for a while that I'd find her and convince her to take me back. That was why I moved.

I couldn't get a job in Dumfries and Galloway anyway. I got one here, and after my day's work I'd park up the wagon, drive into Kelso in the car, and look for her. I thought if I could see her, if I could talk to her, then I could make her see what a terrible thing she'd done and what a big mistake it was. I thought I could show her that I was out now, I was moving past what happened, and she and I could be together again. She'd need to divorce the bastard, but I could wait. I'd wait for her, even though she hadn't waited for me.

It didn't happen. It was like the universe was hiding her from me. How tiny is Kelso? Less than 6,000 people, according to the internet. And yet I never saw her, though I had a few close shaves following women who looked like her. After a while they'd turn and look at me and I'd see my mistake. I thought maybe she'd found out I was around and moved again to avoid me.

So I tried to move on myself. I really did. I did my job, I scraped my rent together, I went out walking a lot. There are a lot of places you can walk round here where you never see a soul. I shot rabbits and pheasants when I saw them. I didn't care who they belonged to – I've always believed animals don't belong to anyone, they belong to themselves, so the idea of poaching is ridiculous. It's made up. And besides, it kept me fed. It kept me sane.

But there's only so long you can spend waking up, driving, getting home, going to sleep, and repeat. Spending days off wandering around the countryside with no real sense of where you're going. I did it for years. But you get depressed, eventually. You can't help it, it's the human brain. I couldn't help it. I tried to hold it off, all the flashbacks, the nightmares, the bad thoughts, the going over and over what had happened with Sophie, imagining her happy with her husband, imagining her never thinking about me.

There's only so much time a person can spend feeling like this, and for me, that time is running out.

13:00

HOUR SEVEN

McLeod didn't knock, he just walked into the office. That was the first sign that something was wrong. The next sign was his ashen face, stark against the collar of his slate-blue shirt.

'Birch,' he said, 'I'm sorry to disturb.'

Birch immediately minimised the browser window on which she'd been scrolling through the BBC News website's live feed, and then felt stupid: she wasn't looking at anything she shouldn't have been. The furtive movement would make McLeod think she'd been on Twitter or something. But she could see from his face that he wasn't interested in her internet usage.

'Sir?' Birch was already halfway out of her chair. 'What's happened?'

'They've found the ex-girlfriend,' he said. 'It's bad. I'm about to take a conference call from the lead officer down there and I'd like you to be in the room. Can you come to my office?'

Birch nodded, mute. Amy had emailed her the screenshots from Hodgson's Facebook page. Something else had happened that morning, besides the shoot-up at the Border Union Show. Either beforehand or afterwards, Gerald Hodgson had – what? No one knew. But Amy and her colleagues had intensified their efforts to identify and locate

Hodgson's ex-partner. It wasn't the easiest job: *Sophie* was all they had to go on.

Birch followed McLeod out into the bullpen, which was now much quieter. She assumed the junior officers wouldn't be briefed until after the call she was about to hear, but there was no mistaking the look on McLeod's face. As she passed, Birch glanced up at the TVs. The newsreader was talking about something unrelated – the *in other news* stuff they were required to do every so often, even in the midst of a crisis – but below his sombre face the tickers streamed on. BORDERS GUNMAN STILL AT LARGE: 'STAY INSIDE' WARNING EXTENDED TO CUMBRIA, DUMFRIES & GALLOWAY.

'They think he's left the region?' Birch asked.

McLeod turned his head a little, but didn't stop walking.

'Hodgson has ties to the Dumfries area,' he said, 'and friends and family near Longtown. We still don't know where he is – just that he's had enough time now to get to one of those places, if he wanted to.'

Birch nodded, though McLeod couldn't see her. She caught Amy's eye across the bullpen, and realised she didn't know what to do with her face.

You okay? she mouthed.

Amy nodded, but pointed at McLeod, and mouthed back, *What's going on?*

Birch glanced at her boss to check he wasn't watching, then looked back at Amy. I don't know yet, she thought. All she could do was shake her head.

In McLeod's office, DI Crosbie – one of Birch's least favourite colleagues – was waiting for them. With him was a specialist firearms officer Birch remembered meeting with a few times during the Three Rivers investigation. She dithered in the doorway for a moment, trying to remember the woman's name.

'Officer Shields,' she said, almost without meaning to, as it came to her. 'Good to see you.'

The woman reached to shake Birch's hand.

'Please,' she said, 'it's Siobhan. And – Helen?'

'Yes,' Birch said. 'It's been a while.' She shuffled further into the room, aware of someone standing behind her.

'Marcello,' McLeod said, waving the man in. 'Thank you for joining us. If you could close the door?'

Birch flashed her biggest smile at Marcello as he joined them. He was one of the geek squad, as they were known: she could see that in his hands he held print-outs of Gerald Hodgson's Facebook posts. Marcello was a gifted analyst and profiler, and for a while, pre-Anjan, Birch had perhaps had a very small crush—

'Right,' McLeod said, and she blinked. 'I'm about to receive a call from someone in the Hawick branch. I haven't been given all the details, but it's not going to be pretty. I need to warn you, this Hodgson thing is about to grow arms and legs, and we're going to be called in to assist.' He looked at Siobhan. 'Firearms are down there already, obviously, but this is about to go beyond just Operational Division. We'll need SCD officers, and very likely air support. It has just become absolutely vital that we track down this bastard.'

Birch realised that everyone in the room was nodding, almost in unison. But before anyone could speak, the phone on McLeod's desk rang. He hit the speakerphone button.

'This is McLeod.'

'Sir, this is Inspector Dacre,' the man on the phone replied. 'Matthew Dacre. I'm Duty Inspector at the Hawick station.'

'Good to hear from you, Dacre,' McLeod said. 'I'm here with a few officers from my team, and from Specialist Crime Division. I've heard a little about what's going on, but everyone else needs to be briefed. Tell us the latest.'

There was a pause, as though Dacre was taking a deep breath.

'About an hour ago,' he said, 'we attended the address of one Sophie Lowther, with thanks to your team for tracking it down.'

McLeod threw Marcello a nod, and Marcello smiled and looked at the floor. That's why he was here, Birch realised. He'd been the one to find Sophie.

'There was no answer at either the front or rear of the property,' Dacre went on, 'but we found the front door unlocked and so proceeded inside, shouting out to anyone who might have been in the residence. There was no answer, and a search of the ground floor turned up nothing. However, there was dried mud on the carpet in the hall and on the lower stairs – mud in the shape of boot treads, which we decided to follow. To cut a long story short, my officers discovered the body of Mrs Lowther in the main upstairs bedroom. She'd been shot in the chest. With her was an unidentified man we're assuming is her husband. He also had a gunshot wound to the chest. I checked his vitals and found he had a pulse, though he was unresponsive. He's been taken to Borders General, but . . .' Dacre trailed off.

'But?' McLeod's voice was like a fist hitting a tabletop.

'I'm – obviously not a doctor,' Dacre said. Birch could hear the tremble in his voice. 'But I'd say it doesn't look good for him. He was . . . he was in really, really bad shape.'

Birch closed her eyes, and set her teeth. She'd been one of the first officers to arrive on the scene at Three Rivers. She

remembered the first floor girls' bathroom, where four female
students had been cornered by the gunman. She remembered
the tape on the floor, marking out where their bodies had lain.
The smell of blood that hummed like white noise under everything, even after the place had been practically flooded with
disinfectant. The first attending officer, PC Dave Leake,
crying as he recalled stepping into that bathroom. He'd
retreated behind a desk for some time, after that.

She felt someone touch her arm, and snapped her eyes
open. Siobhan was standing closer to her now, looking at her
with concern. Birch gave her a reassuring nod: I'm okay. The
other woman smiled, but didn't step back again. Birch
wondered what mental footage *she* was replaying in that
moment.

'The couple were slumped in a corner,' Dacre said, more
brisk now. 'It seems they couldn't have got away. The shots
were obviously fired at close range.'

'Do we know Mrs Lowther's time of death?' McLeod asked.

'All we know is, early this morning,' Dacre replied.
'Before the incident at the showfield. The victim was wearing pyjamas. We're asking that you give us some assistance
with forensics, so we can start to put a clearer picture
together.'

McLeod drew himself up a little taller.

'We'll talk through logistics in a moment,' he said. 'What's
happening with Hodgson?'

Dacre sighed, and the speaker on McLeod's phone made a
rattling noise.

'Things have escalated significantly,' he said. 'We now
believe Hodgson has a hostage.'

'Who?' It was the first time DI Crosbie had spoken, and
Birch jumped. She'd forgotten he was there.

'The Lowthers have a daughter,' Dacre said. 'Elise. She recently turned three.'

Birch closed her eyes. No, she thought. No, no, no.

'We've done a full sweep of the house,' Dacre said, 'and she's nowhere on the property. We found a leaflet for her nursery on the kitchen noticeboard, and phoned to see if she was there, but they say she never arrived this morning. Her bed looks to have been slept in, so I'm afraid she may have been present at the time her mother was murdered. We're trying to contact other family members, and I have officers out driving around the local area – it may be that she ran away in fright. But I'm afraid we have to entertain the possibility that Hodgson took her with him.'

Marcello's lips moved: *Madre di Dio*. McLeod's face had whitened even further: he was hearing this for the first time, too.

'Was there any sign of a struggle?' Siobhan was speaking now. 'Any blood in the little girl's room, or any breakages? Anything to indicate he hurt her?'

'No,' Dacre said. 'And no possessions appear to have been taken. It seems if he took her, he just picked her up and walked out.'

'Any witness statements yet?' Birch was surprised to find it was her own voice she could hear. 'Did anyone see him leave? What's the property like?'

'It's a detached house,' Dacre replied, 'in a cul-de-sac. Two officers from the Kelso station are going door to door. We feel sure someone must have heard the shots, at the very least. We're hoping some curtain-twitching went on, and we'll get something.'

'Right,' McLeod said. His voice was hoarse, and he looked surprised. He cleared his throat. 'This has just become a whole new situation, hasn't it?'

Birch could feel herself swaying on her feet: McLeod had made the understatement of the century. On the phone, she could hear Dacre speaking quietly to someone else at his end of the line. She could also hear advancing footsteps outside McLeod's office door, but it was still a shock when the knock came, loud and frantic. She saw everyone in the room flinch.

'Just a moment, Dacre,' McLeod said, and then, raising his voice, 'Yes?'

The door opened, and Amy's face appeared. Birch had watched DC Amy Kato tackle all manner of difficult situations: she'd been family liaison officer to the gunman's mother after Three Rivers; she'd been on dawn raids and arrested gangsters; she'd delivered the worst possible news to the loved ones of murder victims. And yet, Birch had never seen this particular look on Amy's face before.

'Sir,' she said, breathing hard. 'It's Hodgson. Gerald Hodgson has just phoned reception. He's on the line right now.'

The silence that followed seemed to stretch and drift. When McLeod spoke into it, his voice was crisp as a bell.

'You're sure?'

It was Marcello who answered.

'Yes,' he said. 'If he has a hostage now, he may be calling to make demands.'

'He called the switchboard?' McLeod asked, and Amy nodded. 'Put the line through to this office. Dacre, I'm sorry. I'll call you back.'

He hung up, and everyone stood looking at the phone, waiting for it to ring again.

'DC Kato,' McLeod said, 'can you gather everyone into the bullpen? I'll brief you all as soon as I can after this.'

Amy nodded, and closed the door. The phone rang, and once again, McLeod hit the speakerphone button.

'You've come through to Detective Chief Inspector James McLeod,' he said. 'Am I speaking to Gerald Hodgson?'

There was silence on the line, or not quite silence. The sound of someone letting out a breath they'd been holding.

'You're not who I asked for.' It was a man's voice, quiet, with an English accent. Northern.

McLeod blinked.

'But you are Gerald Hodgson?'

'You know I am,' the man hissed. Birch saw Marcello lean forward. He was taking mental notes.

'And who was it,' McLeod said, 'that you wanted to speak to?'

There was a pause on the line, and then a word that made Birch stagger backward, as though she'd been slapped.

'Birch,' Hodgson said. 'An officer Birch.'

Every face in the room flicked round: Birch could feel their eyes on her like so many bright lights.

'Detective Inspector Helen Birch?' McLeod asked.

'Yes. Her.'

'She's here, Mr Hodgson,' McLeod said, pulling the words out slowly. 'DI Birch is on this call.'

There was a sound that could have been a cough, or a laugh.

'Prove it,' Hodgson spat.

Birch took a step closer to the desk, and the phone. Her knees felt weak.

'Mr Hodgson,' she said, with all the calm she could muster, 'this is DI Helen Birch. I'm here.' She looked at McLeod, who twirled one finger, a *keep going* gesture. 'What can I do for you? Can you tell me where you are?'

'Am I being recorded right now?' Hodgson asked.

Birch glanced behind her, towards Marcello, who leaped forward and slipped behind the desk with McLeod.

'I don't think so,' Birch replied. 'Do you – do you want to be recorded?'

Marcello pressed one button on the phone, and then another. Watching him, Birch realised she'd never thought about what those particular buttons on her own console were for, let alone asked anyone. I probably should have asked someone, she thought.

'No,' Hodgson barked. 'I don't.'

Marcello threw Birch a thumbs up. Tough luck, Gerald, she thought.

'Well, you're just talking to me,' Birch said. 'Me and DCI McLeod, my boss. No one else is listening.'

She saw McLeod raise a finger to his lips, for the benefit of the others in the room. Yeah, she thought, no shit.

Hodgson was quiet.

'Can you tell me where you are, Mr Hodgson?'

'Gerry. Just Gerry.'

'Okay, Gerry. You can call me Helen. It really would help me if you'd tell me where you are.'

'Yeah,' Hodgson replied, 'I bet it would.'

Birch gritted her teeth, and looked around at her fellow officers. Marcello, still behind McLeod's desk, was scribbling on a Post-it. He held it up. The handwriting was a scrawl, but Birch made out, *ask if he is fine*.

'All right,' Birch said. 'Can I ask how you're doing, then? Are you okay? You're not hurt?'

'Why would I be hurt?'

She closed her eyes. I suck at this, she thought.

'We know about – what happened at Springwood Park this morning. And you know, shotguns. They can be dangerous things. I just want to check—'

'I know my way around a shotgun,' Hodgson said. 'Well enough not to hurt myself, anyroad.'

'That's good,' Birch said. Marcello was scribbling again. 'It's been a while since – that incident, though. Are you looking after yourself? Have you eaten?'

Marcello didn't raise his head from his writing, but she could see him nodding. That question was good.

'Not really,' Hodgson said, 'but it doesn't matter. Don't think I could eat, tell you the truth.'

'Oh yes?'

'Too worked up,' Hodgson said.

Marcello held up another note: *what does he feel right now?*

'Worked up how?' Birch asked. 'Can you tell me?'

Hodgson paused. Birch could hear his tongue working in his mouth, the dry crackle of it.

'Scared,' he said. 'Scared, to be honest with you, Helen.'

There was a noise on the line. A distant noise, but something familiar. A low throb.

'I'm not surprised,' Birch said, meeting McLeod's eye, 'with that chopper hovering over you.'

McLeod pointed at DI Crosbie, and then the door. The command was unspoken, but clear: *find out where the helicopters are.*

The line was quiet, apart from the far-off *chucka chucka chucka* of the rotor blades. Marcello made a pointing motion: *stay on it.*

'How long has it been there?' Birch asked. Crosbie was halfway out of the door, moving slowly so as not to make noise. 'Is it doing circles?'

'It keeps flying past,' Hodgson said. 'It goes behind the hill, and turns, and then back it comes.'

'Doing your head in, is it?'

Hodgson coughed.

'It really is. You ought to call him off.'

Birch faked a laugh. It sounded like a door creaking. She realised her entire body was stiff, upright.

'I would if I could, Gerry,' she said, 'but I can't. It's not a police helicopter, you see. That's Mountain Rescue up there.'

Marcello had written down *hill* and was now writing *high ground*.

'Someone lost?' Hodgson asked. Marcello mouthed a theatrical *yes*.

'Yes,' Birch said, 'yes, Gerry, they are. Some climbers. They've been missing since last night. You haven't seen anyone, have you?'

'Not out here.'

'Out where, Gerry? It really would help me to know where you are.'

The line went quiet again. Birch listened as the helicopter faded: *it goes behind the hill, and turns.*

'You must have phoned me for a reason, right?'

'Right,' Hodgson said. Then quiet again.

Marcello held up a note. *Risky*, it read, *but ask about the girl.* Birch's eyes widened. In her peripheral vision, she could see Siobhan pointing at the Post-it: *yes. Ask him.*

'Can I ask,' Birch said, 'about little Elise? Is she with you? Is she okay?'

Silence. Birch watched Marcello, waiting for him to write something else. Tell me what to say, she thought. But Marcello was waiting, too. Beside him, Birch could see McLeod's jaw working. Then there was a noise. Something almost animal.

'Gerry?'

The second time it came, there was no mistaking it: Gerald Hodgson let out a sob. He pulled in a long, rasping breath, and then let out another.

'Gerry,' Birch said, 'talk to me. Let me help.'

'Fuck,' Hodgson said. His voice was wet now. Suddenly, Birch had a vision of her father. He'd cried on her, too, that day around a week ago, when he came to Anjan's for coffee. He'd done it out of the blue, heaved out a huge sob like Gerald Hodgson's, right there on Anjan's sofa. She'd felt stricken, with no idea how to act. She felt that way again now.

'I want to help you,' she said, 'but I can't help you unless you talk to me.'

She listened as Hodgson pulled in another shaggy breath.

'Yes,' he said, at last. 'She's here. The— Elise?'

'Elise,' Birch repeated. 'Her name is Elise. Is she doing all right, Gerry? Can I talk to her?'

Marcello made a swiping motion through the air, and shook his head: *no*. Bad idea. Shit, Birch thought.

'She's in the back,' Hodgson said.

'The back?'

'Of the Land Rover.'

Birch felt her hands and feet go cold. Marcello wrote *Alive????*, though he didn't need to. It was what they all wanted to know.

'And she's okay?'

Hodgson sniffed.

'She's been crying,' he said, 'she's been crying for hours, Helen. I didn't know a kid could cry so much.'

Birch felt the entire room relax, just a little.

'Well, she's only three,' Birch said. 'Only a wee one. She's probably scared, too.'

In the background, the *chucka-chucka* sound ebbed back in.

'There's that chopper again,' Birch said.

'Aye,' Hodgson said. He seemed to be pulling himself together, the sobs easing. 'Really wish he'd buzz off.'

'You know,' Birch said, 'I might be able to find out which helicopter that is, and see if we can move it on. There are a few out, you see, for – for the climbers. Is it coming close again, now?'

'Yeah,' Hodgson said, 'close by.'

'Okay. Can you see any identifying marks on the helicopter? Can you tell me what colour it is, maybe?'

'It's red. And there's a saltire on the side.'

McLeod looked at Siobhan, and then back at Birch. He shrugged: not enough.

'Yep, it's Mountain Rescue, then,' Birch said. 'But that doesn't give me much to go on. If you could just tell me—'

'I won't go back to prison, DI Birch.' Hodgson's tone changed: the tears were gone. 'I won't. I can't, do you understand?'

Birch went quiet. McLeod was glaring at her, waiting for her to speak.

'You were in Low Moss, right?'

She waited, fearing the line would go dead, but it didn't.

'Yeah.'

'I know it well,' Birch said. 'My brother Charlie is in Low Moss prison. He's doing a stretch for – well, for various things.'

'I know,' Hodgson replied.

'You do?'

'Yeah.'

She blinked.

'So . . . is that why you called me? Why you asked for me?'

'Partly,' Hodgson said, 'yeah.'

Birch frowned.

'Do you know Charlie?'

'No. After my time. But I read about him.'

'In the papers, you mean?'

'Yeah. He sounds like just the sort of bloke I'd have been shit-scared of in that place, I'll tell you.'

She tried for a laugh again, and this time it sounded more real.

'He'd like for you to think that,' she said, 'but Charlie's soft as anything. I mean, he's done some bad things, but he's one of the good guys really.'

The line was quiet for a few seconds.

'You're just saying that,' Hodgson said, 'because he's your brother.'

No, Marcello wrote on a Post-it. Then, below it, he scribbled, *benefit of doubt*.

'No, Gerry,' Birch said, hoping she'd interpreted the message correctly. 'I believe everyone deserves the benefit of the doubt.'

Silence fell again. Birch listened as the helicopter made its pass, and then faded. Every so often there was a little fizz or glitch on the line, but nothing else. She couldn't even hear Hodgson's breathing. Marcello was holding one hand up now, palm out, as though stopping traffic. *Wait*, he mouthed. *Wait*.

Birch waited. She listened for the chopper coming back, for the slightest sound from Hodgson. She wondered if he'd laid down the phone and walked away without hanging up. She thought about Charlie, and why Hodgson had asked for her. He thought she'd be more sympathetic, because her brother was in prison? But surely he knew she was still police – why not call a friend, or a family member?

'Look.'

Hodgson's voice coming back on the line made her jump. Marcello's hand was still up, and she didn't speak.

'Look, Helen,' Hodgson said. 'I do need your help. I do. I didn't know about the kid, I swear to you. I had no idea she even existed until today. But then she was just *there*, and I couldn't – I had no choice. I had to take her. And now she's here and I don't know what to do with her.'

Marcello's hand dropped to his side. He nodded: *talk*.

'I can help you,' Birch said. Her mouth was dry after the long silence. 'I promise, I'll help you, I just need—'

'I'm at Seefew,' Hodgson said. There was a click, and the line went dead.

HOUR EIGHT

Justiceforcreatures.org

'The love for all living creatures is the most noble attribute of man' – Charles Darwin

<u>Home</u> > <u>Members area</u> > <u>Forums</u> > Breaking News: Gerald Hodgson Released OPEN THREAD

Breaking News: Gerald Hodgson released OPEN THREAD

This thread was automatically archived on 4 May 2008

<u>WildWelshWolf</u> (**Moderator**)
Posted 10:04 4 May 2007
BREAKING NEWS and very good news, creature lovers! Gerald Hodgson has at last been released from prison, having served almost a full five-year sentence. I know that since he was first charged in 2001, many of you have joined me in protesting Hodgson's innocence, and subsequently campaigning for his early release. I'd like to thank you all for your efforts, even though we weren't successful and Hodgson was unfairly made an example

of. It still seems ludicrous to me that he was given no opportunity for early release, but then, it's absurd that he was handed a custodial sentence at all. Hodgson is a true hero and did the right thing by the animals. I'm happy to know that today, he is a free man.

More details on his release, including a brief statement from Hodgson, at this link.

cre4turec4re77
Posted 10:20 4 May 2007
Fab news Wolfie. Do we know of an address for Hodgson, where we could send letters of support/ congratulations/thanks?

coocattlesanctuary
Posted 10:27 4 May 2007
seconded i would love to send a note of thanks for his actions

WildWelshWolf (**Moderator**)
Posted 10:45 4 May 2007
I don't know of a personal address for Gerald Hodgson but the contact details of the law firm who represented him are here on their site.
I imagine they would be happy to pass on correspondence for him.

John958473
Posted 12:35 5 May 2007
Great news
Very glad to hear he's a free man again
disgusting what was done to him
He deserved much better

caroline_1
Posted 14:55 5 May 2007
Thanks for the link Wolfie. Can't believe it's been so many years since we first protested outside Gerald Hodgson's trial. I've still got the placard somewhere! Also can't believe we didn't convince the bastards. Poor guy, but so glad he's back in the free world and I hope he joins us or another animal rights org to carry on his good work.

I found another paper covering his release in case anyone wants to read more, the link is here.

WildWelshWolf (**Moderator**)
Posted 18:09 17 November 2010
I know this thread is archived but didn't want to create a whole new one just to say: Gerald Hodgson is now on Facebook if any of you are still in contact and/or want to reach out to him that way. I got a friend request from him just now. Here's his profile.

caroline_1
Posted 01:02 18 November 2010
Thanks WWW I've sent a friend request :)

ixhxtzyq104 (**Guest**)
Posted 10 minutes ago
You sickos need to take this down Gerald Hodgson is a murderer!!!

opdfsjwb905 (**Guest**)
Posted 8 minutes ago
This thread is trending on Twitter!!! Suggest you take it down guys not a good look

htusgybd342 (**Guest**)
Posted 7 minutes ago
Freaks

FUcreaturescum (**Newbie**)
Posted 7 minutes ago
how the fuck can u say justice 4 creatures when u dont
care about justice 4 humans
humans r creatures
gh is a murderer

hkljkhiu443 (**Guest**)
Posted 6 minutes ago
lol he goin back to prison now

okokokok (**Newbie**)
Posted 5 minutes ago
Saw this trending on Twitter and can't believe anyone ever
defended this man he is a monster. You should be
ashamed of yourselfs

aajdlnkl004 (**Guest**)
Posted 5 minutes ago
smdh people how is this still up????
delete ur account!!!

FUcreaturescum (**Newbie**)
Posted 4 minutes ago
@WildWelshWolf gerald hodgson is this u?

okokokok (**Newbie**)
Posted 3 minutes ago

@FUcreaturescum @WildWelshWolf It's like his fan site
from years ago
Can't believe it but glad they have not deleted so we can
all see who defended this MONSTER

okokokok (**Newbie**)
Posted 2 minutes ago
OMG they put his Fb on here I'm gonna message him

FUcreaturescum (**Newbie**)
Posted 2 minutes ago
same

WildWelshWolf (**Moderator**) closed comments on this
thread

15:00

HOUR NINE

In a way, it was a relief to get into the car, alone, and close the door. Birch sat in the driver's seat for a moment, pulling in a few long breaths. The last hour had been a frenzy of briefings and preparations and orders. They'd called Dacre back, and waited while he found a Kelso officer who knew what Seefew meant, explained where it was. McLeod had listened as Dacre listed all the things they needed, now: more firearms officers, more uniforms, police air support. They had a brief discussion about the RAF and permission to fly. Dacre wanted to keep Hodgson's Mountain Rescue helicopter in the air: it turned out they'd clocked a Land Rover and had been making fly-pasts for some time, waiting to see where it went. Birch had tried to argue it ought to be called home – its endless circling was making Hodgson jumpy. Dacre said they needed to keep eyes on his position, in case he moved.

'He could move anyway.' Birch had practically spat out the words. 'He's already sick of them hovering over him. And his state of mind is pretty erratic. He's fragile.'

She'd wanted to say, *and he has with him a shotgun and a small child who he's realised is a burden.* She'd looked at Marcello's face, and seen that same anguish written all over it. Dacre had argued back, and she felt her head fill with static. McLeod had taken one look at her and stepped in. The helicopter didn't need to do constant fly-pasts. It could pull back a fair way, and still be able to keep Hodgson's Land Rover in its peripheral vision.

'He thinks they're out looking for missing climbers,' McLeod added. 'Make it look that way.'

Birch had stood next to McLeod as he addressed the bull-pen. She'd tried to focus on Amy, who made horrified but ultimately sympathetic faces as McLeod explained that Hodgson had chosen her, Birch, to reach out to. Then McLeod had explained what was to happen next: the main priority was getting to the rendezvous point. There'd be a better, more comprehensive briefing there.

'Our colleagues in the Borders,' he said, 'have been dealing with this since early this morning. They'll be able to give us more information, and we'll go from there.'

Birch had rather zoned out after that. She couldn't help but think about little Elise. Had she seen Hodgson shoot her parents? Had she watched her mother, still dressed in pyjamas, plead with this strange man who'd burst into the house? She imagined the girl now, crouching in the back of a Land Rover, no doubt still crying though she'd already been crying for hours. Birch couldn't imagine the terror she must be feeling. And her mother was dead, and her father in hospital, likely dying. Even if Elise made it through this – and Birch hoped to God that she would – then her life on the other side of this trauma would be ruined. What would happen to her? Where would she go? How could she ever feel safe again?

Birch didn't really surface from this swirl of thoughts until the car door was closed and she found herself alone. McLeod had agreed she could drive herself to the rendezvous site: she told him she wanted to call Anjan, let him know what was about to happen.

'Like you have any idea,' she said into the car's bubble of quiet, 'what's about to happen.'

What she hadn't said was she also wanted some headspace, some silence. The idea of making the hour-and-a-half-long trip in the back of a panda car, having to do small talk with two uniforms . . . she just didn't think she could do it. McLeod's face had shown he'd understood. He'd be taking his own car, too, and she noticed he didn't offer her a lift.

'Okay,' she said, looking at the steering wheel as though she'd never seen one before. Her voice quivered. 'Okay, Helen. We have to go.'

She turned the key in the ignition. Across the car park she could see uniformed officers milling in and out of the fleet sheds, climbing into the backs of vans. It was tempting to sit with the engine idling, and watch them.

'Come on,' she said. 'Get out now. You don't want to end up in a police convoy.'

The idea of having a van of uniformed officers behind her – each of them watching her driving all the way to Kelso – was enough to make her move. She pulled out of the space, waited at the barrier, and when it lifted, slid out of the car park and on to the road.

'Well done,' she said, negotiating the Comely Bank roundabout. 'Now let's phone Anjan. Get it over with.'

Her phone, set up in its hands-free holster on the dashboard, showed six missed calls from Anjan. Each one came at a fifteen-minute interval, as though he'd set a timer. She'd felt the calls as a persistent vibration at her hip, throughout the crabbit second conversation with Dacre and all through McLeod's briefing. She'd known it must be Anjan, seeing on the news that officers from Edinburgh had been called in to help. Wanting to know if she was going, what she'd be doing, if she was okay. She'd tried not to remember their earlier call, making plans for dinner as though everything was right with the world. Had Hodgson been taunting Sophie Lowther while they talked? Had he shot her dead, at point-blank range, as Birch grinned and flirted and told herself what a good day she was about to have? The thought made her feel sick.

She hit the call button on her steering wheel.

'Call Anjan,' she told the car.

'Calling. Anjan.'

Birch counted the trilling rings. Three.

'Helen,' Anjan said, 'hello.'

'Hey, you.' Birch felt suddenly teary, hearing his voice. Hearing the worry in it. 'I'm so sorry, I know you've been trying to get hold of me.'

'I have. Jennie told me – she showed me the news. You're being called up to help in the Borders?'

'We are,' Birch said. 'Half the station is headed down there. I'm in the car right now, on the way.'

'That means something's changed,' Anjan said. 'They're not saying what, on the news. But something else has happened, hasn't it?'

Birch bit her lip. She'd known this conversation would be hard.

'Yes,' she said. 'The press won't know this yet, but – we know where he is. The gunman, who we think is a man named Gerald Hodgson. We know his location.'

Anjan's long exhale was a clatter in the car's speakers.

'Well, that's a good thing,' he said. There was a pause. Birch knew what was coming: Anjan wasn't stupid. 'But that can't be it,' he went on. 'That can't be why they're asking for back-up.'

'No, it isn't. Obviously I can't give you many details, but – the situation has escalated. Significantly. I can tell you a little, but it needs to be in total confidence.'

'Helen.' Anjan's voice was grave. 'Don't we know each other well enough by now that—'

'Yes, of course,' she said. 'I'm sorry. So, the major issue at stake now is . . .' She pulled in a breath. 'Hodgson has a hostage. A child, a little girl. And we know he's armed, and he's in a pretty bad place. So it's not as simple as just bringing him in. Not any more.'

'A pretty bad place,' Anjan echoed. 'He's made contact?'

Birch winced. She'd known she'd have to tell him, but doing so was hard.

'He has,' she said. 'In fact, he – he contacted me, Anjan. Me, specifically.'

She listened to the shocked silence on the line as Anjan processed this.

'You,' he said, quietly. 'Why?'

'I'm not entirely sure. He said on the phone that he'd read about Charlie in the papers – presumably he means when Charlie was sent down. He was in Low Moss himself – Hodgson, I mean – for five years. It might be that he thinks I'll go easy on him, knowing what the place is like, maybe? But finding out *why me* wasn't really the focus of our conversation.'

'But—' It was rare for Anjan to be lost for words. Birch could practically hear his brain scrambling to make sense of things. You and me both, pal, she thought. 'But – what does he want, then? Did he say?'

'Honestly,' Birch replied, 'I don't think he knows. He said he was scared. He has this wee girl with him, and he clearly has no idea what to do with her. I don't think he was intending to take a hostage, which means we're in really frightening territory. If he doesn't see her as a hostage, then she's not an asset to him. She's not useful. She's a burden. I haven't said this to anyone, not even to McLeod, but I'm really very worried about what he'll do next.'

'But he phoned,' Anjan said. 'He did phone, and tell you where he was. I presume that means he wants help. Isn't it possible he'll just come quietly?'

'I wish I knew. I mean, I hope so. But we're heading down there and taking the entire cavalry with us. He's already pissed off that there are helicopters flying over every two minutes. Now he's about to have every armed officer in Scotland descend around him in a very tight circle. That's enough to freak anyone out – let alone a guy with a hostage he doesn't really want and an itchy trigger finger.'

Anjan was quiet. He wasn't scrambling any more: she could feel the seriousness of what she'd said sinking in. He was quiet for some time. Birch sat at a red traffic light, listening to his breath on the line.

'And you,' he said, eventually. 'What's your role going to be, when you get down there?'

Birch was flooded with a strong feeling: the desire to peel off the main road into some small back street, turn off the engine, close her eyes and go to sleep. To just sleep, right there, sitting upright in the car, for as long as it took for all this mess to be cleaned up.

'I don't know yet,' she said. 'But I'm his chosen contact. It's possible I'll be the person who has to talk to him.'

When Anjan spoke again, his voice was careful, deliberate.

'You're telling me,' he said, 'that you might be about to walk into a hostage negotiation?'

'That's a fairly dramatic way to word it,' she said. She could feel that her teeth were clenched together. You can't lie to Anjan, she told herself. 'But – potentially, yes.'

'Look,' Anjan said, after a brief pause. 'I know I'm having an emotional response to this. You're my partner, and I realise that raises the stakes. But I'm also speaking in my professional capacity when I say that you are not trained for such a thing. I'm sorry, but you're not. It's dangerous. Not just dangerous, it's *reckless*. It's reckless of McLeod to even entertain the idea.'

For a moment, she couldn't decide whether to be touched by his concern, or annoyed by it.

'I'm hoping,' she said, 'that it won't happen. I think we're all hoping that – McLeod most of all. You know how risk-averse he is. There's a specialist negotiator being flown down by helicopter from Glasgow. She *is* trained, and she'll get there before me. I'm hoping that by the time I arrive she'll have taken over, and I'll just get to – I don't know, man the tea urn or something.'

'I know when you're trying to fob me off, Helen.'

Birch was surprised to find herself smiling.

'I know you know,' she said, 'but it's true. Rena Brooks, she's called – R-E-N-A. Google her, I'm sure she's highly credentialled.'

'Let's hope so,' Anjan said. Birch imagined him feeling around for a pen, writing down *Rena Brooks*.

'I'm hoping,' she said, 'that in a few hours she'll be on the news, being hailed as the hero of the hour.'

'Indeed.' He sounded sceptical.

'It's going to be okay.' She was aware she was protesting too much now: she had no idea if it was going to be okay. She thought again of little Elise, curled up in the back of the Land Rover, and shoved the thought away. 'I'm going to be on the bypass in a minute, so I should probably go. I'll try to call you again when I get there.'

'When you get where? Can you tell me where you're going?'

'There's a rendezvous site,' Birch replied. 'In a village about seven miles outside of Kelso.' She glanced at her satnav. 'Town Yetholm, it's called. The guys in the Borders are setting up a command post. From there, we'll run the op to apprehend our man. I'm hoping that command post is as close to Hodgson as I'll ever get.'

'Well,' Anjan said, 'I hope so, too. And I hope you're able to ring me again – or text me, or something. Keep me updated however you can.'

'I will. I promise.'

There was another pause. Anjan was thinking.

'Before you go,' he said, 'would you like me to call Jamieson?'

'Why would you call my dad?'

'Oh,' Anjan said, 'just to let him know that his only daughter is about to walk into a situation wherein it's possible she may be killed.'

'Holy shit, Anjan.'

'Sorry,' he said, 'but you haven't filled me with confidence. I'm worried. I think he'd be worried too.'

Birch was quiet. Her brain had snagged on *only daughter*: she wanted to snort and say, *yeah, that we know of*. But she was also struggling to imagine her father worrying about her well-being. It didn't seem like something he'd ever done before.

'You know I'm right,' Anjan was saying. 'If he's seen the news, he might be worried already. He deserves to know what's going on.'

Birch huffed.

'Fine,' she said, 'but don't you phone him. I'll do it. It'll be better coming from me. Once I've negotiated the bloody bypass, I'll do it.'

'Please do, Helen. He's more invested in you than you think.'

Birch thought again of Jamieson, sitting in Anjan's living room, bursting into tears out of nowhere, spluttering a repeated apology. She'd steered him up off the couch and marched him out into the Meadows for a brisk walk, not wanting Anjan to see what an abject creature her father had apparently become. *He's trying*, Charlie had said to her, that morning. Was that really just this morning, that she was sitting in the Visit Room at Low Moss?

'I'll do it,' she said again. 'I'm at the A8 junction now, though, Anjan. I'd better go.'

'I love you,' Anjan said. His voice was solemn.

'I love you too.'

The bypass was, thankfully, quiet, once Birch had negotiated the merge at Hermiston Gait. Every so often she saw a cattle truck or horse box pass on the opposite side of the carriageway, and she wondered if the people in those vehicles were driving home after being turned away from the Border Union Show. The entire showground was now a crime scene: she imagined it empty, sealed off with police tape. Was anyone there, or had everyone been called away to hunt for Hodgson? Were scene-of-crime officers there? Surely there were scene guards at least? She should have asked McLeod. She should have paid more attention to his briefing of the junior officers.

The conversation with Anjan bothered at her. Surely he was wrong: she couldn't imagine her father worrying about her. All those years she and Charlie and their mother had scraped by without him, he hadn't worried about her. Not when she'd learned to ride a bike – something dads were supposed to care about, she'd heard. Not when she'd gone through a brief rollerblading phase as a teen, broken her arm and been driven to the Royal Vic by her furious mother. Not when she'd learned to drive or got her exam results or when she'd decided to join the police. Somewhere in the midst of all of that, Charlie went missing, and his own father didn't seem to care. He didn't care when his missing son showed up, a fully fledged gangster, to kick seven shades out of him before disappearing again. He'd never thought to raise the alarm, let anyone know: I saw Charlie, he's alive, he's okay. Years of their mother calling him, Jamieson, leaving messages on his old tape-recorder voicemail and waiting for ever to hear anything back. No, Birch thought – shaking her head to try and dislodge the anger – he's never cared about anyone but himself.

But on the other hand, Anjan had a point. Charlie, that morning, had had a point. Whatever he'd done in the past, Jamieson was trying now. He was showing up. He was keeping in touch. He was crying and *apologising*, for Christ's sake. And did she want to sink to his level? Did she want to become like him, by being stubborn and refusing to mention when something huge might be about to happen?

Birch paused. That voice – the scolding voice in her head – was her mother's. It had been a while since she'd heard it, but it was unmistakable. Her mother was years dead, but annoyingly, still always right.

'Oh, *fine*.' Birch sighed, hitting the phone button on her steering wheel once again. 'Call Jamieson Birch.'

'Calling. Jamieson. Birch.' The robot woman said *Jamieson* wrong, stretching out the *e*.

The phone rang for longer than it had with Anjan: this was one of her father's trademarks. She didn't know whether he left his phone in another room, or if he turned the ringer down so it took a while to hear. Or was he just standing with the phone in his hand, staring at her caller ID on the screen, weighing up whether to ignore her or not? *Stop being so suspicious*, her mother's voice said. And then her father picked up.

'Hello, hen.'

'Hi, Dad.'

'Nice tae get a call from ye.'

Birch rolled her eyes. He hadn't seen the news, then. She knew it: he hadn't been worried at all.

'Are you okay to speak just now?' she asked, trying to show him she'd noticed the long pause before he picked up. 'Are you busy?'

'No really, hen. Jist daein away.'

This was how their conversations went, with Jamieson blithely contributing the bare minimum. She found it difficult to get any sense of her father's day-to-day life. He lived on Boswall Parkway, in a rented ground-floor villa with a rectangle of concrete yard at the front. It was meant to be a parking space, but he didn't have a car: instead he sat out on the hard standing in a plastic garden chair, smoking JPS Blacks and watching his neighbours. He called himself semi-retired, which meant he sometimes did odd jobs for blokes he knew – blokes Birch knew were shady but who she hoped were operating above the law. Jamieson mixed and poured cement, unloaded pallets into warehouses, and occasionally drove vehicles. In between he lived off his small pension – more of it these days, he kept saying, since he'd quit drinking and betting – and went to his meetings once a week at the Pilton Community Health Project. She imagined that once upon a time, his life had revolved around the Gunner, the bar he favoured on Pennywell Road . . . but now the Gunner was long gone, demolished in yet another Pilton regeneration. And besides, Jamieson swore he really was sober.

'It's a beautiful day,' Birch said. Suddenly, she had no desire to get into things with her father. If he didn't know what was going on, why tell him? 'Have you been out?'

'Aye, along to the wee Day Today, jist fer ma paper. An I've been sittin oot, ken, in the front.'

Birch imagined her father in his garden chair, leafing through – she shuddered – the *Sun*. She felt a pang of jealousy that surprised her. The lucky swine, able to just sit in the sunshine, not caring in the slightest what's going on in the world.

'No jobs today, then?'

'No, hen, nothing the day. Quiet week this week.'

'That's good.'

Silence hung on the line between them. It wasn't the companionable silence she lapsed into with Charlie. Rather, she could hear her father waiting for her to either say something or wrap things up, though he apparently had all the time in the world. The burden of conversation was, as always, on her.

'So, look,' she said at last. 'Anjan said I ought to call you. It's probably nothing, but . . . well, there's a big case opened up here, and—'

'Is this the mannie who's shooting folk down in the Borders?'

Birch bit her lip. She wanted to swear. He *had* seen the news, and *still* he hadn't been worried about her.

'It is,' she said, counting to ten in her head. 'We've been called in to help. I'm just driving down there now.'

'Mad business,' Jamieson said. 'Sounds tae me like the gadge is touched.'

Birch thought of McLeod calling her earlier, while she sat in the Low Moss car park: *some farmer gone loopy*. If only, she thought. If only it were just that.

'It's pretty serious,' she said. 'That's why they're calling for reinforcements. He's still at large, and . . . well, like I say, it's pretty serious.'

'He'll get himself shot,' Jamieson said, 'if he's no careful.'

'That,' Birch replied, 'or he'll shoot someone else. This is why I'm ringing, really, Dad. Just . . . to talk to you. About what might happen. I mean, it's unlikely, but—'

'Helen.' Her father's voice was louder, suddenly, like he'd put the receiver closer to his face. 'Are ye calling tae say . . . will this be dangerous for ye?'

Yes, she thought. And then, no, Helen, don't be dramatic. You'll be manning the tea urn, just like you said. She pulled in a breath.

'It might be,' she said, 'yes. Maybe. It's possible.'

'They surely cannae send ye near an armed man?'

Birch laughed, though her hands were tight on the steering wheel.

'That's what Anjan said. I'm not trained for this sort of caper.'

'Well, ye're no. Not that I think you're no a professional, but.'

'No, Dad, I know. Look, it'll probably be fine. Like I said to Anjan, I'll probably get there and end up making the teas. Looking after the coats. That sort of thing.'

'They ought to promote ye, hen. Better than that bampot boss o yours.'

Birch grimaced. She'd made a single, less-than-complimentary remark about McLeod in front of her father once, and now he'd since convinced himself they were sworn enemies.

'One day,' she said. Playing along was simpler: once again she was feeling that strong urge to pull over and sleep. 'But yes. I just wanted to say that I'm driving down there, and we're not sure how this is going to play out. Just to let you know.'

For a moment, her father was quiet. She'd have thought he'd hung up, except somewhere in the background she could hear a radio singing to itself.

'Ye're a good lassie.'

She blinked. He'd said the words with such warmth that she wasn't sure it was still her father on the line. She felt a strange stab of pleasure, hearing them, but also the old familiar annoyance that lay just below the surface of everything her father said and did. She wanted to say *you're damn right*, and yell at him about all the things she'd had to do on her own because she didn't have a father around. But now wasn't the right time – there might never be a right time – and besides, her phone was beeping to indicate someone else was calling, and when she glanced at the screen she saw it was a call from HMP Low Moss.

'Shit,' she said. 'Sorry, Dad. I think Charlie's calling me, and if I don't pick up I can't call him back. I have to go, I'm sorry.'

She didn't wait for her father to respond. Instead, she risked looking down at the screen to hang up and switch to the other line. It took perhaps two full seconds, but as soon as the call was connected she looked in the rear-view, as though that police van full of her watchful colleagues might suddenly have materialised behind her.

'Hello?' Charlie was saying, his voice faint. 'Nella, are you there?'

'I'm here,' she said. 'Sorry, I'm driving. You sound a bit like you're down a hole.'

'Hello, hello, hello.' She could hear him shifting around as he spoke, his voice wavering in and out.

'There,' she said, 'whatever you did for your last hello, do that.'

'Oh, right – this okay?'

'Better.'

'Great. Hello.'

'Well, this is a fine conversation.' Birch could feel herself smiling, her mood just that little bit lighter now her father had gone. 'What's up?'

'Gerald Hodgson,' Charlie said. 'I'm guessing he's what's up with you, too.'

'I can't tell you anything,' Birch said, 'and I'm not going to, I just want to make that perfectly clear to anyone who might be listening in to this call. But . . . you're not wrong.'

'You said you're driving?'

'Yeah. I'm . . . I'm more involved now than I was when I saw you this morning.'

'You're being careful, aren't you, Nella?'

'Always, honey.'

Charlie snorted.

'Oh, sure. Stickler Birch, that's what they call you. She *never* puts herself in danger or does anything daft.'

Birch laughed.

'Shut it, you. I'm absolutely not going to be lectured on safety by my criminal fiend of a brother. We can sit here and compare who's done more irresponsible stuff in their lives if you like, but that's not a competition you're going to win, is it?'

'Dunno what you mean. I'm an innocent man, me. Wrongly imprisoned, Your Honour.'

'You know they record these calls and listen to them back, right? That'll give them all a good laugh in the break room.'

'Nah, they get that every day.'

'Hmm. Yes, I imagine they do . . . and probably from even gnarlier types than you. Anyway, enough of your craic. You rang?'

'I did,' Charlie said, though she could still hear mischief in his voice. 'I've been asking around about Gerald Hodgson.'

'After I told you not to.'

'When you knew I would anyway.'

'Right.'

'Right. But don't get too excited. I didn't find out anything much of interest. It sounds like he was basically the world's nicest guy and he got seriously fucked around.'

Birch thought again of Sophie Lowther. If only you knew the half of it, she thought.

'He landed in here,' Charlie was saying, 'in 2002, which I'm pretty sure you know. Back then Low Moss was only for prisoners serving up to thirty-six months, not like now. Hodgson had been given five years but I don't think anyone expected him to serve that long. Hence, they put him in here. First-time offender, clean nose, nice guy, so they sent him to the *nice* jail.'

'Nice?'

'Yeah. By all accounts this place was like a Hilton before they rebuilt it.'

'Hardly,' Birch said. 'I remember it being like Nissen huts. It was like army barracks, wasn't it? Communal living.'

'Dunno. The auld yins in here are just always banging on about how it was better in the old days.'

'Ah, the rose-tinted nostalgia of hardened jailbirds. Quite the thing. Anyway, carry on.'

'Okay, so he lands in here and then someone somewhere has a change of heart. He goes for the early release and doesn't get it. By then the plans were in the works to tear the old Low

Moss down and build this one, so I guess he just ended up staying put.'

'He got out in 2007,' Birch said.

'Yeah, five years. Seems like a lot. For what he did, I mean. But then, it's all relative. Compared to my stretch it seems like fuck all.'

Charlie made a *pfft* sound. Birch ignored it.

'But people have been saying he was a nice guy?'

'That is the resounding feedback,' Charlie said. 'There are a couple of guys in here who just hadn't had enough jail and came back for more – they remember him from their first stretches. Said he was a quiet sort, kept to himself, never spoke. Never made trouble, but also never showed remorse – that type. Maybe that's why no early release. He didn't jump through their hoops.'

'No remorse,' Birch echoed, her voice grim. Her brain cycled round once again to that image of a little girl, curled up on the cold metal floor in the back of Hodgson's Land Rover.

'He wasn't just fucked by the law, though,' Charlie went on. 'These guys told me he was also really messed about by his girlfriend. Or – fiancée? The woman in his life, anyway.'

'So I've been led to believe.'

'She was a lot younger than him,' Charlie went on, 'and supposedly she'd been Hodgson's rock. Stand by your man, that whole thing. Right up until the last day in court, and then she almost literally did a runner. Never visited him, never wrote to him, ignored him entirely when he tried to get in contact. Apparently he pined away in here. They thought he was on hunger strike for something, until they found out about this wifey. I mean, pretty harsh, don't you think?'

Birch squirmed. She couldn't say Sophie's actions had been admirable, but she certainly hadn't deserved to die.

'I guess,' she said.

'He apparently talked about it non-stop,' Charlie said, 'even years into his sentence. It really cut him up. It was like he couldn't get over it.'

'Yeah,' Birch said, 'seems that way. But that's it? Nothing else to report?'

'Not really. The only other thing I've heard is that his case got a lot of interest from animal rights groups. He apparently used to get letters from them, telling him he was a hero, asking him to do interviews or write articles and what have you.'

'And did he?' Birch made a mental note – could they track down some of those groups? Though really, she realised, the time for checking out Hodgson's past was pretty much over.

'Doesn't seem like it. He rarely had visitors or talked to anyone at all, from the sounds. A real bona fide loner.'

'Of course,' Birch said.

'Yeah. Classic, right? Lone wolf gets trigger-happy, settles some scores? It's like something you'd get in America.'

'Charlie.' Birch could hear her voice was sharp, but couldn't help it. 'I'd like to remind you that Scotland has seen its share of that sort of thing, too, and in recent memory. It's no joke.'

Her brother was quiet for a moment.

'Sorry, Nella,' he said. 'I forgot, for a second.'

'It's okay. Just don't be a jerk.'

'Tricky, but I'll try my best. You all right?'

Birch shrugged, then realised he couldn't see her.

'I've had better days at the office,' she said. The spectre of Three Rivers loomed in her mind, summoned by her brother's careless remark. 'But then again, I've also had worse.'

'That's the spirit.'

Birch smiled. The tired feeling was still hovering.

'I just spoke to Dad,' she said.

'Yeah? What's he up to? Let me guess: he's out in his exercise yard watching the natives and wishing he could have a drink.'

'Bingo.'

Charlie laughed a hard-edged laugh.

'He and I, we've got a lot in common.'

'Oh jeez, don't say that.'

'Why?' The mischief was back in her brother's voice now. 'You don't want me comparing myself to an addled old drunk? Or you don't want me comparing him to a failed gangster?'

Birch was laughing now, too.

'Honestly,' she said, 'I'm not entirely sure.'

'I'm glad you two are talking, though,' Charlie said. 'I'm glad you're giving him a chance.'

'I *may* just have hung up on him so I could talk to you instead.'

'Well, obviously. Finest conversationalist in the known world, me.'

Birch felt conflicted, her thoughts still turning over and over. Each time she laughed at one of Charlie's wisecracks, she was reminded of Elise, and what she was driving towards. It was starting to make her feel sick, and she needed to focus on where she was going.

'Be that as it may,' she said, 'I should probably go. I need to get my head in the game, for – well, what's coming.'

'Nella, I know you can't tell me anything. But you will be careful, won't you? If you're going anywhere near this guy, you'll be careful? I may have been told over and over what a nice quiet type he is, but nice quiet types don't suddenly turn into Rambo for no reason.'

'Not usually,' Birch said, 'no.'

'Right. So just go carefully, okay? I'm serious. I don't know what I'd do in here if it wasn't for you. I know I spraff on and wind you up, but I do love you, Nella. You know that, right?'

'I do.' She felt teary again, and got the strong urge – as she did, from time to time – to wrap Charlie in a bear hug. Whenever she visualised this, her brother was around eight years old, having somehow never grown up – too scrawny to escape from her, and only half trying. 'And I love you too, for all your spraffing.'

'Right. Well, just be good, then.'

'And if you can't be good,' Birch said, 'which *you* apparently can't—'

'—then be careful,' Charlie replied.

'I will,' Birch said, swallowing the lump in her throat. 'I promise.'

HOUR TEN

◙ LIVE: Police Scotland close in on Border Union Show gunman

Borders residents can leave homes, but should exercise caution
BBC 16:26
Live reporting
Edited by Alex Paulson

16:25
'We're tightening the net' around gunman, say Police Scotland

Uniformed officers and specialist units from both Edinburgh and Glasgow have been drafted in to assist Borders police in the manhunt for the Border Union Show gunman.

Speaking at a short press conference, a Police Scotland spokesperson revealed that police helicopters and armed response teams had been scrambled to help.

Borders officers received an initial report that a man was randomly firing a shotgun in the Border Union Showground at Springwood Park in Kelso early this morning. The first officers arrived on the scene at around 8.45 a.m.

The gunman has been at large for around nine hours, but police are 'tightening the net', the spokesperson said. Borders residents had been advised to stay in their homes as the manhunt went on. It is now safe to leave the house, police advise, but they stress that locals must exercise caution.

At one point the warning was extended to Cumbria and Dumfries and Galloway, amid worries that the gunman might have fled beyond the Borders region. There is now 'no risk' to people outside the Scottish Borders.

16:18

Gunman is white, male, and driving a green Land Rover Defender

The identity of the gunman has yet to be officially confirmed, but earlier in the day Police Scotland appealed for anyone who knew the whereabouts of a Gerald Hodgson, of Cessford near Kelso, to come forward. They also reached out to anyone who might have seen a green Land Rover Defender driving erratically.

Hodgson, 59, is a livestock haulage driver who works around the Scottish Borders region. He was previously an inmate of HMP Low Moss, convicted of a series of charges in a landmark case amid the 2001 foot-and-mouth outbreak, which decimated farms in the Borders and Dumfries and Galloway. He was released in 2007.

HOUR ELEVEN

The closer Birch got to Kelso, the quieter the roads had become. If the news that it was safe to go outside had filtered through, people weren't acknowledging it. The town's suburbs were ghostly: no cars, no dog walkers. Birch passed the tall, blank windows of the deserted high school; an old-fashioned ice rink and curling centre, its car park an empty gravel lot. She passed a petrol station with a square of cardboard taped in the window: CLOSED TODAY. The people of Kelso were taking no chances.

Instead of following her satnav, Birch had peeled off to follow signs for the town centre. This was procrastination, she knew – getting to the rendezvous meant passing the point of no return, and although she couldn't turn the car round and drive back towards the good day she'd promised herself when she first woke up, she could stall for time, just a little. She'd been to Kelso before, albeit years ago. But as she drove through the streets, she remembered it: the quaint, French-looking square, its domed clock tower with the powder-blue face. She remembered the cobbled roads, the big, slightly shabby hotel painted mint green. Outside it, five small hatchbacks were parked in a row, their windows wide open, an urgent thud of bass passing back and forth along the line. Boy racers, it seemed, didn't pay much attention to warnings about armed and dangerous men.

Birch looped through the one-way system, out of the square and off the main drag. On one side of the road were pub yards, empty kegs stacked shining against walls, awaiting pickup. On the other side, a dark green graveyard full of twisty old yews. The sun slanted through them, making little rooms of light among the stones. At the turning, the famous Kelso abbey loomed above the car, its sandstone ruins the colour of honeycomb against the blue sky. Gerald Hodgson felt like the bogeyman: a scary story invented as a prank to keep everyone indoors. Though Birch had spoken to him herself – every so often her pulse stuttered at the thought of the little girl he'd abducted – she was finding it hard to believe that what had happened so far was real. That there could be worse to come, even on this gorgeous day.

Birch crossed the stone bridge and realised, noting its nameplate, that she was passing above the River Tweed. Here, there was activity. At the other end of the bridge, a side road slanted off to the right. A marked police car was positioned diagonally across the white lines, its lights flashing. Two male uniformed officers in yellow fluorescent overcoats leaned against its side. Birch slowed her CID Mondeo to a stop, and zipped down the window.

'DI Helen Birch,' she said, as one of the uniforms approached. She fished for her warrant card. 'I've come down from Edinburgh.'

The uniformed officer bent to look at the badge, then straightened up so rapidly that she thought he might salute.

'We're just on traffic duty, marm,' he said. 'Keeping locals away from the scene.'

Birch glanced past him. She'd been distracted by the panda car, but now she saw the sign behind it: *Springwood Park. Border Union Show traffic follow A699.*

'That's the showground?' She gestured past him, but couldn't see much: a sandstone perimeter wall, and above it, scrubby trees.

'Yeah. One corner of it. The main gate is down there.' He waved a hand towards the road his car was blocking. 'We've been told to grant no access to the showfield, and we're stopping anyone using the access road, just as a precaution.'

'Are there many officers here?'

The man made a sort of huffing sound.

'Only a few of us,' he said. 'The also-rans, you know.'

'I'm sure that's not true,' Birch said, though she knew it probably was. Dacre and his colleagues would have sent their best out looking for Hodgson. 'You're playing a vital role, here.'

The uniform grinned. He didn't believe her. He could only be about nineteen or so, Birch thought.

'You're not here for us, though, are you, marm? You're on your way to the rendezvous.'

'Yes,' she admitted, 'I am.'

The uniform raised one neon arm and pointed vaguely.

'Follow this road round,' he said, 'and then go straight until you get to the roundabout at Sainsbury's. Third exit, the B6352 – then just keep driving. The road'll take you right there. It's about seven miles.'

'Thanks,' Birch said. 'I appreciate it.'

The uniform grinned again, and then brought his hand down once, twice, on the roof of her car: that *off you go* thing she thought policemen only did in films. She smiled, watching in her rear-view mirror as he sloped back to his partner beside the panda car. I was an also-ran once, too, she thought.

She did as he'd told her, following the road round in a wide sweep as it began to climb above the river. She passed a low

wall with a sheet flung over it, the words 6TH JUNE ANGIE
B = NAUGHTY FORTY sprayed across it in wobbly blue
aerosol. She passed a shuttered funeral director's, a car wash,
and a couple of turn-offs that seemed to lead into industrial
estates: signs for companies with names like Scotmas and
Keltel. As the big orange siding of Sainsbury's crested into
view, Birch spotted a figure on the side of the road. The appa-
rition made her jump. An elderly man was sitting beside the
pavement, perched on top of a yellow council grit bin. He
appeared to be soaking up the sun, one arm leaning on a walking stick, and one foot sticking out, the toe pointed like a balle-
rina's. He was older than her father, but Birch was struck by
how much he reminded her of Jamieson, sitting on his plastic
chair in the front yard. As she passed, the man raised one
hand in greeting, and Birch waved back. She'd made it beyond
the roundabout before she wondered if he'd seen the news – if
she ought to have pulled over, offered him a lift home.
Someone might be wondering where he was – his daughter,
maybe. His daughter who found him infuriating beyond
words, but, if she was honest with herself, still loved him. Still
wanted him in her life.

The buildings stopped abruptly, and Birch was in open
countryside. The road was empty, the sky seemingly huge,
and she opted to invalidate her air con and open the car
windows, let the warm June air inside. She drove past potato
fields with their regimented green rows, then on through
wheat, catching its dry, powdery smell. The road climbed
slowly but steadily: the crops fell away, replaced by grazing
land. Birch drove under ancient beech trees, their leaves' hiss
audible over her engine, and when she came to a rise in the
road her breath caught as, just for a moment, a vista of
Cheviots opened out in front of her. The way dipped and

twisted, the side roads off it growing smaller, their signposts for farms rather than settlements. Birch savoured the names: Blakelaw, Cherrytrees, Lochtower. The sun was still high and the hedges were tall and almost blindingly green. This was a beautiful place. But it was also bleak, she noted: houses were few and far between, the roads were quiet and the fields huge. Stands of beech and fir and old woodland broke up any long line of sight. This was a sparse place, perfect for evading capture. No wonder Hodgson had slipped her colleagues' net. She shuddered to think how long he could have stayed hidden, had he not decided to pick up the phone, and ask for her.

Town Yetholm appeared round a sharp bend: suddenly, Birch was slowing to thirty and steering her way under chestnut trees, past whinstone houses with colourful front doors. There was no mistaking where she should go: up ahead, a cordon had been erected right across the road. Beyond it, she could see the village's one main street was littered with police vehicles.

Birch pulled up in front of the cones. As with the roadblock in Kelso, the cordon was manned by two youngish uniformed officers, both men. Feeling a degree of déjà vu, she made her warrant card visible through the already open car window.

'DI Helen Birch,' she said. 'I'm from the Edinburgh contingent.'

The officer who'd crossed to the car this time didn't stand up straighter, but she watched as the light of recognition came on in his eyes.

'Oh,' he said, 'it's you. You're here.'

Birch gave him a look. She felt like he was smirking at her.

'The chosen one,' he went on. 'The one Hodgson wants to talk to.'

'Listen, it's not a role I particularly cherish.' She couldn't help snapping. The officer's tone had an edge of nastiness in it. 'Are you going to let me through?'

The uniform looked as though he might say no, but then seemed to change his mind. He stepped back from the car and gestured to his partner, who walked across the cordon, lifting cones out of the way.

'Go all the way along the village green.' The smirking uniform had raised his voice, so his partner could hear him now, too. 'When you get level with the pub, take a right. Someone'll help you park.'

As Birch steered through the gap in the cones, she glanced back in her rear-view mirror. The two officers were replacing the cordon, laughing together about something.

'I don't need any help to park, *thank* you,' she said, annoyed she'd let the smirk get to her.

The main street was straight and wide. On one side ran a long green: more chestnut trees, benches, a little blue hut she assumed was a bus stop. Beyond the green was an old-fashioned garage, more terraced whinstone, more brightly painted doors. On the other side of the road were more cottages, these ones newer, sandstone or pebble-dash. A craggy hill loomed over the village: Birch realised she was now at the feet of the fells she'd seen on the way in from Kelso.

The road was choked on both sides with panda cars and police vans, black Land Rovers with discreet police livery, a few off-road vehicles of various types marked Mountain Rescue. Birch drove with her window still open, hearing the thick fizz of radio static as the officers talked or listened on their various channels. She could feel her pulse quickening: this felt chaotic. She'd hoped to arrive at a rendezvous point being run with such military precision that her own small input couldn't possibly be required. But the officers she passed looked jittery, all of them waiting for something. As the pub – the Plough, a long, low, whitewashed building with black lintels – came into view on her left, she felt an urge to keep driving, out past the cordon at the other end of the village, up and up into the hills. This, she realised, was what Hodgson must have done: she was close to him now. Town Yetholm was the last point of civilisation he'd passed before he headed for Seefew.

But of course, Birch did as she'd been told, and turned right. Here, the green widened and she could see a temporary control centre had been created. Yet more vehicles were clustered around, but there were also white gazebos, marked vans with all their doors open, officers climbing in and out. As the officer at the cordon had promised, another uniform approached the car, waving one arm. She would indeed be helped to park, it seemed.

'DI Birch?' The uniform bent down to look at her through the window.

'That's me.'

'Well, thank Christ you're here. We've saved you a parking space. Just over to the left there.'

Birch followed the direction of the man's waving arm. *Parking space* was a bit of a stretch: there was a narrow strip of grass between two vans, into which she could probably just about squeeze the Mondeo, if she was careful. She took a deep breath. This would *not* be the time to scrape her paintwork, with all these people around.

But the uniform wasn't watching, having already turned his back to attend to some other task. Birch tightened her grip on the wheel and inched the car on to the grass, nose first, not thinking about how she'd get it out again. The vans rose up on both sides, their flanks blinding white under the afternoon sun. It felt like parking in a polytunnel. She turned off the engine and sat for a handful of seconds, listening to her own breath. This was it. *Thank Christ you're here*, the uniform had said. Yes, she was here. No going back.

Birch shimmied her way out of the car and along the thin channel between the Mondeo and the van on her driver's side. She could practically feel the dry dust of the road she'd just driven peeling off the two vehicles and on to her new jeans. She regretted wearing them now: in her jeans and blouse and thin-soled flats she couldn't feel as authoritative as she might have in a suit. Her jacket was on the passenger seat but she'd squeezed out now, and didn't relish the idea of slithering along by the other van to retrieve it. She'd just have to make do as she was, dressed for drinks with Anjan, wholly unprepared to be flung into the midst of – well, whatever this was about to be.

She headed for the cluster of gazebos in the centre of the green. The uniform who'd shown her where to park was standing underneath one of them, pointing at her. Beside him was a man wearing full tactical gear, including a shouldered G36 carbine rifle. Birch knew without asking that this was the commanding officer, and made a beeline for him.

'DI Helen Birch,' she said, extending a hand as she reached him. 'You're the CO?'

'Jamal Leigh,' the man said, shifting his grip on the gun in order to shake her hand. 'Specialist firearms officer. And this is my little kingdom, yes. Though I'm deferring to the Borders teams, obviously. This is their turf.'

'And you've come in from—?'

'Glasgow,' Leigh replied. 'We flew in to help with tactical support. I'm with what was the counterterrorism unit of

Strathclyde Police, before we all became one big happy family.'

'Rena Brooks is with you, then. The negotiator?'

'Yep, she's one of my flock, and she's around here some-where. We'll get the two of you talking. I must say, I'm bloody glad you've got here, DI Birch.'

'Helen.' Birch was trying to ignore the assault rifle in his hands, though something in her yearned to look at it.

'Right. Our man Hodgson seems very keen to speak to you.'

'You've been in contact with him?'

'We've been at the scene. We helped establish the perimeter at Seefew.'

'Of course,' Birch said. She glanced around, realising now that most of the officers here at the centre of things were Leigh's team, dressed in flak vests and heavy boots. 'Tell me how it looks out there.'

Leigh made a face.

'Well,' he said, 'Hodgson must know the terrain. He's chosen just about the worst possible place to camp, from our point of view. Seefew is a grazing pasture, with no road access, about five miles or so from here up the Bowmont Valley. When you get there, you'll see why it's called that. The pasture is sort of a bowl, surrounded by hills on all sides. You can't see in, and you can't see out. And there's nothing up there but fucking sheep.'

'Nothing,' Birch echoed. She was trying to ignore the *when you get there*, holding on to the hope that there might still be a tea urn somewhere with her name on it. 'Nothing at all? Why—'

'No,' Leigh cut in, 'I lie. There's a building. Or, there *was* a building. It's a ruin, now. The farmer whose pasture it is reck-ons it was a shepherd's cottage, and the cottage's name would have been *Seefew*. But it's not much more than four broken walls now. Hodgson's using it as cover. He must have known it was there.'

'Did you see the little girl,' Birch asked, 'when you were there?'

'No sign of her,' Leigh said, his mouth making a line. 'Hodgson wouldn't be drawn on where she was, or how she was doing.'

Birch closed her eyes. Please, she thought, please say she's still alive.

'We need to get you in front of Rena,' Leigh was saying. When Birch opened her eyes again, she saw he was casting about for someone in the crowd of vehicles and bodies. 'That's the most important thing right now, I think. Let me go and find her. Meantime, you've had a bit of a drive. Why don't you wait in the shop over there? The ladies who run it are doing teas.'

Leigh motioned with one elbow, not letting go of the rifle. Birch looked in the direction of the gesture, and saw beyond the vans and gazebos to a retro little shopfront in the bottom floor of one of the whinstone cottages. A dark green awning stuck out above the door, the words *Yetholm Village Shop* printed on it in old-fashioned cursive.

'Thanks,' she said. 'I could murder a cuppa.'

The words were out of her mouth before she could stop them, and she winced, but Leigh had already turned away, looking for Rena Brooks. Birch straightened up, and picked her way across the rendezvous site, trying not to make eye contact with anyone.

Inside, the shop felt cool and dark after the glare of the sun and the many white vehicles outside. Birch found herself in front of a stand of newspapers, expecting to see Gerald Hodgson's name in the headlines. But of course, it had only been a few hours. It felt like an eternity since she'd stepped out of the shower that morning.

'Can we help you, hen?'

Birch jumped. Standing behind the shop counter were two elderly women, wearing matching tabards. The one who'd spoken had a badge pinned to hers. It read *Pearl, Manager*.

'I'm—' Birch's eyes adjusted to the gloom. She could see now that at the back of the shop a space had been cleared among the shelves and displays, and a row of mismatched kitchen chairs laid out. Several of these chairs were occupied by her colleagues, uniformed and not. They were talking in low voices, holding white polystyrene cups. 'I just got here,' Birch said. 'I was told there were teas and coffees?'

She waited while Pearl looked her up and down.

'You dinnae look like polis,' she said.

Birch attempted her best charming smile.

'Kind of you to say so,' she said. 'I'm a Detective Inspector, so I'm plain clothes.'

Pearl's expression didn't change.

'Well, pardon me,' she said. 'You'll be down fae Edinburgh, then.'

Behind Pearl, the other woman had begun to shuffle on her feet, eyeing the opening in the shop's back corner which, Birch assumed, led to the kitchen.

'I am, yes.'

'Plain clothes, ye said.'

'Yes.' Leigh hadn't mentioned that the cup of tea would come with an interrogation.

'I'm surprised they let ye come tae work in such a skimpy wee hing as that blouse,' Pearl said.

Birch blinked. She could feel her cheeks beginning to burn. The woman's rudeness barely registered: she was right. Listen,

I had the morning off, Birch wanted to say. It was supposed to have been a light day. A good day.

'Look,' she said, 'I just came in for a cup of tea.'

'Evie.' Pearl glanced back at the other woman, and nodded.

'How d'ye take it, hen?' Evie looked glad to round the corner of the counter and move towards Birch. 'We've only full fat milk, I'm sorry.'

Birch smiled.

'Full fat's just fine. And one sugar, please.'

'Right ye are.' Evie smiled a mousy smile, and leaned forward, dropping her voice to a whisper. 'An I think that's a bonny blouse.'

'*E*vie.' Pearl's eyes had narrowed. Evie straightened up, and turned on her heel towards the kitchen. For a moment, Birch stood in Pearl's icy glare, neither woman speaking.

'We're keeping you busy,' Birch said, nodding at the officers huddled on their kitchen chairs. Pearl sniffed.

'Happy tae help,' she said, not sounding it. 'Besides, the hale village is locked down, so we've no customers. We'd no want tae be idle.'

'It's very good of you.'

Pearl gave a stiff nod.

'It's no the way o things here,' she said. 'In this village, we all ken one another. We dinnae lock our doors at night. It's no right, folk being told to stay in their hooses. Aw this fuss.'

Birch didn't want to argue with this woman, but she felt her eyes widen.

'It's for everyone's safety,' she said. 'There's an armed man on the loose.'

Pearl looked away. Birch thought the older woman might even have shrugged.

'Poor soul,' she said.

'I'm sorry?'

'Well.' Pearl held up her hands. 'I'm no saying whit he did at the showfield was right, but . . . ye can understand, can ye no? How someone can . . . lose it. Go mad. Efter whit happened tae the poor soul. Whit he saw.' Pearl met Birch's eyes again. 'Dinnae look at me that way, missy. You lot had better treat him kindly when ye catch up tae him. It's no like anyone's deid, is it?'

Birch's mouth had been open, ready to speak, but now she closed it again. Of course. The press didn't know yet about Sophie Lowther. They didn't know yet about Elise.

'Do you know Gerald Hodgson?'

''Course not. But I remember him, remember reading aboot him, whit he did. Folk who arenae from here – you Edinburgh types – you dinnae ken whit it was like back then. Back when that sickness came. That horrible time.'

'The sickness – you mean foot-and-mouth?'

'Aye.' Pearl stabbed one index finger down on to the counter. 'See this place? This is a farming place. If you're no from a farming place, ye willnae understand. There's only one road up that valley' – Pearl pointed above Birch's head, out of the shop towards the hills – 'an the same road back oot. Can ye imagine whit it wis like? They were sitting ducks up there, all they farms. No way tae avoid it. They were aw just waiting fer the sickness tae arrive.'

Birch frowned. A memory swam through her head, distant and slow. A red, churning sky. A long pall of black smoke.

'I'll admit,' she said, 'I remember it being on the news. I remember it, but . . . you're right, from where I was seeing it, it didn't seem that bad.'

'It wis *bad*,' Pearl snapped. 'It wis worse than any o us thought it might be. They said it wis coming in oan vehicles, right? The government said. Think how many vehicles come oan and off a farm every day. Feed trucks, transport trucks, the farmers themselves, their Land Rovers. Quad bikes. Ye cannae stop the feed trucks coming in, or the animals starve. Ye cannae stop the school bus driving up the valley tae get the farm weans tae school. There were roadblocks everywhere, guys wi buckets stopping every car, every truck, scrubbing their wheels down wi disinfectant, the whole palaver. This shop stank wi that disinfectant for weeks, walked in oan aw the farmers' boots. But the sickness still came. They couldnae stop it.'

'Och, it wis terrible, though.' Evie had reappeared at Birch's elbow, a cup of thick, milky tea in her hand. 'See if even wan sheep got the sickness? That was the whole herd had tae be slaughtered. Every animal on a farm. Even the dogs, I read somewhere.'

'An no jist that,' Pearl said, 'no jist the farm that *got* the sickness. Aw the farms around it, within a radius. If you had pasture that bordered the pasture o a sick farm? It wis you, too. Your animals.'

Birch took the tea from Evie, felt the slimy coating of the polystyrene.

'I'll never forget,' Evie said, her voice quiet, 'the wan time – Pearl, remember? That couple up at Hownam.'

Pearl nodded, her face grave.

'Their farm got the sickness,' Evie went on, 'an the wife – she wis just a wee girl really – she came in here that day in tears. She said she'd come intae the village because she couldnae stand tae be there while they did it. While they slaughtered the animals. See, the farmers didnae even get tae dae it themselves. It wis aw men employed by the government, ken. Shipped in fae all over. Strangers. Can ye imagine? Coming tae yer home an taking over that way? Destroying yer livelihood.'

Pearl was still nodding.

'An the animals,' she said. 'The poor animals. They didnae ken they had the sickness. They didnae have a clue. Folk in these parts, they love their animals. A farm can have five hundred head o sheep – the farmer still kens every one, I swear to ye.' She nodded towards Evie. 'Oor family were farming stock, we've seen it, haven't we, Evie? The thought o seeing someone come in an slaughter the lot, an nothing tae be done. It wis awful. It wis the worst time we've ever seen here. Worse than anything.'

Evie was nodding now. Birch looked back and forth between the two women.

'Worse,' she said, slowly, 'than the coronavirus?'

Pearl snorted.

'That,' she said, 'wis jist people. This wis animals. This wis money. Community. This wis people losing everything they'd ever had. Everything their families had built over generations. I'll say it again, missy. That sickness wis the worst time we've ever seen here.'

'And Gerald Hodgson?'

'Well,' Pearl said, 'he blew the whistle, did he no? He wis wan o the folk they hired tae dae their dirty work. The government. He wis wan o the guys they hired tae kill the flocks. He saw it, how bad it was. How traumatic fer those animals. How traumatic fer the farmers. An he did the right thing. He protested. He tried to pit a stop tae it.'

Evie placed a hand on Birch's arm. It felt dry, impossibly light.

'We're no saying,' she said, 'that whit he's done today is right. Are we, Pearl? We're no saying that at aw. But . . . when ye think whit he must have seen. The poor soul, he cannae be in his right mind. An it's been years now. Amazing it didnae happen sooner, if ye ask me.'

In spite of herself, Birch had begun to nod. She heard a noise behind her, in the shop doorway, and caught herself.

'But nothing justifies a shooting,' she began, Three Rivers looming once again in her mind. 'Nothing can—'

'DI Birch?'

Jamal Leigh was standing in the doorway, the huge gun still in his hands. Behind him, Birch could see a woman: petite, curly-haired, and also boxed into a flak vest. Birch flashed a smile at Evie and Pearl.

'Ladies,' she said, 'thank you for telling me all of that. It's really helped me get a sense of the context of this. I appreciate it.' She nodded towards Evie, who smiled at her. 'And thank you for the tea.'

Leigh moved aside, and Birch stepped back out into the bright June day. Rena Brooks held out a small hand.

'Rena,' she said, as they shook. 'You're Helen Birch.'

'That's me.'

'Gerald Hodgson told me about you.'

Birch glanced at Leigh, then looked back at Rena Brooks, whose face was kind, though furrowed with concern.

'You've spoken with him?'

'Yes,' Rena said. 'Once the perimeter was set up, I tried to start a dialogue with him. He was a way off – they wouldn't send me closer, so I had to use a loudhailer. It wasn't entirely satisfactory. But I got him to answer me, to shout back. I thought I might be able to get somewhere.'

'You thought?'

'I'm afraid it didn't go very well,' Rena said. 'Hodgson is adamant. He wants to talk to you.'

Birch felt her knees sag beneath her.

'No,' she heard herself saying. 'Surely he'll talk to you, won't he? If we keep trying? You're an expert in this stuff, and I'm—'

'He's decided he can trust you,' Rena said. Her voice was soothing – Birch could see how she'd be good at calming someone down. 'It's not ideal, I know, and I'm not sure why you've been chosen, but I'm glad he's latched on to someone. I'm hopeful that, when we get you to the scene, we can get some meaningful communication going.'

Birch hauled in a breath. Keep it together, Helen.

'I'm really not cut out for this. What if I mess up? Say the wrong thing? There's a child's life at stake here, and—'

Rena raised one hand towards Birch's, though she didn't make contact. Again, the effect was calming: Birch realised it was the kind of gesture you might make towards a growling dog.

'I'll be at the scene with you,' Rena said. 'I can talk you through things. Advise. We won't let you struggle with this on your own.'

Birch nodded, and tried to straighten up again. She imagined a scenario wherein Rena Brooks stood at her side, feeding the correct lines into her ear, while she repeated them into the loudhailer. Okay, yes, Birch thought. That, I could probably do.

'Tell me what you've observed about Hodgson so far,' she said. 'How does he seem?'

Rena dipped her head to one side.

'Agitated,' she said, 'but more frightened than anything. Out of his depth, I'd say.'

'Which makes him dangerous,' Leigh cut in. 'Nervy, that's the word I'd use. That's how he seemed to me. I think he's on edge, liable to make snap decisions.'

But Rena Brooks was frowning.

'I'm not so sure,' she said. 'He's made a lot of snap deci-sions today, and they've all backfired on him. They've all got him into deep water he doesn't know how to get out of. If anything, I think he'll be inclined to go more carefully now, take his time. Especially if that idea is put into his head. I think we can encourage him to calm down, slow down. I think he'd welcome that.'

Leigh was nodding, though she'd disagreed with him.

'That's why we're taking our time here,' he said, as though repeating something Rena had explained to him earlier. 'We haven't rushed you along to the scene. We need to make sure you're ready, and you're properly supported.'

Birch realised her face must be a picture, because Rena reached out again, and this time squeezed her arm.

'You're going to be okay,' she said, 'I promise. You can follow my lead the whole way.'

Leigh was still nodding.

'We'll get you kitted out, of course,' he said, knocking on his flak vest with one knuckle, 'and we'll wait for your DCI to arrive. He'll come with us up to Seefew.'

Birch blinked. She'd temporarily forgotten about McLeod. She tried to imagine him standing in the middle of a sheep pasture, and found she couldn't. But the idea of her boss coming along with her *was* comforting, she realised.

'He should be here any minute,' she said, looking out over the green and the roofs of the many police vehicles towards the road, as though by doing so she could make her boss and his sleek, slate-grey Insignia appear. 'He can't have set off long after me.'

Rena smiled.

'Don't worry,' she said, 'like I said, we're taking it slow. The calmer everything looks to Hodgson, the less erratic he'll be.

And the better chance we have of bringing Elise out of that ruin alive.'

Birch pushed her shoulders back. Yes, she thought. This is about her. Elise. This isn't about you. You can do this. You *will* do this. You'll do it for her.

'Right,' she said. 'Right. So, where do I get my flak vest from?'

HOUR TWELVE

TRANSCRIPT: initial contact with suspect, Gerald Hodgson
Hostage & Crisis Negotiator: Rena Brooks
Location: Seefew, Bowmont Valley, Scottish Borders
(map co-ordinates 55.466802, -2.318763)
Date & Time: 4 June 16:23

RENA BROOKS: Mr Hodgson, my name is Rena Brooks. Can you hear me okay? If you can hear me, then do something to let me know.

GERALD HODGSON: Who are you?

RB: My name is Rena Brooks, Mr Hodgson. Rena.

GH: I've said I won't talk. Not to you.

RB: I just want to speak for a minute, and check you're doing okay, Mr Hodgson. Gerald? Or Gerry, can I call you Gerry?

GH: You needn't call me anything, I'm not talking to you.

RB: Not to me, not talking to me? Who *would* you like to speak to, Gerry?

GH: I spoke to her on the phone before. Helen Birch.

RB: Helen Birch is on her way here, Gerry, but she's coming from Edinburgh. It's going to take her a little while to get here. Will you speak to me in the meantime?

GH: How come you're here and she's not?

RB: I'm sorry, I didn't catch that, can you say again?

GH: I said how come you're here, and she's not?

RB: Helen's driving here, but I came in one of the helicopters, so I got here first. You sound quite tired, Gerry, are you?

GH: I told her I wanted rid of the damn helicopter and now you people bring more of them here.

RB: I'm sorry about that, I didn't know you'd told Helen you wanted rid of the helicopters. They're just a necessary evil, I'm afraid. I wanted to get here and see if we could sort this out quickly. Can you tell me how you're doing over there?

GH: I'm not telling you anything. I'm not talking to you, I don't know you.

RB: You don't know me, no. Do you know Helen Birch, Gerry?

GH: Go away. Until she gets here I'm not saying another damn thing.

HOUR THIRTEEN

Birch scrolled through the transcript on an iPad Rena had handed her. The light was dim in the back of the police Land Rover, and the vehicle jostled on the twisty road. She had to clutch the screen with both hands. She could feel the sandwich she'd eaten at the rendezvous site – solid from the shop's overly cold fridge – coagulating in her stomach. Beside her, she could tell DCI McLeod was reading over her shoulder.

'I see what you mean about *didn't go very well*,' he said.

If Rena was offended, her face didn't show it.

'It wasn't the best start,' she said, 'but I wasn't especially surprised. When the person in crisis has identified a specific person to contact, it's pretty standard for them to be angry when someone other than that person tries to take over. You'll see I didn't push it – it was fairly obvious Hodgson wasn't going to budge.'

Birch was still staring down at the words on the screen. Her vision swam, making the lines fuzzy.

'I can see you doing things here,' she said, not looking up. 'I can see you communicating in a particular way. Always ending with a question, for example. Is that something I ought to be doing?'

Rena tilted her head to one side.

'I always try to keep them taking turns in the conversation,' she said. 'It's something we're trained to do, especially with people in suicidal crisis. If you can make them talk back, you're keeping them alive. Questions are a good way to keep the conversation flowing. But I didn't have a lot to go on, having only just arrived, and with this being our first interaction. The more you know about someone, the more sophisticated the questions you can ask.'

Birch was nodding, still looking at the screen. She didn't want to pull her gaze away, look out and see the progress they were making along the narrow road up the Bowmont Valley. She didn't want to know how close they were to the scene.

'What else should I know?'

There was a pause before Rena replied.

'It's tricky,' she said, 'to give specific pointers, because every situation is different. Obviously there's no magic bullet. But, a few small things. Try not to use the word *talk*. It'll be the word you really, really want to use – talk to me, I just want to talk to you, can we talk, etc. – but you should try not to. You'll see in the transcript I only ever use *talk* when I'm repeating him saying it. Otherwise I always say *speak*. I don't know why, but people see talking as trivial, whereas speaking carries more gravitas. They like to think they're being spoken to, not talked to.'

'Got it,' Birch said. 'No talking.'

'Obviously I don't have much to go on from that quick exchange,' Rena went on, gesturing at the iPad screen, 'but I suspect Hodgson is also not the type of person to be won over by expressions of concern or care. Telling him you care about him, you care about what happens to him – I don't think that's going to wash with him. He's dealt with the police before, and it landed him in prison. He knows from experience that the police won't handle him with care. If you try that line, I suspect he'll throw it back at you. He won't believe it.'

'What about the girl?' McLeod asked. 'Surely he'll believe we care about her well-being?'

'That's a bit of an unknown quantity,' Rena said. 'At the moment, I'm not sure how *he* feels about her, so it's hard to know how to play things. This is why I'll be next to you, Helen.' Rena turned towards Birch. 'As you talk with him, and things develop, I'll be better able to advise on how to proceed.'

'Okay,' Birch said. She risked glancing up at Rena, who was smiling at her. Birch found she couldn't smile back. Her teeth were set against one another, her jaw stiff.

'One thing I would say,' Rena went on, 'is, it's a good idea to humanise the little girl as much as you can. Call her by her name, say Elise, wee Elise, little Elise. But humanise him, too. Hodgson. No matter what he's done, he's a human being with feelings and fears. And there are outcomes he's hoping for from this situation. He's been up in that pasture a good while now, and he's had time to think. He'll be going over possible scenarios – the worst of which is probably his own death – in his mind. But he'll know there are options other than that, there are various ways this could play out. What we'll try to do is get him to reveal some of the things he expects to have happen, if not the things he wants.'

McLeod sniffed.

'We have to care,' he said, 'what this man wants?'

'We have to find out,' Rena said, 'because his expectations could inform the way we react. A man who's certain that he'll be shot before the negotiation is out has the capacity to be more reckless, more ruthless, than a man who thinks he might be able to strike a deal, or de-escalate things. I feel strongly that Hodgson is the latter – he's a clever man.'

'Not that clever,' McLeod said. 'He's trapped in a blind alley in the middle of nowhere and surrounded by police.'

Rena was smiling again, though her expression had changed from one of reassurance to one of mild amusement.

'The thing is,' she said, 'I don't think Hodgson intended to escape, to disappear. Certainly not once he took Elise. I think he's probably always known that there'd be a reckoning. He's actually chosen a spot that's very convenient for him, and very inconvenient for us. I don't think he's run down a blind alley at all. I think he's stepped into a spotlight. I think he wants an opportunity to say his piece. Air his grievances.'

'I just don't know why me,' Birch said. The Land Rover hit a pothole, and her stomach lurched. She thought for a terrible half-second that she might be sick all over McLeod. 'I just don't get what I have to do with all this.'

'Now I've met you,' Rena said, 'I'm not at all surprised that you're the person Hodgson chose. You're straight-talking, but you're not aggressive. You seem fair-minded, and you're a young, modern sort of police officer. You're probably quite different to the officers Hodgson dealt with twenty years ago, when he was arrested.'

'That's kind of you,' Birch said. She didn't dare look at McLeod to see what he made of this appraisal of her character. 'But Hodgson has never met me. How can he know any of that?'

'You'd be surprised by what we can intuit about someone just from seeing a photograph of them,' Rena replied. 'Hodgson might have seen your photo online, and thought you looked like the right sort of person. He wouldn't want to talk to a man – he spent five years in a men's prison. He's seen the worst of what men can be like. And he's likely chosen you because he thinks you'll be sympathetic towards him. We know he's aware that your brother is in jail. There might be something about his experience inside that he wants to talk about, and he thinks you're better equipped to understand, because of Charlie.'

Birch thought of her brother, grinning at her across the Visit Room table that morning – and again she was struck by how long ago that seemed, though it was only a handful of hours.

'Bloody Charlie,' she muttered.

'But I'm getting ahead of myself,' Rena was saying. 'All will become clear, I'm sure, once you get him talking.'

'Or speaking,' Birch said.

Rena laughed.

'Speaking,' she said, 'yes. Very good.'

She held her hand out for the iPad, and Birch passed it over. Now she had no choice but to look out of the window and see where they were going. It was a beautiful evening in the Bowmont Valley: the light had begun to lengthen, and it hung dappled and gold in the trees. The Land Rover passed tall hedges which gave way occasionally to gateways and farm tracks. Birch caught glimpses of fields tufted with grazing sheep, and every so often, the Bowmont Water. As the road climbed higher, the hedges fell away: they were properly in the hills now, only a few scant drystone walls delineating the land. Now she could see gorse still in flower on the higher ground, yellow flags of ragwort and patches of hard rushes in the places where the road curled nearer to the river. She caught the distant smell of a barbecue. Even here, it was a perfect June evening.

The Land Rover came to a sharp turn in the road, at the apex of which was a pale, stony track that forked upwards. The vehicle slowed. Birch glanced behind to see the convoy of others behind it slow, too: police fleet filling the road for what looked like a quarter of a mile. Now the engine was idling, she could hear the steady beat of a helicopter somewhere over-head. They were close, she realised. She was about to meet Gerald Hodgson for the first time.

There was yet another cordon at the end of the track, manned by uniforms. The convoy was quickly waved through, and the Land Rover left the road, beginning its shaky ascent on the pale dirt track.

'We'll try to get Hodgson on the phone,' Rena said, fixing Birch with a level look. 'That'll make for a much easier discussion. Once you're on with him, you should always try to sound engaged. Use minimal encouragers as he talks – those little mm-hmms and yeahs and okays. You probably do this naturally when you're on the phone to someone, so just be yourself. Don't overdo it, just make sure he knows you're listening.'

Birch bit her lip.

'Nudge me if I don't,' she said. 'I have this bad habit, on the phone, of nodding, even though the person can't see me.'

Rena raised an eyebrow.

'Okay,' she said, 'I'll nudge you.'

'Anything else?' Birch pressed her palms together, and found they were slippery. 'Anything at all, really. I feel clueless, going into this.'

'Well,' Rena replied, 'rather than asking him outright how he feels, try telling him. I know that seems strange, but it's something we call emotional labelling, and if you can get it right, it gives the person you're talking to a sense that you're able to empathise with them. So don't say *are you angry*, say *you sound angry*. Make sense?'

'Yes,' Birch said. 'I just hope I can hold all this in my head.'

'The key thing,' Rena said, 'is to take your time, and be understanding. Try to understand where he's coming from, really try. If you can't understand what he's saying, or how he's feeling, then say that. Ask him to tell you more. Keep him talking. And remember, I'll be right there with you.'

'Good,' Birch said. To her surprise, she felt DCI McLeod lean over and carefully pat her knee.

'I have every confidence in you, Birch,' he said. 'You've been in much scarier situations than this before. You know how to handle yourself.'

Birch grimaced. She couldn't help it. She knew he was referring to Three Rivers, her arrival on the scene, that bathroom—

'Due respect, sir,' she said, 'I think only I can be the judge of how scary I find something. And right now I feel more scared than I ever have, if I'm honest.'

'That's because you're not there yet,' McLeod said. 'The unknown, and all that. We'll arrive in a minute, we'll get you set up, and you'll see the lie of the land. Then you'll feel more in control, I have no doubt.'

You can't possibly know that, Birch wanted to say, but instead, she gave her boss a watery smile. He was just trying to help.

'I think DCI McLeod has a point,' Rena said. 'You'll see the perimeter we've got set up around the house. The ruin. Hodgson feels a long way off. He doesn't feel especially threatening at that distance.'

'He has a shotgun,' Birch said. She felt stupid as soon as she'd finished the sentence, stating the obvious like that.

'Yes,' McLeod said, 'but the evidence suggests he's a bad shot at any distance. No one from the showfield was fatally hit.'

'That might only tell us he didn't intend to kill anyone there,' Birch replied. 'We know from his social media posts that he's a poacher. That suggests he can hit a moving target at long range. And he's already killed one person today, possibly two. Is there any update on Elise's dad?'

McLeod shook his head.

'No change,' he said. 'All I know is, he's in surgery. We'll know more when he gets out.'

'I don't think you need worry,' Rena said, 'about being shot. I mean, you're right to be cautious, but . . . you're Hodgson's chosen contact. He's unlikely to want to take you out of the equation.'

'Unless I really piss him off,' Birch said. She'd tried to say it as a joke, but the words came out hard and spitty. 'Besides, I'm not just worried about me. I'm worried about everyone. Elise, all of you, everyone here. I don't want to see anyone shot. I've seen enough of that for one lifetime.'

For the first time, Rena's face looked less than calm. Birch watched as she exchanged a glance with McLeod, just for a second, that said, *is this woman up to the job?* But the look was gone as soon as it had appeared.

'No one's getting shot,' Rena said. 'No one else. Not if I have anything to do with it.'

The dirt track had run out: Birch felt the terrain under the Land Rover's wheels change. Now they were rolling over grass. They'd arrived at the pasture.

'Here we are,' Rena said. 'Just check your vest is secure, before you get out.'

Birch patted herself down. Leigh's team had given her a plain black sweatshirt to go underneath the vest: it was too big, but she was glad to have an extra layer over the filmy fabric of her blouse. The Kevlar vest was uncomfortable, but reassuring. Birch tapped on it once, twice, as though knocking on wood. The Land Rover came to a stop.

'Here we go,' said McLeod.

Birch stepped down on to the soft grass, and got her first look at the scene. The Seefew pasture was beautiful, and also bleak. The ruined cottage in the bottom of the pasture's bowl only served to make the hills around it look higher, their sides painted orange and gold by the evening light. She could see the dark figures of firearms personnel camped on high ground at various positions on those slopes, each team of two officers crouched around a single gun which was mounted and trained on Hodgson's position. The noise of helicopters was a maddening pulse overhead: Birch could see two choppers with police markings making wide circles over the pasture. But most of her colleagues had formed a crescent-shaped perimeter around one side of the cottage: they were clustered there, slightly uphill from Hodgson, and she could tell Leigh's team had picked this vantage point carefully. Leigh appeared at her side now, having climbed out of the Land Rover behind her own.

'So,' he said, 'you see the set-up.'

Birch nodded.

'We're going to need light soon,' Leigh said. 'While you and Rena make contact, we're going to work on erecting some floodlights.'

'You think it'll take that long?' Birch asked. 'You think we'll be here into the night?'

Leigh looked at Rena.

'Could be,' she said. 'It really all depends on how this goes.'

Birch swallowed. Her mouth was dry, and the nausea she'd felt on the drive up showed no signs of abating.

'No pressure,' she said.

Rena led her to the front of the gaggle of officers, where a perimeter line had been taped to plastic stakes pushed into the ground. Standing with that tape brushing the knees of her jeans, Birch could look out over the expanse of grass that stretched between her and Hodgson's cover. McLeod had been right: it did help to see it, to take in the scale of things. Her breath was fast, her hands still slick with sweat, but Birch tried to focus on the scene in front of her. She noticed now that Hodgson's Land Rover was parked on the other side of the ruin, only its front fender visible at the building's corner. She could see that the ruin had no roof, and that old timbers stuck up out of it at odd angles. Though a slab of rotten wood – possibly the building's original door – had been propped across the doorway, the windows were devoid of glass, the frames gone: all that remained were holes in the crumbling walls, like eye sockets in a rotten skull.

Someone had handed Rena a police loudhailer. She nudged Birch.

'Are you ready?' she asked.

Birch pulled in a long breath, and smelled sheep's wool, sheep shit, dry earth.

'Ready as I'll ever be,' she replied.

Rena nodded, and then lifted the loudhailer.

'Gerry,' she said, 'it's Rena again, from before. I'm happy to say that Helen Birch is here with me now, and she'd like to speak to you.'

Birch gave her head a little shake: it was weird, hearing Rena's regular voice beside her, but also the distorted crackle of a voice that came out of the loudhailer. Rena kept the mouthpiece to her lips, and Birch felt the entire cohort of officers hold their breath. She could see that the sun had moved out of the ruin: the inside of the building was in shade. There was no movement in the windows, and no sound. Nothing to suggest that anyone was inside.

Birch expected Rena to call Hodgson's name again, but instead, she lowered the loudhailer and held it out.

'I guess he already told me he wouldn't speak to me,' she said. 'Better that you give it a try.'

Birch put out her hands, and saw they were shaking. Come on, she thought. Pull yourself together. She took the loud-hailer, surprised at the weight of it, and held it up, bringing the mouthpiece close to her face.

'Gerry?' she said. The two syllables echoed back and forth off the sides of the hills. 'Gerry, it's Detective Inspector Birch. It's Helen. We spoke on the phone this afternoon.'

Once again, the gathering of officers waited. Once again, there was no answer. No movement in the windows of the ruined house.

'You asked for me,' Birch said, 'and now I'm here. I've come to speak to you, like you wanted.'

'He probably doesn't like this particular set-up,' Rena hissed. She was whispering, though Hodgson could never have heard her, fifty yards or so from the perimeter and behind a wall. 'I sure as hell hate talking through that godforsaken thing.' Rena gestured at the loudhailer. 'His phone seems to be off, we've tried it. But ask him if he'll turn it on to speak to you. Speak, remember.'

Birch nodded, and raised the mouthpiece once again.

'Look,' she said, 'this feels wrong, shouting at you like this. Can we speak on the phone? Can you turn your phone on, Gerry, so I can call you?'

Behind her, Birch was vaguely aware that Leigh was hold-ing a mobile phone, ready for her to use if Hodgson acqui-esced. But her attention was caught by a brief movement in one of the ruin's windows: just the slightest pale flash. Was it a face, risking a look at her?

'It's good to see you're still here,' Birch said. 'I thought for a minute I was stood here talking to myself.'

She was surprised at how well the loudhailer was able to convey the warmth she'd pushed into the sentence. Rena was nodding: good. Still, once the echoes – *talking to myself, myself, myself* – had faded, there came no reply.

Birch dropped the mouthpiece.

'What now?' she whispered to Rena. She realised the whispering was instinctive, not logical. But Rena was holding up one index finger.

'Wait,' she said. 'Just give him a moment. Slow and steady, remember.'

Behind her, Birch heard the familiar sound of DCI McLeod huffing air. Leigh waved a hand to catch her attention, and when she looked round she could see he'd dialled Hodgson's number. The line hadn't connected: the phone was still off. Birch raised the mouthpiece again.

'Come on, Gerry,' she said. 'Can you turn your phone on for me?'

This time, there was an answer: one so clear that Birch jumped a little, making her teeth clatter together.

'No,' Hodgson yelled. Once again, his face was visible in the window, just for a second. 'I can't.'

'Why not?' Birch called. 'You surely can't enjoy being bellowed at through this thing?'

There was a pause.

'No,' Hodgson shouted again. 'The fucking phone's run out of battery.'

Birch looked at Rena.

'But he wants to speak?' she whispered.

'But,' Birch repeated into the loudhailer, 'you do want to speak to me, is that right?'

Again, there was a pause.

'Not like this,' Hodgson called. 'Only in person.'

'I don't know what you mean, Gerry.'

This time, the answer was fast.

'I mean what I bloody said – in person. I mean put that bloody bullhorn down and walk over here and talk to me. Can you do that, DI Birch?'

Birch dropped the mouthpiece and looked at Rena, but Rena wasn't looking back. She'd turned to look at Leigh, and Birch followed her gaze. McLeod had come to stand at Leigh's elbow, and both men were wearing the same expression. Birch couldn't help but articulate it, since no one else seemed able to.

'Well,' she said, 'that's a whole new ball game, isn't it?'

HOUR FOURTEEN

'I'll say it again.' McLeod was shouting now: Birch was pretty sure Gerald Hodgson would be able to hear him. 'I will *not* jeopardise the safety of one of my officers. Not when there are other options.'

Jamal Leigh's mouth was a hard line.

'And *I'll* say again,' he said, 'that I don't think there *are* other options. Not right now. Not the ones you're talking about.'

'I don't understand,' McLeod replied, 'why you can't just surround the house. There are dozens of you, all armed – he's no match for you.'

'There are several possible outcomes to that scenario,' Leigh said, keeping his voice level. 'And sure, one of them is that Hodgson realises he's beat, and comes quietly. We take him in, we recover his hostage, and we all go home happy.'

'Right,' McLeod said.

'But personally,' Leigh went on, 'I think it's far more likely that Hodgson will feel trapped, and turn the gun on the little girl.'

'I don't believe he'd shoot a child.' McLeod turned to Rena. 'Do you think he's capable of that?'

Rena was quiet for a moment, thinking.

'There's a difference,' she said, 'between whether he's capable of shooting a child and whether he would. I fully believe he's capable of it – he's already shot both of her parents at close range, apparently without hesitation. Whether or not he *would*, though – that's the unknown factor.'

'Exactly,' Leigh said. 'We can't gamble a little girl's life on the idea that he wouldn't be able to bring himself to go through with such an action. What's more, he could also turn the gun on himself. That's another possible outcome – a likely one, I think.'

McLeod made a noise of exasperation. Birch knew him well enough to know that he wanted to say *so what?*, but he also realised he couldn't.

'And we absolutely do not want a fatality outcome, here,' Leigh went. 'It doesn't matter who.'

McLeod rallied.

'My point exactly,' he said. His voice was getting louder again. 'If you don't want a fatality outcome, how can you justify sending an unarmed officer into that building alone?'

'I haven't said that we should definitely do that,' Leigh replied. 'I just think it's the best option we have.'

Birch looked at Rena. She was watching the exchange carefully, her head tilted to one side. Also watching was Duty Inspector Matthew Dacre, who'd arrived further back in the convoy. He'd introduced himself to Birch after she'd stepped back from the initial exchange with Hodgson at the perimeter, and since then, he hadn't spoken at all. Now, he cleared his throat.

'Look,' Dacre said, pausing while the two senior officers turned to look at him. 'I realise I don't know anything about this, but . . . couldn't we just do nothing? Starve him out, as it were? It's going to get dark and cold in there. He's going to get hungry. Can't we just wait, and see if he gives himself up?'

'That is an option,' Leigh said, 'yes. But Rena isn't keen on it, and I tend to listen to what Rena has to say.'

'It's the little girl,' Rena said. 'We don't think Hodgson intended to take a hostage, so he doesn't see her as a bargaining tool. We can argue all night about whether or not he'd be willing to shoot her, but I'm fairly sure he's not equipped to take good care of her, even if he wanted to. We don't know what she's wearing, but I suspect she's not kitted out for a night in the open. On the phone, Hodgson told DI Birch that he hadn't eaten and didn't want to eat. That's fine, but he's a grown man. Elise is three. She needs to eat and drink and be kept warm. She's been with him since early this morning, so I suspect she's dehydrated already. We also haven't ruled out the possibility that she might be in some way hurt, and in need of medical attention. I'm keen for us to be patient, and not rush – but at the same time, we do need to get her out of there. She's very vulnerable.'

'Okay,' Dacre replied, stepping back a little as though hoping to disappear. 'Fair points. I just thought I'd ask.'

'It's also just good to be talking,' Rena went on. 'I'm worried that we haven't been in touch with Hodgson enough, thus far. We still don't know much about what he's thinking. He's been here hours already. In an ideal world, we'd have been talking to him this whole time.'

Birch looked at McLeod.

'Sir.' There was a tremor in her voice. That was annoying: it undermined what she wanted to say. 'I'd like to do it. I'd like to go in and talk to him.'

McLeod closed his eyes.

'Birch,' he said.

'Really,' she said. 'I want to. I think it's the best option, as Jamal says. Rena says we need to be talking to him, and I agree. Plus, if I went in then I could immediately assess the situation with Elise. See how she is, if she's hurt, what she needs. I could take some food and water in for her. Rena thinks it's unlikely Hodgson will shoot me, and even if he does' – she paused to knock on the Kevlar vest again, as she had earlier – 'I'm wearing this. I'm better protected than Elise is.'

McLeod had opened his eyes again, and was pointing at Leigh.

'No fatality outcome, he just said. I don't mean to be indelicate, Birch, but what if he shot you in the head?'

Birch gritted her teeth.

'Well, then I guess I'd die, sir. But there's a difference between a civilian fatality and me, isn't there?'

She looked at Leigh for support.

'I mean, technically,' he replied, though she could tell the question made him uneasy. 'But no one wants that. I promise, no one wants that. We're really between a rock and a hard place, here.'

'And running low on options,' Birch said. 'Options that all suck, as we've established. But this one, I think, sucks the least.'

'To coin a phrase,' McLeod said. His tone was bitter. He could tell he'd been overruled. 'I am very, very unhappy about this state of affairs, I just want to make that known.'

Yeah, Birch thought, we've established that.

'The question is,' she said, addressing the group as a whole now, 'do you think I'm up to it?'

Rena was nodding before she'd even completed the question.

'In my opinion,' she said, 'if anyone's going in, it has to be you. I'd like to be able to talk to you through an earpiece, so we can—'

'I doubt Hodgson will allow that,' Leigh said. 'He'll clock an earpiece straight away, and that could be enough to anger him. Make him do something stupid.'

There was a moment of quiet.

'We do want him calm,' Rena said. 'The calmer the better.'

Leigh looked at Birch, and straightened up.

'Personally,' he said, 'I think this can work. Hodgson has chosen you, he wants to talk to you. Keeping that talking going is all you'd have to do.'

Birch attempted a smile.

'Speaking,' she said, 'not talking.'

Leigh smiled.

'Right. Speaking.'

Birch turned to look at McLeod. He was rocking back on his heels, a sure sign of vexation. She pasted on a smile, trying to show confidence she didn't really feel.

'You reckon I'm up for it, guv?'

McLeod fixed her with a look.

'Helen,' he said, 'I have complete and utter faith in your abilities. You're a damn fine officer, and if I may say so, highly adept at getting just about anything you want. I can't think of a better person to send in and talk to a raving madman.' He nodded at Rena. 'Present company excepted,' he added.

Rena wore the same amused expression Birch had seen on the way up the track in the Land Rover. She gave a little bow of the head.

'Of course,' she said.

'My reservations,' McLeod went on, 'are nothing to do with you, and everything to do with him. Hodgson. How he might react.'

Birch's pasted-on smile had become a real one: McLeod barely praised anyone. She was sure she'd annoyed him almost to the point of him transferring her to another station on more than one occasion. She regularly disagreed with him, and he knew it – and yet, it was gratifying to hear him call her a damn fine officer. In front of people, no less.

'I know, sir,' she said.

Around them, the light changed, like the flick of a switch. Birch turned back towards the perimeter, to see the floodlights Leigh had mentioned being illuminated, one by one. Although there was still daylight – the hilltops around them were bathed in evening sun – the pasture seemed to grow darker as each light was turned on. The hum of the generators matched the pitch of the helicopters, still circling in the sky overhead.

Rena shook Birch's arm.

'There's movement,' she said, 'in the ruin.'

Leigh was already pushing his way back to the perimeter, and Birch followed, with Rena at her elbow and McLeod not far behind. The ruined walls of the cottage looked sharper, spotlit by the floodlights. Birch could see more clearly now the ragged shards of the roof, the black mouths of the windows, the gaps between the stones. Inside, Hodgson was shouting.

'What's he saying?' McLeod was right behind Birch: his voice in her ear made her jump.

'He says, he didn't ask for any light,' Rena replied.

Yes, Birch could hear it now, over all the background noise – now that Rena had made sense of the sound.

'I didn't say I wanted light!' Hodgson yelled. 'I didn't ask for light!'

Birch cast around for the loudhailer. Leigh, realising what she was looking for, darted away and returned with it, passing it to her over the heads of Rena and McLeod.

'Careful,' Rena said, as Birch lifted the mouthpiece. 'He sounds angry.'

'Gerry,' Birch said, 'It's Helen Birch again. I'm going to come in and speak to you in a sec. We're just getting things ready.'

Hodgson was quiet for a moment, as though absorbing what she'd said.

'What do you need those damn lights for?' he called.

Birch rolled her eyes.

'It's getting dark, Gerry,' she said. 'Soon, you won't be able to see your hand in front of your face in there.'

'I don't care,' came the reply. 'I'd rather have it that way. Better than those lights.'

'Well frankly,' Birch said, 'I have to disagree.'

Beside her, Rena sucked air through her teeth. Birch ignored it.

'I'm going to have to walk across half a pasture to get to you,' she went on, 'and I don't want to fall over and break my ankle because I can't see where I'm going.'

'Come now, then,' Hodgson shot back. 'Turn those lights off and come now; there's still daylight.'

'I need to get ready first, Gerry.'

There was another pause.

'Get what ready? What do you need to get ready?'

'Well,' Birch said, 'I won't be armed, but my team want to make sure I've got a radio, and—'

'No,' Hodgson yelled. 'No radio.'

'Gerry—'

'No radio,' he said again. 'Just you. No back-up, no radio, no nothing. Just you. I just want to talk to *you*. And turn those damn lights off, I said.'

'He's really not happy,' Rena whispered.

I know that, Birch thought.

'How about a compromise?' she said, into the loudhailer. 'How about we turn off *some* of these lights, but leave some on so I can get down to you in one piece?'

Again, Hodgson was quiet.

'We shouldn't compromise with *him*,' McLeod muttered, 'he should compromise with *us*.'

'One light,' Hodgson shouted. 'You can leave one light on. I want the rest turned off. And no radio, DI Birch. Just you, on your own. No communication.'

Birch looked at Leigh, who nodded.

'Okay,' she said, into the mouthpiece. 'We can do that.'

No answer came, and Birch opened her mouth to speak again. But then Hodgson shouted something else that she didn't catch.

'Oh great,' McLeod said. 'This again.'

Birch frowned.

'What did he say?'

'He asked,' McLeod said, 'about the helicopters.'

Birch lifted the loudhailer once again.

'Sorry, Gerry,' she said, 'I didn't catch what you said then. What about the helicopters?'

'I asked,' Hodgson yelled back, 'why they're still up there. You said you'd try and get rid of them, DI Birch.'

Again, Birch looked at Leigh.

'He does have a point,' she said.

'No,' Leigh replied, firmly. 'We need eyes up there. Hodgson has total cover from every other angle – we need to be able to see him from somewhere.'

Birch squinted skywards. The helicopters swam back and forth in the same repeating pattern: one made a tight circle, while the other pulled back and disappeared behind the hills. Then they switched places: one always overhead, the other always hanging back.

'Okay,' she said, still watching the insect-like machines in the sky, 'but . . . why are there two?'

'I'm sorry?'

She looked back down at Leigh's face.

'Why do we need both? I'm not on his side or anything, it's just a genuine question. Is it necessary to have two up there, making double the noise and presumably using twice the fuel?' She pointed up at the retreating chopper, heading off to do its sweep of the next valley. 'And they're flying like that because they're avoiding each other, aren't they? Giving each other room. Is it necessary?'

Leigh blinked. He was quiet for a moment, thinking.

'You have a point.'

Behind them, McLeod made a noise of exasperation.

'Oh come on,' he said, 'we're surely not going to start making tactical decisions based on what that man has decided he wants?'

'Actually,' Rena said, 'we are. He's asked for the lights to go out, so we're putting the lights out. If we ground one of the helicopters, that's another compromise. We're showing we're capable of listening, that our negotiator isn't just saying empty words. These are tangible things that will make him feel understood – they could make him more likely to co-operate.'

'Plus,' Leigh said, 'DI Birch is right. We don't necessarily need two choppers in the air just because that's what we were sent. One, yes, because we can't see Hodgson any other way. But the other we can bring down, I agree.'

Birch gestured with the loudhailer.

'I can tell him?' she said. 'You're sure?'

Leigh nodded.

'I'll get the team on to it.'

Behind them, McLeod sighed. Birch ignored him, and lifted the mouthpiece again.

'Sorry for the wait there, Gerry,' she said. 'We can't ground both the choppers, but we can take one of them out of the equation. Another compromise, okay?'

There was a pause, and then Hodgson shouted, 'Do it quickly, would you?'

'Fast as we can, I promise.'

'And get yourself down here, if you're coming.'

'I will,' Birch said. 'I'll be with you shortly. I'll give you another shout on this thing before I set off down to the house, okay?'

She waited, listening to the thud of the choppers overhead. Hodgson didn't answer.

Eventually, it was McLeod who spoke.

'No radio,' he said, 'and no light.' He gestured at the closer of the two helicopters. 'We'll be able to see the top of your head, and hear absolutely nothing.'

'No,' Leigh replied, 'he said no radio. But if we put a wire on DI Birch here, then we'll be able to listen in to everything. We won't be able to talk, but we'll be able to listen, which is the more important thing, I think.'

Rena put a hand on Birch's arm.

'You have to try not to anger him,' she said. There was a sharpness in her voice that hadn't been there before. 'You shouldn't have answered back about the lights. Arguing with him isn't a good idea.'

Leigh had walked away, presumably to start the ball rolling with the lights, the helicopter, food and water, a microphone. Birch shrugged, unable to help herself.

'I didn't think I was arguing,' she said, 'I thought I was bargaining with him. That's a bit different, isn't it?'

'We're going to be pretty much blind, Birch,' McLeod said. 'It's going to get dark out here. Not just Edinburgh dark

– countryside dark. I mean *dark*. Without those lights we won't be able to see a damn thing.'

'There'll be one light,' Birch replied. 'He said one light could stay on.'

'Well, let's hope it's enough,' McLeod snapped. 'Once you're in there, we'll need to figure out how we're going to extract you. I'm not overly keen on the idea of sending armed officers down there in almost total darkness.'

'My hope is,' Birch said, 'that an extraction won't be necessary.'

McLeod scoffed.

'So you're going to get him to walk out of there, hands up?'

'Isn't that the plan?'

Beside them, Rena was wincing.

'This isn't great,' she said. 'I'm sure I don't need to tell you, this isn't great. Hodgson has far too much control, and we have none. We don't have a coherent approach up here. We don't even have a clear chain of command. You can talk about extraction, DCI McLeod, but who's going to authorise it? Are you better placed, because of your rank, than a specialist firearms officer with years of experience in this sort of scenario? I don't know the answer – I don't think any of us do. But I can tell you right now, we're mishandling this. None of what has happened so far is how this is supposed to go.'

Birch looked at McLeod, who didn't speak. She realised that the rush of confidence she'd felt earlier had ebbed away again, and she was back to feeling as nauseous and uncertain as she had in the Land Rover. She couldn't think of any coherent way to respond to what Rena had said, but she felt the truth of it sink through her, all the way to her bones. She thought of Anjan telling her on the phone that she wasn't trained for something like this, and her agreeing. She thought of how naïve she'd been, only a few hours ago, assuming that she might be allowed to just stand to one side and serve teas, hold coats, be useful. She realised she'd been assuming, right up until the moment Rena stopped speaking, that she'd get home tonight and sleep in her own bed. Now they were talking about darkness, about being here for many more hours. None of us have eaten properly, she wanted to point out. None of us have had a proper break. She recognised the ghost of her mother in these thoughts, and then found herself wishing, irrationally, that her mother were there on the pasture with them. If anyone could figure this out, Birch thought, then she surely could. No doubt by marching down to the ruin and dragging Hodgson out by his collar. That particular method had always worked when extracting an underage Charlie from inappropriate house parties.

'DI Birch.' Leigh was back at her side. She flinched at the sound of his voice, and turned to find him holding an empty flak vest in his hands. 'If you can swap this out,' he said, 'for the one you're wearing, then we'll test to check the mic is working. It should be.'

Birch shook her head slightly, as though waking from a dream.

'Sorry,' she said, as though she'd been speaking the vision of her mother and Hodgson aloud to the assembled group. 'Okay, give me a sec.'

Rena reached out to help with the fastenings. It felt like a peace offering, though Birch could feel the other woman's anxiety fizzing off her, like static.

'I hope this works,' Rena said, quietly, as the vest peeled away from Birch's sweatshirt like a shell pulled off a snail. 'I really hope this works.'

Birch manoeuvred the new, identical vest on.

'Where's the mic?' she asked. 'Where should I aim my voice?'

Leigh pressed his index finger to a tiny open point, almost invisible in the black fabric.

'You don't need to aim anywhere,' he said, 'it'll pick you up just fine. If you turn your back on Hodgson, though, we'll struggle to hear him. Try to stay facing him at all times.'

'I won't be turning my back on the guy with the shotgun, I promise you.'

'Good.' Leigh stood back. 'Right, we just need to see if it's working.' Birch watched as he unclipped a radio pack from his belt. 'If you talk,' he said, holding it up, 'we should be able to receive you through this.'

'Okay,' Birch said, and the radio crackled. 'Testing, testing, one, two, three.'

The voice that came through was distorted by a whine of feedback.

'It'll be clearer,' Leigh said, 'once you're further away.'

'Let's hope,' McLeod muttered. Around them, the flood-lights began to go out, one at a time, each one making a sort of flashbulb noise. The natural light in the pasture seemed to flicker in response.

Dacre appeared behind Leigh. Wedged under his arm was a shrink-wrapped case: six bottles of water. His hands crack-led. Birch saw they were full of cereal bars.

'I don't know,' Dacre said, 'if a three-year-old will eat these, but . . .'

Rena cut in.

'She'll be starving by now,' she said. 'I'd guess she will.'

Dacre held out his hands towards Birch. For a moment, she just stared down at the clutch of cereal bars as though she couldn't quite place what they were. But then she shook herself, reached out. She tucked two bars in each of the back pockets of her jeans, and then another two in each of the front pockets. Only one remained.

'You lot can fight over the last one,' she said, wanting desperately to crack the brittle atmosphere that was developing between them all. No one laughed, but Dacre gave her a weak smile, and swung the water bottles out from under his arm.

'Good luck,' he said, holding them out to her.

Birch took the case of water, and pulled in a breath. She realised her pulse was rising: this was it.

'So,' she said, 'are we a go?'

Rena put a hand on her arm.

'If in doubt,' she said, 'listen to him. Let him speak. Don't rush it.'

Birch smiled, but she felt the smile fade as soon as it appeared.

'If I fuck up,' she said, 'I'm really, really sorry.'

Rena gave her arm a squeeze.

'You can do it,' she said. 'Like I say, don't rush. Easy does it. As long as little Elise isn't hurt, then we've got time.'

Leigh turned to Dacre.

'Matthew,' he said, 'this is your turf, your case. I want your blessing. Are we doing the right thing?'

Dacre's face contorted. Birch tried to imagine what he was thinking. Considering a career change, perhaps, or wishing he hadn't got out of bed that morning. You and me both, pal, she thought.

'It's really not my place—' Dacre began.

'Nonsense.' McLeod leaned over the smaller man. 'No matter what happens next, you know damn sure there's going to be an inquiry over this. I certainly don't want it said that I overruled the wishes of local officers – that anyone did. You know the terrain here. You've been dealing with this man since this morning. It's entirely your place.'

Poor guy, Birch thought.

'Well then,' Dacre replied, 'as I see it, this is the best way forward. We have to get the bairn out of there, soon as we can.'

Leigh nodded.

'I agree,' he said.

McLeod turned to Birch, and placed a hand on her shoulder. The pressure felt strange, through the hard surface of the vest.

'You know my thoughts,' he said, 'but I'm confident you can do this, Birch. Bring this one home for us, okay?'

'Yes, guv.'

'Good girl.'

Rena picked up the loudhailer, and handed the mouthpiece out to Birch.

'Good luck,' she said, and her voice sounded exactly the same way Dacre's had when he'd said it. Leaden. Tinged with fear.

Birch nodded, shook out her shoulders, and then took the mouthpiece in her free hand. For a moment, stood listening to the crackle of her own breath in the receiver. Then she spoke.

'Gerry, it's DI Birch again. I'm on my way down to you now, so don't be alarmed. I'll knock on the cottage door in just a few seconds, okay?'

This time, she didn't wait for an answer. She realised she was sick of the loudhailer, sick of standing beside the flimsy tape of the perimeter, waiting while nothing happened. Like Hodgson, she was sick of the helicopters' oppressive patrols overhead, sick of the milling of bodies and vehicles and opinions and worry. She felt what she realised Rena must feel: a genuine desire to sit face to face with Hodgson and just hash things out. That conversation stood between her and her car – still sandwiched, she remembered, by white vans on the Town Yetholm green – and the long drive home to her little house, where she imagined herself eating toast standing up at the kitchen worktop before falling into bed. Her whole body yawned towards that now, towards the chance to do those normal things. She handed the mouthpiece back to Rena, and swung one leg up over the perimeter tape.

She looked back at McLeod.

'If I die,' she said, 'which, I know – I'm just saying, if I do – please can you find my dad, and tell him . . . I don't know. Tell him I'm glad he came back.'

McLeod frowned at her.

'I will,' he said. 'But if you don't mind, DI Birch, I'd rather you didn't die on this occasion.' He smiled at her. 'The paperwork would be a bloody nightmare.'

Birch grinned back.

'Roger that,' she said. She swung the other leg up over the tape, shifted her hold on the case of water bottles, and turned her back on her colleagues. Focusing on her own feet, she picked her way through the scrubby grass, downhill, towards the ruin.

HOUR FIFTEEN

The ruin was surrounded by a rough oval of bare earth, where sheep had worried the ground with their hooves and pressed against the walls in bad weather. Birch could feel the bite of stones through the cardboard soles of her ballet flats, and wished, not for the first time that day, that she'd worn boots. She'd walked down the pasture in the beam of the single remaining floodlight, and as she neared the cottage, she watched her own huge shadow shudder and dwindle against its walls. Overhead, the choppers stirred and stirred the air: it had begun to feel cool, as the last direct sunlight pulled back from the peaks and everything began to turn blueish. Birch stopped about six feet from the ruined door, and looked back. Beyond the bright, wide-open eye of the light, she saw her colleagues as a cluster of dark figures with pale faces, all turned in her direction. She felt impossibly small amid the ring of hills, every human eye for miles and miles watching her, waiting.

'Gerry? I'm outside now. It's just me, and I'm unarmed. Can you move this door, and let me in?'

Birch's hands were shaking, and there was a shudder in her voice as she spoke. Every nerve in her body told her to turn and run, but she stood her ground as, inside the ruined walls, a scuffing started up. She squinted at the door, which she could now see was sort of wedged in the remains of its frame.

The wood crackled as it moved, and she saw more than one pale sliver fall away as Hodgson wrenched it aside. He was being careful: at no point did he move into the gap he'd made. All Birch could see were four white fingers, gripping the door at one side, then disappearing from view.

'Can you get through that?' Hodgson's voice sounded hoarse, tired – Rena was right, he was tired. Tell him *you seem tired*, Birch reminded herself. Don't ask him *are you tired?*

He'd opened a slim gap in the doorway, a little over a foot. Birch studied it for a moment. Let's not have *that* headline, she thought: crisis negotiation ruined by police officer wedged in door.

'I'll try,' she said, and stepped on to the ruin's threshold on trembling legs. She wanted to look back again, but knew it was a bad idea. The urge to run was too strong. If she looked back, she might obey it.

Instead, she pressed the palm of her free hand against the door, and then leaned into the wood with her chest. The flak vest scraped against the wood as she shimmied sideways into the gap.

'Just about,' she said, reaching that same hand out into the darkness inside the cottage, feeling around on the inner wall for something to get hold of. Something touched her and she jumped, flinching away and whacking her elbow against the stone.

'Shit,' she hissed. She almost let go of the case of water, but managed to hook it into the room through the narrow opening.

'Sorry.' It was Hodgson: Birch's eyes adjusted to the dim grey light inside the ruin. He was holding out his hand to her, to help her through the gap. 'Sorry,' he said again.

Birch took a moment to look at him. Amy had shown her pictures, back at the station, but the man who stood before her now was older, greyer, and his eyes looked dull. The hand she took hold of was as damp as her own, but it was cold. Hodgson was cold. She realised he wasn't wearing a coat.

'There,' he said, as she righted herself. Her elbow pulsed with pain. Birch remembered the microphone, and hoped to God that her dragging of the flak vest across the wood of the door hadn't wrecked it. 'Now, if you don't mind, I'll just . . .'

Hodgson ducked behind her and braced himself against the back of the door, his arms spread wide as he scuffed it back into place. Get his gun, Birch thought, now, while he's occupied. She cast around for it, scanning the walls and floor for the long black line of the shotgun. But the light in the ruin was weird and glitchy: the two empty windows let in the fizzy white glow of the floodlight, casting square spotlights on the inner back wall. The whole building was one room: any dividing walls there had been were long gone now. The end beyond Hodgson and the door was filled with rubble and rotted timber, presumably the remains of the building's roof. At the other end, Birch could make out an old stone fireplace – in the unlit grate, a pale bundle of something. Overhead, ragged timbers criss-crossed precariously, silhouetted against the purple evening sky. There was no sign of the gun.

'Right,' Hodgson said. He appeared at her side, breathing hard. 'You should sit.'

He waved an arm in the direction of the fireplace. Birch stepped forward, through one of the two beams of light thrown into the room by the lone remaining floodlight. She paused there, looking out of the window, imagining her face lit up and visible to her waiting colleagues. She watched as Hodgson ducked low, scuttling under the window to remain unseen. It surprised her, seeing a man of his age move that way, with apparent ease.

The light had left a bright print on her retina, but as she stumbled forward, she discerned the outline of a folding canvas camping chair, propped up in the corner by the fireplace. Hodgson was in the opposite corner, standing now in the darkest part of the room. Birch felt rather than saw as he took the shotgun from its hiding place: the alcove at the corner of the chimney breast. He knew she'd never have spotted it there, in the shadows. She could hear the metallic noises of the gun moving and settling in his grip. He didn't point it at her, but held it up, diagonally across his chest, so she could see it.

'I brought water,' she heard herself say. She lifted the bottles and held them out. The glow of the floodlight refracted through them. Hodgson didn't move. 'I've brought some food, too,' she went on. 'Nothing fancy, just cereal bars. But you must be hungry.'

Still, Hodgson didn't move. Birch's arms began to sag, but she kept the water held aloft. It felt almost like a shield, a makeshift barrier between her and the guy with the gun.

'I didn't ask for anything,' he said.

'No, I know. I'm sorry.' She couldn't believe she'd just apologised to him. 'But you must be thirsty, even if you're not hungry.'

He made no response, so Birch lowered the case of water and bent to set it on the floor of the ruin, her neck bent awkwardly so she could keep her eyes on the gun.

'I'll leave it there,' she said. 'And the bars. They're in my pockets, so . . .'

There was a pause, and then Hodgson twitched the shotgun in his hands, as though getting a more accurate grip.

'Slowly, then,' he said.

Birch complied. It felt like she was doing some sort of strange tai chi, moving her hands in slow motion through the air to reach into her own back pockets. She held up the bars so he could see what they were, before placing them in a pile on top of the water. Once she'd done all eight, she lifted her hands, palms up, to show she was done.

'Sit,' Hodgson said.

Birch took a step backward, and lowered herself into the camping chair, which creaked. She was relieved that the food-and-water dance was over, but she wished she'd put them further away from the chair. She didn't like the idea of him getting any closer than he already was.

'Okay,' Hodgson said, and let out a long breath. She could sense he was relieved: he'd got her into the ruin, he'd got her sitting down. They could begin.

In the fireplace, the pale bundle moved. Birch realised she'd been so fixated on the door, the gun, her bruised elbow, the microphone, the water, that she'd almost forgotten about Elise. Now she looked at the bundle, she could see it was a tiny body, the little girl curled into a comma shape, her back to the room. She was shivering.

'Elise,' Birch whispered.

'She's sleeping,' Hodgson snapped.

Birch put her hands on the arms of the chair, ready to lever herself up again.

'I just want to—'

It took half a second for Hodgson to level the shotgun at her.

'Stay where you are,' he said. 'She's sleeping. Leave her be.'

Birch put both hands up, imagining what they must look like in the gloom of the ruin: two pale stars of surrender.

'All right, all right,' she said, 'I'm not moving. I just want to know if she's okay. Is she hurt?'

'Are you saying I've hurt her?' Hodgson's face was barely visible now, the gun and his cocked elbow obscuring it. Birch tried not to look down the barrel, but ignoring it was hard work. Her heart felt like two fists battering against the inside of her chest.

'No,' she said, slowly, 'I'm not saying that at all. I just know how easily wee ones get hurt, is all. They're fragile. And it's a bumpy ride up that track in the back of a Land Rover. I'm a grown woman, and I didn't enjoy it.'

Hodgson made a snorting noise.

'She's fine,' he said, from behind the shotgun. 'She's not hurt. I just don't want her waking up again, not after the racket she's made.'

Birch heard Rena's voice in her head: *try to understand him.*

'I get that,' she said. Her hands were still in the air – she couldn't seem to lower them, not while the gun was still pointed at her face. 'I understand that, Gerry. It's part of why I've never had kids myself. I can't stand the sound of a crying baby. It's distressing, isn't it?'

Hodgson didn't lower the gun, but his pose seemed to relax, just a little.

'I haven't been able to hear myself think,' he said.

'I'm sorry about that,' Birch replied. 'I suppose you have a lot to think about right now. A lot of important stuff.'

'I suppose I do.'

Silence fell between them. A helicopter passed overhead, directly above the cottage. Birch felt the timbers of the old door rattle, the thud of the rotor blades vibrating through the walls. She realised she could only hear one now: Leigh had ordered the other chopper down. She couldn't look away from the gun, from Hodgson's hunched figure in the corner. She realised how right Rena had been, how important it was to keep the other guy talking. She had no idea what to say, no idea what was right, and for a moment, she imagined that they might stay like this for ever, frozen in this impossible pose of mutual fear.

'Maybe we can think it through together,' she said, eventually. 'Talk it through, you know?'

The words were barely out of her mouth before she kicked herself – *speak! Not talk!* – though Hodgson seemed unmoved.

'They say two heads are better than one,' Birch added, keen to move on from her mistake. 'And that's why I've come down here, after all. To . . . speak to you. To hear what you have to say. To hear what you're thinking.'

She felt absurd, babbling with her hands in the air. Part of her hoped the mic *was* broken, so Rena couldn't hear how badly she was screwing this up.

'I don't know,' Hodgson said. 'I feel like I can't think. I can't make sense of anything.'

'Why don't we start with the basics?' Birch said, hoping this was the right tack. 'Open up that water and have something to drink. Something to eat. It might help you think more clearly.'

Again, Hodgson made no response. His face was indistinct beyond the gun's long barrel. He *had* to be hungry and thirsty, surely. Birch had the brief, absurd thought that he might think she was trying to poison him.

'Or if you don't want to,' she said, 'at least let me give something to Elise. The poor wee scone must be starving.'

Hodgson nudged the gun, as though reminding her it was there, pointing at her. Like she could forget.

'I told you,' he said, his voice raised now, 'you're not waking her up. I'm not having it. I have to be able to *think*.'

'Okay,' Birch said, 'that's okay. We can just talk for now, that's fine. But I'll be honest with you, Gerry, I'm finding it pretty hard to think myself, when there's a gun pointed at my head. I promise you, I won't move from this chair. I won't do anything you don't want me to. Can you please just put the shotgun down? Then maybe we can both start thinking.'

Hodgson didn't move.

'Please?' Birch could feel tears in her eyes, and gritted her teeth to try and keep them back. 'Please. I came down here, like you asked. Unarmed, and no radio. I got them to turn off the lights. And listen.' She balled one of her upturned hands, and then pointed at the sky. 'There's only one helicopter now. I've done as much as I can. So please, I'm asking you. Just lower the gun. You can keep hold of it, just . . . I can't concentrate on anything else when it's pointed at me like that.'

She realised she'd convinced him before he moved: she felt something shift in the air between them. Hodgson lowered the shotgun's barrel, and then, after a moment of hesitation, propped it back across his chest.

'Thank you,' she said.

He let out a ragged breath, then stepped towards the chimney breast, and leaned against it. She could see his body sagging in the middle, the pose of an exhausted man.

'Do you want this chair?' she asked.

Hodgson shook his head.

'You stay where you are. Where I can see you.'

Birch thought about insisting, about telling him *you seem tired*, but then she remembered Rena's instruction not to argue with him.

'Okay,' she said. 'Okay. So . . . what are we all doing here, Gerry? How did all of this get started?'

Hodgson made a sound that Birch realised was a bitter kind of laugh.

'You want the whole of it?' he asked. 'The long version?'

Birch glanced at Elise, still shivering in the dark gap of the fireplace. She hadn't yet ascertained for sure that the child wasn't hurt, that she didn't need anything. But the relief of no longer having a gun levelled at her was strong. She could sit with that feeling for a little while, at least, before she pushed him again about Elise.

'I mean,' she said, 'it seems we have time. Tell me.'

'2001,' he blurted: it was as though he'd been waiting for permission to say it, to start relaying his story. 'It started in 2001. Or . . . 2000, really. But 2001 was when the shit hit the fan.'

'So I've heard.'

'Don't you believe what you *heard*,' Hodgson spat. 'Especially not if you heard it from the papers, or any of your lot, for that matter. There's been a lot of lies told about me.'

'So tell me the truth.'

He let out a sigh.

'In the year 2000,' he said, 'I was thirty-eight. Still a young man. Still fit. I had to be, with the work I did. I don't know if you've ever lifted a sheep, DI Birch, but it's not easy. It's probably hard for you to believe, but I liked my job. The driving, the route I had, the stops along the way. I drove one of those pain-in-the-arse lorries people hate on the A75 to Stranraer. But I was content. I lived simply, and I was fine with it.'

'And then what happened?'

'I met . . .' Hodgson paused. Birch wondered how it felt, trying to say the name of a woman you'd recently murdered in cold blood. 'Sophie,' he said, his voice cracking on the *o*.

'Tell me about her.'

Hodgson sighed again. He wanted to do this, she could tell, but it was as though the whole process – standing, thinking, speaking – was taking all the energy he had.

'She was training as an auctioneer,' he said, 'at the livestock mart in Longtown. That was my base camp. It's in England, just, but it sits sort of at the corner where Dumfries and Galloway and the Borders meet. I covered both regions, and delivered to that auction mart a lot.'

Birch nodded. The name *Longtown* stirred up that same memory she'd had in the village shop, while Pearl was talking about the foot-and-mouth outbreak. The black smoke, and a red sky.

'Sophie was only twenty-two,' Hodgson went on. 'I didn't think she'd look twice at me. Asked her to go for a drink anyway, reasoning I'd nothing to lose. But I was bloody shocked when she said yes.'

'And you became a couple?'

'Not at first,' he said, 'not really. I was off driving a lot, so we were just a casual thing. I assumed she saw other men – you know, men her own age. But then she fell out with her house-mate, and ditched out of the place she was living. She'd nowhere to go, and asked to move in with me.'

'You were happy about that?'

Hodgson sniffed.

'Couldn't believe my luck at the time,' he said. 'Lads in the haulage yard used to yip at me about it something awful, *cradle-snatcher,* all that stuff. She was a bonny lass, DI Birch. I was made up.'

'But then . . .?'

'Then,' Hodgson said, 'came the bloody sickness.'

'The foot-and-mouth outbreak.'

'Yes. That bastard disease. They found it down south first, Essex. I don't know if you remember. The government put restrictions in, but we all knew it would spread. Folk like me, we move animals all the time. We see how far they travel, how much they mingle with each other, the conditions they're in. And like I say, it's a bastard disease. Once it takes hold, there's no containing it.'

'And it came to Scotland.'

'Yeah. Came to my backyard, in fact: two farms in Dumfries and Galloway got it, and one of them was a farm I worked with. So immediately there's a focus on my truck, on me. When was I last there? When did I bring animals in, and where from? These government guys came to the haulage yard and questioned us all. They were hoping it was just us, just our firm, something they could contain. They wanted it to be just those farms. But of course it wasn't just those farms.'

'It had already spread.'

'You bet it had. They didn't tell us, but that day they came to speak to us there were already five other farms with suspected cases, probably a lot of others worried they had it but not saying anything yet. I remember that night, after work. That night, the farm in Canonbie – that farm I'd stopped at – burned the bodies. You could smell the smoke all the way over in Longtown, ten miles away. A couple of days later the government guys were back, and they were asking us if anyone wanted some extra work.'

'They asked if you'd be part of the . . . clean-up?'

'You could call it that,' Hodgson said. 'The writing was on the wall pretty quickly for us: they wanted to restrict our travel, limit the movement of animals around the place. When we did go out, the trucks were constantly stopping to be hosed down with disinfectant, and the wheels scrubbed. It was about the worst day job to have at that time. Except for being a farmer, of course.'

'So you agreed?'

'They said it was freelance. Temporary. It was well paid. We knew our way around animals, and we knew the farmers. It made sense for us to go in and help, they said. And I guess it did on paper.'

'But not in practice?'

Hodgson huffed out a grim laugh.

'Picture the scene,' he said. 'Some farmer you've been working with for years finds out he's got the sickness on his farm. Tested positive, no question about it. He's going to have to slaughter every animal he has; he can't get out of it. If there's another farm bordering his, he has to ring his neighbour up and tell that farmer that *his* animals have to be slaughtered, too. Both of them are about to have their entire livelihood go up in smoke. And who turns up wielding the bolt gun? Some government pen-pusher, and muggins here. The guy who that farmer suspects probably shipped the bloody sickness into his farm in the first place.'

'Farmers blamed you?'

He shrugged.

'Plenty of farmers are dirt poor at the best of times,' he said. 'A lot of them reckoned if they got it, it would finish them off. Their whole business would go pop. And for a lot of them, it came true. So yeah, they were looking around for someone to blame. Me, my workmates, the company. I decided it probably made them feel better, so I was kind of okay to be blamed.'

'That's very magnanimous of you,' Birch said, 'but it must have made your job even harder. The clean-up job, I mean. Work that I imagine was already very hard to do.'

Hodgson was quiet for a moment.

'Lassie,' he said, quietly, 'honestly, it was like working in a circle of hell.'

'I'm sure.'

'No,' Hodgson said, 'you're not sure. You can't have any idea what it was like. Rounding up hundreds of animals – most of them perfectly healthy – and then killing them, one by one, methodically. You very quickly get to feel like you're a machine. Your hand holds the bolt gun for long enough, and it develops muscle memory, so even after you're done for the day you can still feel it in your palm. I still dream about it most nights. In my dreams I'm killing anything that comes near me: animals, people.' Hodgson nodded towards Elise, curled up in the fireplace. 'Children, even. I dream I'm a machine that murders things.'

'I'm sorry, Gerry,' Birch said, though a cold shiver had passed through her as he spoke. 'That sounds horrendous.'

'That's one word for it. And that was just the slaughtering. Once the slaughtering was done, there were hundreds of bodies to deal with. Some farms didn't even have the space for them all . . . we were burning cattle on airfields before long, with army overseers telling us we weren't going fast enough. I tell you, DI Birch, I've seen hell. It looks like five hundred cows on a pyre. And it smells like nothing I can even describe to you. That was probably the worst part about the whole thing, the smell. I can always call it to mind. I can smell it now. Like it got into my skin all those years ago and no matter what I do, I can't get it out.'

Birch was quiet, unable to think of anything to say. She recalled the footage on the news at the time: piles of carcasses with dead animals' legs sticking out along the top like grim fencing. She remembered the red sky.

'Forgive me,' she said, 'for asking this question, but ... could you have quit? Told them you'd had enough, and walked away?'

Hodgson shrugged.

'I've thought about that a lot,' he said, 'since it all went down. In prison, I thought about it every single day. Why didn't I just walk away, if I objected to it so much? People threw that question at me often, during the trial, so I spent a lot of time considering it. But the answer is, I don't know for sure why I carried on. I suppose I felt like the farmers already hated me. They already blamed me. *They* had no choice but to stand by and watch it all happen. What sort of coward would I have been if I'd left them to it? At least I was a local, and so I understood how devastating it all was. The army guys they shipped in, they didn't know. Didn't seem to care. But I cared. If it had to be done, I cared that it was done right.'

'It became a moral thing for you.'

'It was from the start,' Hodgson snapped. 'It was a moral thing from the very beginning. And an emotional thing. I drove home in tears every single night, and I couldn't watch the news on TV, or it'd set me off.'

'And eventually, you'd had enough.'

Hodgson pushed against the chimney breast, and teetered upright. Birch watched the gun, but he kept it hugged across his chest. He began pacing back and forth, two steps in one direction, then a turn, and two steps back.

'Look,' he said, 'I wasn't the only one who snapped, okay? There was that woman – you'll remember this from the news – with the fancy-breed sheep. God, what was her name? She was out in Glasserton, and she raised Dutch Zwartbles. She had a smallholding; they were pets, really – but they got the order. Pre-emptive cull. She went to court over it and lost, so she got all the sheep in her living room with her and barricaded herself in the house.'

Birch nodded, slowly.

'Now you mention it,' she said, 'I do remember that.'

'Didn't fucking work,' Hodgson spat. 'She held them off for five days, but in the end they dragged her out and killed the animals anyway. They weren't even sick.'

Birch looked over at Elise. Her little body was shivering in the stone grate. How she was managing to sleep there, with the two of them talking and Hodgson getting increasingly agitated, Birch had no idea. Never mind the clatter of the helicopter passing over every five minutes. She glanced up through the ruined beams as it chugged overhead once again.

'Then there was that guy,' Hodgson went on, 'Hubbard. You'll remember him, too. Turned his bolt gun on another slaughterman on a big job down in Cumbria. Shot him in the head.'

'Yes, I remember that.'

'It killed him,' Hodgson said. 'I mean, as it would. Those things are designed to kill a cow that weighs half a ton. Poor sod stood no chance.'

'I remember the trial,' Birch said. 'They talked about the stress they were under, the slaughtermen. The stress you were under.'

Hodgson stopped pacing. He jostled the weight of the gun, releasing one hand so he could point his index finger at her. Birch flinched.

'That's just it,' he said, practically shouting now. 'That's just *it*! He got off in the end, that guy, and he killed another human being! I didn't kill anyone, did I? I wanted the killing to *stop*. I was under the same bloody stress as he was, doing the same horrifying, shitty work he was, under the same conditions. I was going home and taking three showers every night, trying to get the smell off me. I was waking up in a cold sweat with the nightmares, or having Sophie wake me up because I was shouting in my sleep. I was crying all the time, and I never used to cry. Hadn't cried since I was a kid, and then I found I couldn't stop it. I was in the exact same boat as that guy! And what happens to me?' Hodgson was stabbing the air with his finger. 'I get royally *fucked*. By *you*. By people just like *you*.'

Birch held her hands up again, though it was only his finger he was pointing.

'I'd like you to calm down, Gerry,' she said. 'I'm here to listen to you. To try and understand. And so far I agree – it sounds like you went through a terrible ordeal.'

Hodgson lowered the pointing finger, and his voice, though when he spoke again, it was still a snarl.

'You're damn right I did,' he said, 'and what did I get in return? I got thrown in jail. Locked away to rot.'

Birch opened her mouth to speak, but there was a noise from the fireplace. A sort of snuffling, that turned into a thin wail and then a full-blown cry. The bundle in the fireplace uncurled, and Elise rolled over in the grate. In the dim light, Birch saw the child's face for the first time as the little girl heaved in a ragged sob.

'Elise,' she whispered.

HOUR SIXTEEN

'Jesus,' Hodgson spat, 'that's the last thing I need.'

Elise had levered herself into a sitting position in the dark mouth of the fireplace. Any natural light was almost gone: though the sky overhead was still a purplish blue, pale stars could now be seen between the ruin's splintered rafters. The main source of light was the weird, diffuse beam of the lone floodlight. But Birch could see now that the little girl was wearing pale-coloured pyjamas, smeared with dirt and soot down one side, where she'd been lying in the grate. Her feet were bare, and she was crying in earnest.

'I can quieten her down, Gerry,' Birch said. 'We can keep talking.'

Hodgson stood for a moment, watching the child as she rubbed her eyes and sobbed. Birch hadn't been lying when she'd told him she found a baby's cry distressing: already she was finding it hard to stand the mournful sound Elise was making. She wanted to quiet her, too, though not so she could hear herself think. The sound tugged at something inside her. It made her want to cry as well.

'Please,' she said, and she heard a crack in her voice. 'Let me calm her down a bit.'

Hodgson returned to his position at the corner of the chimney breast. As though only just realising he was there, Elise looked up at him, and flinched. Her crying intensified. Birch could see she was frightened of him, and no wonder.

'Fine,' he replied.

Birch shifted her weight in the camping chair, and reached one hand out towards the little girl.

'Elise?'

It took a moment for the child to look at her. For a moment, she kept her eyes on Hodgson, as though she didn't trust him enough to look away. But then she turned, and there was a pause between sobs as surprise registered in her tiny body. Someone else was here. Someone new.

Birch tried for a big smile, though she didn't know how distinctly the kid could see her in the dim light, and with tears in her eyes.

'Hello, Elise,' she said. 'My name's Helen. Do you want to come over and sit with me for a minute?'

She realised she was holding her hand out the way you might do towards a wary cat. It felt patronising, even to a child, but she didn't know how much more she could move without upsetting Hodgson.

'It's okay,' she said. 'I know you don't know me, but I'm a friend. In fact, I'm a police officer. Do you know what a police officer is, Elise?'

The little girl stole another look at Hodgson. She was still crying, but her sobs had subsided: they sounded hiccupy now. Birch could see her ribcage juddering.

'Go on,' Hodgson said, a new note of sadness in his voice. 'Go and . . . see the lady. Say hello to the lady.'

Birch watched as Elise pushed the palms of her hands into the sooty floor of the fireplace, and pushed herself unsteadily to her feet. She looked down at herself with an expression of disdain, taking in the dirt on her pyjamas, the grubby stones around her. In a motion that almost made Birch laugh, she wiped her little hands down the front of her pyjama trousers, obviously feeling that they were gritty and black. Then, with some uncertainty, she picked her way out of the grate and across the uneven floor of the ruin, until she stood at Birch's side.

'Hello,' Birch said, relief palpable in her voice. Elise could walk. She could move her arms. She didn't seem to be badly hurt: Hodgson had been telling the truth earlier. 'Hello, Elise.'

The child was close enough now for Birch to be able to reach out and place her outstretched palm on the top of her head, but she didn't. Elise was eyeing her with suspicion.

'You're not a police lady,' she said.

'I'm sorry?'

Elise took a big breath, and then repeated herself, much louder.

'I said *you're* not a police lady.'

'I am so,' Birch replied. 'I promise, I am. Why do you think I'm not?'

'Because.' Elise's lip was still quivering, as though she hadn't fully decided to finish crying yet. 'You're not wearing a police lady hat.'

Birch laughed, but the laugh came out twisted, as though she herself were holding back tears.

'You're a clever girl,' she said. 'You're right, police officers do sometimes wear hats. But I don't wear one.'

Elise screwed up her face.

'Why?'

'Well, because . . .' Birch paused. She wasn't sure she had the capacity to explain what CID was to a three-year-old, and besides, this wasn't exactly the time. 'I'm not wearing my hat,' she said, 'because I left it in my car by accident. Wasn't that silly of me?'

Elise undid her frown.

'Yes,' she said, solemnly. 'Silly.'

Birch smiled.

'But I promise,' she said, 'I am a police officer. Wait a second, I'll look in my pocket and find my police badge.'

Birch twisted in the camping chair, awkward in the boxy flak vest. The unmistakable clack of the shotgun made her realise her mistake. Hodgson had levelled the barrel in her direction once more, and the panic that seized her felt fifty times more urgent now that Elise was also standing within the shotgun's range.

'Don't even think about it,' Hodgson snarled. Elise's tears returned immediately, like a flicked switch.

'Okay, Gerry,' Birch said. She realised her hands were already aloft: she'd raised them without a thought. 'I don't have anything, I promise. I told you, I'm not armed. I just wanted to give her my warrant card to play with, but it's fine. I don't have to. It's fine.'

'I'll decide what's *fine*,' Hodgson replied. He showed no sign of lowering the gun, and Elise had begun to wail again, loudly. Birch decided to take a risk.

'Oh, *now* look,' she said, forcing herself to fling her hands down in exasperation. She realised how instinctive the *hands up* gesture was: doing anything other than that felt border-line impossible. 'I'd just got her quiet and now she's bawling again.'

Hodgson snorted.

'This is how it's been,' he said. 'I had this for hours.'

Birch reached out to Elise once again, and this time, touched her on the shoulder. Elise looked at her hand, but didn't move. Birch felt, through the fine fleece of the pyjamas, how cold the little girl was.

'I think,' she said, 'that she doesn't like the gun. I'm not saying that for my own sake, though I really don't like it either. Genuinely, I think she'd be happier if you put it down somewhere. Put it back in the corner there, or something.'

'Oh sure. You'd love that. Have me disarm myself.'

Birch rolled her eyes: she couldn't help it. She tried not to think of Rena up at the perimeter, listening.

'Come *on*,' she snapped, 'hardly. You could put that gun just about anywhere in this room and still get to it before I got out of this chair. I'm not here to be a hero; I'm not going to wrestle you to the ground. I'm the poor fool they sent in to hear you out. This is a police operation, it's not . . .' Birch scrabbled around for an example she knew Hodgson would get. '*Die Hard*. It's not a movie. I'm not going to get up from this chair until we work all this out, I absolutely promise you. Apart from anything else, it's more than my job's worth.'

Hodgson lowered the gun, though only by about an inch. It was dark, but she could feel him peering at her over the barrel.

'What do you mean?'

'Exactly what I say,' she replied. 'You know that after something like this, there'll be an inquiry. If they were to find that I'd used unnecessary force against you, or put this little one in danger, then I'd be out of a job faster than you could say Jack Robinson.' Birch still had one hand resting on Elise's shoulder. She could feel the sobs moving through her like small waves. 'I'm here to listen to you. To sit here, and listen. That's literally it.'

Hodgson didn't move, but once again, Birch felt something change in the air between them, something soften.

'So there's really no need,' she said, 'to have a gun trained on me. Especially when it's upsetting Elise.'

No one spoke. The helicopter sounded distant, out at the widest apex of its circle. The loudest noise now was Elise, hauling in snotty breaths and then spitting them out again.

'For Christ's sake,' Hodgson said at last, 'shut her up.' He swung the gun into one hand, pointing the barrel at the floor. Birch allowed herself to let out the breath she'd been holding.

'All right, Elise,' she said. Her hand was still on the girl's shoulder, and now she gave it a small squeeze. 'I know, you're not happy, are you? It's cold and dark and not very nice in here.'

Elise swiped at her runny nose with one sleeve, and nodded.

'Why don't you come and sit on my knee for a bit?' Birch ventured. 'It'll warm you up.'

Elise paused for a moment, blinking her tears away so she could study this strange woman in the camping chair. Keep a hold of that, Birch thought, that natural suspicion. Don't trust anyone easily, not in this shitty world.

'It's okay,' she said, quietly. 'Promise.'

At this, Elise held out both arms, the universal little-kid gesture for *pick me up*. Birch bent forward in the chair, but the bottom edge of the flak vest cut into her thighs. She glanced at Hodgson. He was watching her, holding the shotgun loosely against his thigh. She didn't dare stand up.

'Wait,' Birch said, 'hang on. I can't give you a proper cuddle wearing this thing, can I?'

She looked again at Hodgson.

'Gerry,' she said, 'I am going to take off this vest, all right? In fact, I'm going to take off my sweatshirt as well, so I can wrap Elise in it. That's all I'm doing, there's nothing dodgy going on. Is that okay with you?'

He made no answer.

'Please. This isn't a trick. I'm making myself more vulnerable here.'

Hodgson grunted.

'If it quiets her down,' he said, 'then fine.'

Birch fiddled with the fastenings of the vest. It was easier to do in the light, ideally with a mirror or someone to help you. It took her a while to get everything loosened, and Elise's sobs grew louder.

'Hey,' Birch said to her, in as soothing a voice as she could muster, 'I'm sorry, wee scone. This is just fiddly, okay? I'm nearly done, then you can get up here and coorie in. Just a minute—'

She slid the vest off over her head, and leaned it carefully against one side of the camping chair. She hoped it didn't look too obvious: she wanted the microphone angled out, facing Hodgson. She felt relief at being free of the vest's restrictive grip, but her fear ticked up, too: she *was* more vulnerable now. She slipped the sweatshirt off, and felt goosebumps rise on her arms.

'Right, wee one,' she said, trying to sound buoyant. 'I'm ready now. You climb up here.' With the hand that wasn't clutching the sweatshirt, she patted her knee, realising again that she was treating Elise like a pet, rather than a child. It worked, though. Once again, the little girl held out her arms, and this time Birch scooped her up and on to her lap, where Elise curled into a ball against her chest.

'Shoogle this way a bit,' Birch said, manoeuvring the sweatshirt around the child's small frame. 'You get in under this and get cosy. That's better.'

Elise pressed her face against Birch's collarbone, tears smearing on to her blouse. Almost immediately, the crying eased off into a quiet whimper.

'There we go, Gerry,' Birch said. 'Is that better?'

Hodgson had started pacing again, swinging the shotgun in long arcs that matched his strides. With his free hand, he was rubbing his face, as though trying to get something out of his eyes.

Seeing him distracted, Birch ran a scuttling hand over Elise's arms. She wasn't entirely sure what broken bones felt like in a body this small, but she was pretty sure there weren't any. She'd seen the little girl walk: her legs seemed fine. She ran her fingers over the small dome of Elise's head. Her hair was thin and wispy, and smelled like talc. There were no swellings, no injuries.

'She's doing remarkably well,' Birch said, raising her voice so the microphone could pick her up. 'Elise, I mean. There doesn't seem to be a scratch on her. And it's good that she's had a wee sleep. Though how she could sleep in that hard fireplace I've no idea.'

'This wasn't in the plan, you know,' Hodgson barked.

'What wasn't?'

'The kid. Having the kid with me. Having anyone with me.'

'No,' Birch said, 'I know. I mean, I guessed. Gerry, has Elise had anything to eat or drink, since—' She paused, trying to think of the most diplomatic wording. 'Since she's been with you?'

Hodgson shrugged: Birch saw the gesture as he paced. The weird light made his movements appear juddery, like a villain in an old black-and-white film.

'I gave her a bottle of water,' he said, 'in the Land Rover. I don't know if she drank any.'

Birch squinted down at the bundle in her lap. She curled a hand around each of Elise's feet. They were freezing cold.

'Are you thirsty, Elise?'

She felt rather than saw as Elise shook her head, but Hodgson must have seen it.

'There,' he snapped, 'she's fine.'

Birch squinted over at the crate of water, still sitting a few feet away on the floor of the ruin.

'I think she's just being shy,' she said. Elise had buried her face in the thin fabric of Birch's blouse. 'I'd like to try and give her some of that water, if that's okay.'

'You'll stay in that chair, and not move.'

Birch pulled in a breath. Don't get flustered, Helen. Stay calm.

'I'm happy to,' she said, 'but if you could just open up the plastic and then roll me one of the bottles . . .'

Hodgson huffed out a sigh, and kept pacing. Birch assumed he'd refuse, but then he darted forward, fast, making her flinch. He passed the gun into his left hand, then hooked two fingers under the plastic wrap of the water crate. The cereal bars scattered in all directions, one landing a few inches from Birch's foot. Hodgson stepped back, away from her, returning with the water to the corner by the fireplace.

'Thank you,' Birch said.

She watched as he leaned the gun in its hiding place, then braced the crate against his chest, pulling at the plastic. He fumbled, and she realised he wasn't watching what he was doing. His eyes were fixed on her.

'We'll give you a wee drink anyway, Elise,' Birch said, keeping her face turned to Hodgson, but angling her voice down at the bundle in her lap. 'And maybe something to eat.'

Hodgson prised a bottle out of the crate and half threw, half rolled it across the floor towards her. She twisted an arm out from under Elise, and stretched down to reach it.

'There,' he spat. 'You happy?'

His words landed like a slap. Birch was beginning to see how erratic he was: calm one minute, agitated again the next.

'I'd be happier,' she said, hearing the crackle of plastic as she twisted the cap from the bottle, 'if you'd help yourself to one of those, too.'

Hodgson had dropped the remaining bottles in the corner, and now snatched up the gun once again.

'I'm *fine*.' His voice was cold.

'Okay,' she said. She paused, wondering whether or not to push the issue, but she still wasn't sure what to make of Hodgson, or how good an idea it might be to bargain with him. Besides, Elise had squirmed round in Birch's lap and held out both hands for the bottle of water. She tipped it up to her little face, and although a fair bit of liquid ran down her chin on to her pyjama top, she drank.

'Let's just carry on our conversation, then,' Birch said, swiping spilled water away from Elise's face with the sleeve of her blouse. 'You were about to tell me what happened. In 2001. What . . . went wrong.'

'Right,' Hodgson said. His tone was suddenly businesslike – she could tell he wanted to get on with his testimony. 'I was. I expect you've heard the official version. The *police* version.'

'I've been given the vague details,' she said, 'but to be honest, I didn't have much time earlier today to look into it. I've only had bits and pieces. So why don't you tell me the full story?'

Hodgson was nodding.

'The true story,' he said.

'Sure.' Elise had stopped drinking, and Birch looped her fingers around the plastic bottle, so it wouldn't spill. The little girl's breathing had evened out, though she still sniffled every so often. 'I want to hear it.'

Hodgson lifted the gun, resting it back across his chest again, as though this were a necessary ritual, part of the storytelling. She thought he might start pacing again, but he didn't.

'One day,' he said, 'I lost it. I've always admitted that – I snapped. Lost control, whatever you want to call it. It was May, then. I'd been doing that godawful work for nearly two months, and I just couldn't take it any longer.'

'You decided to take action.'

'Yes. Yes, you could say that. I was called to this farm that had been earmarked for slaughter. They'd had no positive tests, but they were just-and-so within the three-kilometre radius of another farm that had. I knew the guy who owned the place, I'd been moving animals of his for years. He was devastated. Told me when I showed up that once the pyre was built, he'd throw himself on it too. You have to understand, it was harder for the farms who got it later: they'd already spent weeks worrying they might be next. They'd had time to do the sums, figure out just how fucked they'd be if they had to slaughter. This guy had done the maths. When he told me he'd climb on the pyre with the cows, I believed him.'

Birch blinked. 'Wasn't there government assistance?' she asked. 'Didn't the farmers get reimbursed for the losses they suffered?'

Hodgson snorted.

'Supposedly,' he said, 'but they weren't given out fairly. One bloke got four million, I remember that being in the papers. Others got what amounted to a slap in the face. And you seem like a smart lassie, DI Birch – you must be able to see it's more complicated than that. Money doesn't pay back all those weeks of anxiety, worrying you'll be next. Money doesn't pay back guilt over losing a heritage flock your family's been tending for generations. Money doesn't pay back the way it must feel, watching your animals get shot in the head one by one and piled up. Understand – it was about so much more than the money.'

'And this particular farmer,' Birch said, 'you felt for him.'

'I felt,' Hodgson said, 'that his herd should never have been slaughtered. He was within the radius by a few feet. He'd appealed it, but been refused. It was madness.'

'Tell me what you did.'

Hodgson flexed his shoulders: Birch heard them crack.

'When I got there,' he said, 'I found I was on my own. Normally there were at least two of us, usually more. Me, and other slaughtermen like me – how many depended on the size of the job. Sometimes the army showed up, sometimes not. But there was always a government bod. Some bloke in clean wellies and a clipboard, checking up on us.'

'But not that day.'

'No. That day, the bod didn't show. Turned out he was sick. Turned out I should have got a call: job postponed. But I heard nothing. So I drove over there, and it was just me and the farmer. I've thought a lot about that moment, the moment he told me there'd been a mistake. I've thought about what my life might have been like if I'd gone *well okay then*, turned around and driven away again. But I didn't. I went into his kitchen, and we had a drink.'

'A *drink* drink?'

'Whisky,' Hodgson said. 'I was drinking a fair bit then. It didn't make the nightmares stop, but it helped me to forget them, in the daytime. I was driving, so I thought I'd only have the one. But he was in such a state. He was on his own – once he'd got the call to say his farm was on the cull list, he'd sent his family away. Didn't want them seeing it happen. He was a mess. And he kept drinking, so I kept drinking. I'd been there about an hour when I had the idea.'

'You had the idea,' Birch said, 'not the farmer?'

Hodgson stabbed his finger at her again.

'Don't you start with that,' he said, 'don't you try to make it his fault. They tried to do that when they brought me in for questioning, tried to make me grass him up. I wouldn't do it then, and I won't now. That poor bastard. It was all me, all my doing, and you'll never get me to say different, you understand?'

'I do,' Birch said, trying to keep her voice level. 'I'm sorry.'

Hodgson pulled back his pointing hand, and curled it around the barrel of the shotgun.

'Good,' he said. 'My thought was, what if they come back tomorrow to slaughter the herd, and find there's no herd to slaughter? It started as a sort of fantasy: I was a few whiskies down and I thought, *God*, I wish I could make those cows disappear, just for a day. But then – well, the brain does what it does. I started to think, okay, how could I make that happen? And I hatched this plan that I honestly thought was foolproof.'

'Because you were drunk.'

'Drunk,' Hodgson said, 'and desperate. Miserable. I was sick of killing things. I wanted to have a go at saving things, instead.'

'So what did you do?'

'I sent the farmer out on his quad bike. Out to the site they'd agreed on for the pyre. I told him to find anything he didn't want that we could burn. Made it sound like we did this everywhere: used old junk off the farms to make a base for the carcasses. He went off collecting bales, tyres, logs. I told him to take them up to the pyre site and sort of lay them out in a long strip. The farmers knew by then what the pyres looked like – they'd seen them enough on the news. I knew it would keep him busy. And off he went.'

'And you went to find the herd.'

Hodgson nodded.

'They didn't take much finding,' he said. 'His was a small-ish farm. He'd got them all in a barn, and you could have heard them for miles. It wasn't what they were used to, and they were spooked. They knew something wasn't right, and they were hollering like crazy. I knew as soon as I got into that barn, I wasn't coming back tomorrow to do the job. I wasn't going to kill another animal, and they couldn't make me. I was going to save that herd.'

'So you put them in your lorry.'

'As many as I could,' Hodgson replied. 'They wouldn't all fit. But I got as many as I could into the truck, yes.'

'Must have been hard to do,' Birch said, 'on your own.'

Hodgson swore.

'I told you,' he said, 'I did it all myself. He wasn't involved, and no one can prove that he was.'

'I just said it must have been hard.'

'I know what you meant by it. But it doesn't matter now, anyway. I did it. I put the cows in the truck. The others I let run, and hoped they wouldn't get caught. Then I got into the driver's seat, and off I went.'

'You stole the herd.'

'I saved them.' Hodgson's voice was sad. 'Or, I thought I had. For just a brief couple of hours, I actually thought I'd saved them.'

'You drove south?'

'Yeah. Into Cumbria. Of course, I realise now that was the worst possible idea. Cumbria was in the thick of it then, they had more roadblocks than anywhere else, more disinfectant stations. I should have gone up the coast road, west and then north. I'd have got a hell of a lot further that way.'

'But someone stopped you.'

'Yeah. Initially it was just to disinfect the wheels. They would have let me go on, if I'd got my story straight. It was my truck; I was employed by the company. I could have been legit. But I lied when I told them what farm I was coming from, and where I was going. They had a database, and I didn't check out. Then one of the policemen there noticed I'd been drinking. Once the breathalyser came out, it was game over.'

'What happened to the cows?'

Hodgson was quiet for a moment. He passed one hand over his eyes. Birch wondered if he was crying – it was too dark to tell.

'They took them back, of course,' he said. 'I knew they would, which was why I struggled. That was why I hit the guy. I suddenly realised they were going to take them back, and they were going to kill them all anyway. I realised what I'd done, and that I'd done it for nothing.'

'You hit a guy?'

'One of the police officers,' Hodgson said. 'I'm surprised you didn't know that. One of the charges they got me on was resisting arrest. They'd tried for assaulting a police officer, but my solicitor did something. Got it ... downgraded, or whatever you'd call it.'

'I hadn't realised that,' Birch said. 'I thought you were tried for perverting the course of justice.'

'Yeah,' Hodgson said. 'That was for taking the cows. For moving them. I went against the government regulations. I put other farms at risk. I endangered lives, blah blah blah.

Those cows were healthy; they couldn't have spread the disease. But they didn't care about that. They cared that I'd broken ranks – that I'd dared to mess with their fucked-up systems.'

Birch looked down at Elise. The little girl was breathing slowly now, falling asleep in the nest of the sweatshirt. Birch gently lifted the half-empty water bottle, hooked it over the arm of the camping chair, and placed it on to the dirt floor.

'They were trying to protect people,' she said. 'It's hard, but no blanket measure can ever be perfect. You can never make things right for absolutely everyone – I should know. You have to do what's best for the majority. They had to slaughter that herd, so others could be saved.'

She expected Hodgson to shout at her again, but when he spoke, his voice was quiet.

'So you *have* had the official version, then. You'd made up your mind about me before you even walked in here.'

'Not at all. I didn't even know about one of your charges, remember. I haven't had any version; I barely know what happened. I'm just saying, in my experience—'

'They got me on a drink driving charge, too,' Hodgson said. He didn't seem to want to hear what she had to say. 'The prosecution really loved that, really revelled in it.'

'I can imagine.'

Hodgson fell quiet again. Birch wondered what could have been going on in his mind, as he hatched the plan, and as he carried it out – as he actually drove his hazardous cargo south-bound. She didn't believe for a moment that the farmer hadn't helped him, hadn't known. Had it been the farmer's plan, and Hodgson had been convinced? Would someone really go to jail for five years to protect a man they'd just met? What on earth had been in his mind?

'Can I ask, Gerry – what did you plan to *do* with those cows? Where were you driving them to?'

Hodgson's shoulders sagged.

'I dunno, really,' he said. 'I honestly don't know. While I was driving, I had a whole load of different ideas. I thought about taking them somewhere remote and letting them go. There are big open pastures up around Caldbeck, in north Cumbria – they're remote, not many folk go up there. I thought about that. But I also thought, I could drive this truckload of cows all the way to Central London. I could drive them to Westminster and let them out on the lawn outside the Houses of Parliament. I could turn this into a real protest, you know? Show the government what they were doing.'

Birch was nodding. She wondered if Hodgson could even see her, in the strange half-dark.

'I thought about this a lot in prison,' he went on, 'and I realised after a while that I'd done it for myself as much as for the animals. I wanted to feel like I'd done something good, after all the badness. All the killing and the burning. I wanted to know I'd also done something pure and compassionate. Something good.'

Birch couldn't stand it any longer. She could feel the words forming in her mouth, and she thought of Rena, of how she might be about to make a hell of a mess for herself, for everyone. But she couldn't prevent it – the question tumbled out anyway.

'That's all very well,' she said, 'but now you've killed again, haven't you?'

HOUR SEVENTEEN

'Can someone please explain to me,' McLeod said, 'why we're all still sitting here?'

The pasture was now completely dark. Overhead, the sky was a deep navy blue, fading to lilac in the west. The circling helicopter swung like an airborne Christmas decoration, pinpricked by red and white light.

'Caution,' Jamal Leigh replied. 'That's why.'

The ruined cottage looked like a stage set in the beam of their single floodlight: two-dimensional, like it was made of paper or painted on cloth. Along the perimeter line, officers huddled around radios, in spots of mobile lighting, to listen in on Gerald Hodgson as he talked. To listen in on Birch as she questioned and cajoled.

'The man's an egomaniac,' McLeod retorted. 'He thinks what he's done today is justifiable.'

'No, actually,' Rena said, 'I don't agree.'

McLeod blinked.

'I beg your pardon?'

Rena lifted the radio in her hand.

'They've been talking for nearly two hours,' she said, 'and you'll notice Hodgson has barely mentioned Sophie Lowther. He hasn't mentioned his actions this morning at all. I'm theorising, of course, but I believe that earlier today, Hodgson had some kind of mental health episode. He's been living with

PTSD since 2001, and from the sounds of things, he's received no support at all since he left prison. I think what happened this morning was some sort of severe break for him. Given how he's talking, I'm not sure if he even remembers what he's done.'

McLeod spluttered.

'That,' he said, 'or he's aware he's speaking to a police officer, and doesn't want to incriminate himself.'

Rena shrugged.

'Maybe,' she said, 'but my experience tells me that people who commit violent acts and then find themselves in crisis want to talk about those acts. Talk *around* them. Try to make sense of them. Try to explain, if not justify them, as you say. Hodgson hasn't actually done any of that. It's very clear to me that he spends a lot of his time inside his head, thinking about 2001. That's almost all he's talked about so far, in two whole hours. The things he did then, the things he was made to do. The things he remembers. Bear in mind, he's been out of prison for a lot of years, and been completely law-abiding as far as we know, until today. Why is that? If he consciously wanted to hurt Sophie, he could have done it before now, and he didn't. But he's been alone with his thoughts an awful lot. If he's been trying to deal with his PTSD on his own, trying to shove those memories away into some back corner of his mind, then he's always been a ticking time bomb. It could only ever have been a matter of time before he had some sort of mental health emergency.'

'You think he shot two people and then wreaked havoc in a showground . . . and he doesn't remember?'

'I can't be sure, of course,' Rena replied. 'But the more I listen, the more I think that, at the very least, Sophie Lowther's murder this morning wasn't premeditated. Hodgson's social media posts never stated he was going to kill her. Never even really said he'd hurt her.'

'Nonsense,' McLeod said. 'Those posts were threatening; you can't deny that.'

'But were they? Or did they just seem that way because by the time we read them, Hodgson had already opened fire at the showground? I think it's possible that he really did just want to see Sophie, just wanted to confront her. I mean sure, his intention was to make her feel threatened, assert his dominance. But I think he got to her house, and ended up being triggered in a way he didn't expect. It might have been seeing her for the first time in many years, or it might have been something she said to him. But I think something happened in that house that flipped a switch in his brain.'

McLeod raised an eyebrow.

'And now?'

'Now,' Rena said, 'he seems very erratic. Part of that is the context he finds himself in, of course. But if you listen to how he's talking, you can hear that he's mainly reliving the events of 2001. He remembers them in intricate detail, though we're two decades on. He's spent so much time in those memories that he knows every facet of them. I might even venture to say, he's walked back into those memories now because they're – well, not safe, but *known*. They're almost a comfort zone.'

McLeod opened his mouth to speak, but Leigh stepped between them and gestured towards the radio.

'Listen,' he hissed. 'She's asking him about it. About this morning.'

They fell quiet. Everyone on the perimeter was quiet, listening. All they could hear was the vague buzz of static.

McLeod nudged Leigh.

'What did she ask him?' he whispered.

'She said,' Leigh replied, '*now you've killed again, haven't you?*'

The radio swished, as though someone were moving around near to the microphone.

'Why isn't he saying anything?' McLeod hissed.

'To be fair,' Rena whispered back, 'it's a hard thing for him to hear. It's not what I'd have said, at this juncture. Not at all.'

Leigh held up a hand.

'Wait,' he said.

But there was silence in the ruin.

'See,' Rena said, 'this backs up my theory. The question's confused him. He won't remember very well what happened this morning.'

They listened while Birch waited a little longer for Hodgson's reply. Then she tried a different tack.

'You said you hadn't planned,' Birch said, her voice crackly in the radio, 'to have Elise with you. This wasn't how you expected today to go. Am I right?'

A pause, and then Hodgson said, 'Right.'

'So . . . how *did* you think today would go, if you don't mind me asking?'

Rena nodded.

'That's a better question,' she said. 'Less of a difficult question.'

Again, there was a pause before Hodgson spoke.

'I went to see Sophie,' he said. His voice was slow, as though he were recalling a clouded memory. '*That* was my plan. As soon as I found out where she lived, I'd been thinking about it. I felt like . . .' His voice faltered. 'I felt like . . .'

'Angry?' Birch asked. 'Did you feel angry with her?'

'Yes.' Again, Hodgson's answer was slow, drawn out. 'But not in the way you'd think. When I was still in prison, and I first worked out she'd ditched me, I was enraged. I mean, after I'd finished being gutted, being sad. I loved her, and she wasn't in my life any more. But yes, I was angry. Back then, I was angry in the way you're imagining.'

'I don't understand what you mean.'

'You think,' Hodgson said, 'that I was vengeful angry. That I'm still vengeful angry. And I'm saying I was, in prison, but then it changed. I've had a lot of time to think. And the desire to hurt Sophie back, to get revenge: that went away. What replaced it was a desire for justice. Or rather for her to see that what she did to me was unjust. Hurtful. I wanted her to see that what she did made my life a lot worse. They gave me five years in prison, but she added many more years of loneliness on to that. I wanted her to understand what she had done, what it felt like. That was all.'

'So you went to see her. This morning.'

'I did.'

'And can you tell me what happened?'

There was silence on the radio once more.

'You know what happened,' Hodgson said, at last.

'Not really,' Birch replied. 'Not in detail. I have an idea, but I haven't heard your side of things. Just like I didn't know everything that happened to you in 2001. I've only heard a version of events.'

The helicopter made its pass, across the thin crescent moon brightening in the sky. Rena shivered.

'I can't,' Hodgson said, and even through the radio his voice sounded changed, thickened. 'I can't.'

Rena looked at McLeod.

'He doesn't remember,' she said. 'Not fully. You see?'

McLeod was shaking his head, but before he could speak, Dacre appeared at his elbow.

'Sir,' he said, 'I'm sorry to interrupt.'

'No, no.' McLeod waved a hand at Rena as though he hoped he could dismiss her. 'It's quite all right, Dacre. What have you got for me?'

Dacre flicked on the screen of his phone, and held it out to McLeod.

'We've been fact-checking Hodgson's story so far,' he said. 'He's not telling her any fibs. We've found a paper trail for just about everything – the haulage firm, the freelance work he did as a slaughterman. We've found the address he lived at in Longtown with Sophie Lowther. It's all true.'

Beside them, Rena sniffed.

'Of course it is,' she muttered. McLeod ignored her.

'What about the people at the showground?'

Dacre nodded.

'We've followed up with several of the witnesses,' he said. 'Including the gentleman who believed Hodgson targeted him deliberately. His name is Bob Veitch.'

'This is the farmer? The one Hodgson had an enmity with?'

'Yes, sir. I'd say a *supposed* enmity – it seems it was rather one-sided.'

McLeod frowned.

'What's the story?'

'Veitch has a farm called Yellow Sike, out in the middle of nowhere between Newcastleton and Langholm,' Dacre replied. 'In 2001 he wrote to the haulage firm Hodgson worked for to complain about the livestock lorries passing close to his farm. See, there's a tiny road that comes off the A7 at a place called Arkleton, and passes through Yellow Sike's land.'

'And?'

'And,' Dacre went on, 'Veitch claimed the lorries were using this road in order to avoid being stopped at various disinfecting stations along the A7 and other larger roads. He claimed they were flouting the rules and putting his animals at risk.'

'And Hodgson got upset?'

Dacre shook his head.

'There's no evidence Hodgson knew about the complaint,' Dacre replied, 'though we do know the haulage firm issued a memo to all employees about always using designated routes.'

McLeod sighed.

'Sorry, Dacre, but . . .'

'There's more. Veitch claims that shortly after his complaint, someone left a dead sheep in the track where his property met the road. He decided it must have been one of the drivers, upset that he'd shopped them to their employer. A day later, Gerald Hodgson was apprehended on the M6 with a truck full of stolen cows.'

Rena leaned in.

'Let me guess,' she said, 'Veitch therefore assumed Hodgson also planted the dead sheep.'

Dacre nodded.

'He phoned the papers.'

Rena snorted.

'Of course he did.'

'"Deranged haulage driver who stole infected cows also left grisly remains in farmer's driveway", that kind of thing?' McLeod asked.

'Practically word for word, sir.'

'Right.' McLeod batted away Dacre's phone, its oblong of light still hovering between them. 'So now he thinks Hodgson deliberately shot at him?'

'He's saying he wants to press charges for attempted murder,' Dacre replied.

Rena pressed one hand to her forehead.

'Isn't it more likely,' McLeod said, 'that Hodgson never knew this farmer even existed?'

'Of course it is,' Rena snapped. 'We're almost certain he was firing randomly in the showground today. He wasn't in any state of mind to go and look for some farmer who complained about him twenty years ago! This was a spree shooting, a rampage. If Hodgson had wanted to hurt Veitch specifically, why didn't he drive to his farm and do it?'

'I mean,' Dacre replied, his voice chastened, 'I wouldn't say we encouraged Veitch on the attempted-murder front. But he's taking the old *go to the papers* line again.'

'My four least favourite words,' McLeod said. 'Stall him, will you? Let him think we're taking it seriously until we can get out of this damn field. I don't have time right now for some farmer with delusions of grandeur, and I definitely don't have time for the tabloids poking their noses in.'

'Right you are,' Dacre replied. He hovered at McLeod's elbow.

'It's not midnight yet,' McLeod said, pointedly. 'I'm sure Veitch is still awake.'

'Right, right,' Dacre said, backing away. 'I'll call him now.'

McLeod turned back to face Rena, who was listening to the radio. Birch was speaking softly to Elise: the sound of the little girl grizzling could be heard over the radio static.

'We need that child out of there,' McLeod said. 'She's been in there too long.'

'At last,' Rena said, 'something we agree on. Though I suspect you're thinking of the PR implications, while I'm thinking about the last time she ate something.'

'I didn't realise,' McLeod said, 'that crisis negotiators were also trained in mind-reading.'

Rena ignored the coldness in his voice, and chuckled.

'Do you have any children, DCI McLeod?'

McLeod stood a little taller, puffing out his chest.

'Two boys,' he said, 'Ruaridh and Sandy. Alexander.'

'How old?'

McLeod paused for a moment, as though doing the maths.

'Twenty-five,' he said, slowly, 'and just turned twenty-three. They're fine lads.'

'What do they do?'

'They went into the forces together,' McLeod said. 'Sandy's still training, but Ruaridh's at Catterick. He had a tour in Afghanistan last year, one of the last Scottish soldiers to serve in Helmand.'

'Impressive,' Rena said.

'I'm very proud of them.'

Birch was making shushing noises at Elise. Over the radio the sound was like distant leaves in the wind.

'What would you be doing now,' McLeod asked, 'if you were in there? What would you be saying?'

Rena tilted her head.

'Don't get me wrong,' she said, 'DI Birch has done pretty well thus far. She's let him talk, and done a good job of keeping the conversation going. The problem is, I can't feel a rapport building, particularly. He called her in there, but I sense he's still uncertain as to whether or not that was a good idea. I'd like to see him feeling like *okay, yes, I was right to ask for this person. This person is definitely going to help me.* But he still doesn't trust her.'

'Is this man ever going to trust a police officer?'

Rena shook her head.

'Probably not,' she said, 'and that's part of the problem. DI Birch is police. She thinks like police; she talks like police. She even sided with the police at one point, while they were talking – that was a mistake, to show sympathy for the police over Hodgson. She's not neutral, and she can't make herself neutral.'

'And you *are* neutral? You work for Police Scotland, too.'

'Yes,' Rena said, 'but my priority is always the person in crisis. That's what I mean about the difference between you and me, Detective Chief Inspector. You're worried about what people will say about how the police have handled this, if little Elise is found to be severely dehydrated, if she needs hospital treatment. You're worried about PR, about your job and the jobs of those around you. I'm actually worried about Elise herself. And I'm worried about Hodgson. To her credit, I think DI Birch is, too. Or she's starting to be. And I think that's bothering her. I think that's why she pivoted to asking him about the shooting this morning. Part of her realises she's empathising with him, so the police side of her brain is telling her not to lose sight of the fact that this man is a killer.'

'Precisely what I'd expect of her,' McLeod retorted. 'That's what she's trained for.'

'And that kind of training is a problem, if you ask me,' Rena said. 'I'm not saying that what Hodgson did this morning doesn't matter, and I'm not saying Sophie Lowther doesn't matter. But in this moment, Hodgson is a person in crisis. Everyone's primary objective right now should be the resolution of that crisis, in as humane a way as we can possibly manage. We should be saving the crime-and-punishment element for later.'

'Look,' McLeod said, 'I agreed with Leigh earlier when he said we don't want a fatality outcome. No one here wants that, trust me.'

'I know,' Rena said, 'but managing not to kill someone in the resolution of a crisis isn't a success. *Look, we didn't kill him* is a very, very low bar.'

McLeod looked down at the radio.

'I'm not sure what you'd like me to say.'

Rena threw him a sad smile. Her teeth glinted in the dim, artificial light.

'It's not you,' she said. 'It's the whole way we do things, really. It's like DI Birch in there, defending the police without thinking. It's all the things I had to unlearn, all the way back to my basic training, in order to get good at this job. And I'm still not perfect. It all goes very deep.'

McLeod still didn't look at her.

'I apologise,' he said, 'for using the word *maniac* earlier. It was probably inappropriate.'

'You're right,' Rena replied. 'It was.'

McLeod looked like he might speak, but in his trouser pocket, his phone rang. He moved awkwardly to answer it, reaching under the hard edge of his Kevlar vest. He swiped to answer the call.

'McLeod.'

Rena turned away, looked out over the pasture at the eerie face of the ruin.

'Anjan?' McLeod said into the phone. 'I'm sorry, the reception here is terrible. You're where?'

The helicopter passed again, looping low over the ruined cottage before turning in the same spot for what could have been the hundredth time.

'I'm sorry,' McLeod was saying, 'I can't authorise that. I can't let civilians past the cordon, no matter who they are. It would be a breach of—'

Rena looked up at him, her interest piqued.

'You're not a special case, Chaudhry,' McLeod said, his voice louder now. 'You of all people ought to know that. And her father isn't either. I can't, I'm sorry.'

He'd closed his eyes now. Rena was listening, but couldn't have heard Anjan's voice on the other end of the line, quiet as always, but speaking urgently.

'You can wait at the cordon,' McLeod said, after a moment. 'That, I can authorise. But I can't bring you up to the perimeter. I'm sorry, there's just no way.'

He hung up the call.

'Birch's partner,' he said to Rena. 'He's apparently got as far as the final cordon, down at the bottom of the track, though Christ knows how. He shouldn't have made it into the village, even. I'll need to knock heads together.'

Rena sighed.

'The man's a lawyer,' McLeod went on, 'he ought to know better than this.'

'He's only a lawyer when he's at work,' Rena said. 'Right now he's just a worried partner, I imagine.'

'Trust me,' McLeod said, beginning to cast about for someone, something. 'Anjan Chaudhry is *always* a lawyer.'

HOUR EIGHTEEN

'Why don't I tell you,' Birch said, 'what *I* think happened this morning.'

Hodgson was back at the chimney breast. He'd braced one forearm against it, and pushed his head into the crook of his elbow. In the darkness, his vague silhouette was that of a man weeping, or else of a man asleep standing up. Birch couldn't see the shotgun any more, which worried her.

'Since you don't seem to want to tell me,' she added.

Hodgson let out a low moan.

'I told you,' he said, 'I can't.'

Birch stifled a yawn. The adrenalin she'd been running on for the past few hours had waned enough for her to realise she was exhausted. Hodgson must be, too – she hadn't seen him sit down in almost three hours. Elise was fast asleep once again, her breaths dry and raspy from crying.

'Well,' Birch said, 'we know you went to see Sophie. It was early – you get up early every day, right? For work.'

'Right.' His voice was weary.

'So you drove into Kelso, to Sophie's house. Maybe you sat in the Land Rover for a little while, psyching yourself up to it. Did you take the gun to the door with you? I suppose you must have – you wouldn't have gone back outside for it, that might have given her time to escape.'

'Please,' Hodgson said, 'it isn't like you think. It wasn't . . .'
He fell silent.

'It wasn't what, Gerry?'

'The gun,' he said. Again, Birch wondered if he was crying
– his voice sounded wet, but it was hard to tell in the gloom of
the ruin. 'The gun was only to frighten her.'

'I must say, that's hard for me to believe,' Birch said, 'having
read some of your recent Facebook updates. They sound
pretty threatening.'

He moved his head, fast and erratic, his hair a sudden blur.
He nodded, but didn't immediately speak: Birch imagined his
mind whirring, trying to recall the posts she was referring to.

'Threatening, yes,' he said at last, 'okay. I'll admit, I wanted
to show her I knew where she was, where she lived. Shake her
up a bit. But that's all.'

'Less than a week ago you posted that time was running
out. You'd had enough.'

'I had,' Hodgson said, his voice plaintive, 'I *had* had enough.
But you have to understand, I had a plan. All along, I had a
plan, and the plan was to frighten her. Mess up her perfect
new life a bit. Let her get blindsided, so she could see what it
felt like. That was all.'

Birch cocked her head. For a brief second, she thought of
Marcello. Marcello would have been able to look at the words
Hodgson had written, and determine whether or not these
protestations checked out. He'd be able to pick up the invisible thread of premeditation, if it was there. Marcello would be
so much better at this than her.

'Maybe.' She tried to keep her voice level, stay firm. 'Maybe,
at the start. But then what happened? What happened to
change that?'

'I don't know. I don't.'

'Something,' Birch went on. 'Something she said to you, maybe? Or was it seeing Elise? Seeing she had a child now? Seeing just how far she'd moved on?'

'Please stop.' Hodgson was whispering now. 'Please don't say any more.'

'Then tell me what happened, Gerry. Tell me what she said to you. Tell me how it went down.' Birch could feel the adrenalin kicking back up now. She wasn't negotiating any more, she was interrogating – the change felt like static building in her chest. For the first time since she'd squeezed in through the broken door, she felt like she was in charge, and the feeling was exhilarating. 'Tell me how you ended up cornering your ex-partner in her bedroom and then shooting her and her husband through the chest. Tell me how you ended up killing two innocent people, after all you've said to me tonight about never wanting to kill anything ever again. *Tell* me, Gerry.'

'Stop, I said *stop!*'

There was a clatter, and Birch jumped. The shotgun, which had been leaning against Hodgson's legs, fell to the floor. Instinctively, Birch pressed Elise's body closer to her chest, and the little girl stirred awake. But Hodgson didn't reach for the gun. He fell to his knees on the rough, rocky floor of the ruin. Out of his mouth came a long, animal sound, a sound with spit and misery in it. The sound emptied his lungs, and he hauled in a tattered breath before making it again, every bit as long and loud. A twisted sound. The sound of desperate grief.

'Okay, Gerry,' Birch said. She could feel her own eyes were wide. Her heart was hammering. 'Okay, I've stopped.'

Elise twisted her head in Birch's grip to look at the source of this strange, new noise. She didn't cry again herself: Birch could feel the child's little eyelashes flickering against her wrist as she blinked, curious, trying to see in the dark.

'You're all right,' Birch whispered to her, 'you're all right.'

Hodgson was not all right. In the weird light, Birch could see his back heaving up and down. He was now on all fours – the gun somewhere beside him – crying and retching. She wondered if he'd throw up, then remembered he hadn't eaten for many hours. Neither had she, for that matter: Birch realised her head felt light, her limbs swimmy. She wanted very badly to sleep now. She didn't know how much longer any of this could go on.

'Gerry, I—'

Hodgson dragged in another breath.

'I killed them?' he said, and it took a moment for Birch to realise it wasn't a statement, but a question. 'I killed Sophie?'

Birch couldn't think of anything to say beyond the obvious, so she said the obvious.

'You didn't know that?'

Hodgson was coughing now, and she could hear how raw his throat was. He shook his head, hard enough that she could see even in the strange near-dark.

'But . . .' Birch glanced down at Elise, hoping she wasn't taking in any of what was being said. 'But you shot them both at point-blank range. They had no chance.'

Hodgson spat on to the floor of the ruin. He was breathing hard.

'So yes,' Birch said, annoyance rising in her again, 'yes, you killed them. And what's more, you then drove to the showfield at Springwood Park and shot several other people.'

He pulled in another long breath.

'Yes,' he said, his voice thick and sodden, 'yes, I did that. I did that, I remember. But Sophie—'

'You're telling me you don't remember shooting Sophie?'

Hodgson rolled back off his knees, pushing himself up with his palms. Birch's heart lurched, assuming he'd reach for the gun again. But instead he rocked backward into a sitting position, pulled his knees up to his chest, and hugged them. Now, he was a roundish mass in the dark: the fuzzy glow from the floodlight illuminated only the wisps of hair on top of his head. He looked like a boulder with a halo, she thought.

'I wasn't . . .' He seemed to be trying to bring himself under control again – it was as though he'd curled into a ball to try and prevent the sobs from bursting out of him. 'I wasn't sure.' His voice came out like rapid-fire now, punctuated by wet inward breaths, like a man whose lungs were giving out. 'What happened. It was like. I'd watched it. But hadn't done it. Like I'd watched. Someone else do it. I remember flashes. I can't explain. Like – a bad dream. Like a nightmare. Screaming. And the shots. But I can't. I can't see them. I can't see Sophie. Her face.'

'What *can* you see?'

Hodgson hacked out another cough.

'Her,' he said. 'The kid. Turning round. She was standing. In the doorway. She'd seen it. I hadn't known about her.' He was bringing his breath under control now, managing longer strings of words between his sobs. 'I hadn't known they had a child. It scared me, turning, seeing her there. I couldn't look back to see what I'd done. I couldn't look away.'

Birch's head buzzed. She couldn't think straight. Had Hodgson really not realised he'd shot Sophie and her husband? She didn't want to believe that someone could commit such a decisive act without fully realising – and yet, she also wanted to believe him. She didn't think such anguish could possibly be faked.

'Why did you take Elise with you, Gerry?'

Hodgson was wiping his face with the back of his sleeve, now. Birch could feel he was calming down again, but something in the air between them was different. Something about him had changed.

'No choice,' he spluttered. 'I couldn't leave her there. Not after . . . what happened. What I thought I might have done. I couldn't.'

'You didn't think about shooting her, too?'

Hodgson's voice made her jump so hard that the legs of the camping chair scraped on the ground.

'No!' he yelled. 'No! No, you can't say that. You *can't* say that!'

Birch heard his voice crack on the second *can't*, all the air from his tired lungs pushed into that yell. The sound was frightening.

'Okay,' she said, 'okay, Gerry, I'm sorry. I shouldn't have asked that.'

'I never wanted to hurt her.' He was still shouting. 'I never wanted to hurt her, or anyone. You understand? No one.'

Of course I don't understand, Birch thought, though she wasn't sure if he was referring to Elise now, or Sophie.

'I'm trying,' she said. 'I'm trying to understand, I promise. That's all anyone up here wants. To try to understand what happened.'

Hodgson pressed his face into his pulled-up knees. Birch wondered if he thought he could curl up small enough to disappear. She could see his shoulders still quaking with sobs.

'Just breathe,' she said, in as soothing a voice as she could muster. 'Just breathe.'

On her lap, Elise squirmed.

'Want my mummy,' she said, in a small voice, and when Birch didn't respond, she said it again, louder. 'Want my mummy.'

Birch tried to swallow the lump in her throat.

'I know you do, wee scone,' she said. 'I know. But just stay with me for now, okay?'

Elise made a few little clucking sounds, pushing her face back into the creased front of Birch's blouse.

'Please don't. Please don't cry, Elise. I'm sorry, I can't do anything. I can't—'

Across the room, Hodgson lifted his head.

'You're saying I really killed them,' he said. His voice was suddenly much calmer – colder, more like it had been before. 'Him too.'

Birch hesitated. Her information was hours old. She had no idea if Elise's father was alive or dead – only that his prognosis at the last update hadn't looked good. As she thought about how to answer, a light came on in her mind, as though someone somewhere had opened the door to a bright room, just by a crack.

'Yes,' she said. 'Yes, that's what I'm saying.'

Hodgson made another sound – it took Birch a second to realise it was a creaking sort of laugh.

'That's it, then,' he said. 'I'm done for.'

Elise was grizzling into Birch's chest, the sound muffled.

'Done for?'

'Life,' he replied, the word sharp in his mouth. 'I'll get life. More than life.'

The crack of light widened in Birch's mind.

'Maybe,' she said, 'but nothing's certain yet. There are still things we can do.'

Hodgson sniffed, and she heard the phlegm rattle in his chest.

'Bullshit,' he spat. 'I've done it now. I'm fucked.'

'No. I mean – I won't lie to you, Gerry, you've got some big questions to answer. But this isn't over. You still have ways to make things right.'

He laughed again – there was venom in him now.

'Like fucking *what*?'

Birch placed a hand on top of Elise's little head, though she guessed Hodgson probably couldn't see.

'You can let this little girl go, for starters.'

Hodgson said nothing. Birch held her breath, waiting for him to refuse her. He didn't.

'Think about it,' she went on. 'You said yourself that you didn't want her with you. You took her because you didn't want to leave her there, after – after what happened. That was an act of kindness, right? Any jury would see that. You didn't hurt her, and you didn't leave her. You wanted her to be okay. You can show you still want her to be okay, by letting her go. If you let her go, my colleagues will be able to confirm she isn't hurt. You haven't harmed her in any way. She's tired and thirsty, nothing more. If you let her go now, it'll improve things for you, Gerry, I guarantee it.'

Still he didn't speak. Birch hoped that was a sign it was working: he was considering it.

'Also,' she said, unable to stop babbling now, 'you don't need her, because you've got me. In terms of, you know, having a hostage. Having leverage. I'm here, now. And I'll make you a promise: I don't leave this house until you do. How does that sound? Whatever happens from now on, happens to both of us. I promise.'

She paused. He still wasn't arguing.

'So,' she said, 'you don't need Elise, do you? You can let her go and get warmed up. She can have something to eat. She can be taken care of. You can show that you still want what you wanted when you first saw her, back at the house: for Elise to be okay.'

Birch heard a voice in her head that she realised was Rena's. *Enough now. Stop talking.* She remembered Marcello, standing behind McLeod's desk, one hand raised, palm flat: *wait.* She waited.

It felt like many minutes passed before Hodgson spoke.

'You really think,' he said, 'that would make a difference? When you're telling me for sure that I've killed someone. I've murdered someone.'

Birch took a long breath in before answering.

'So have lots of people,' she said, 'and it's almost always complicated. Everything has to be taken into account, right? Every decision made. Whether or not there was intent. Whether or not there's remorse. It's all evidence. It's all considered. And anything can make a difference.'

Hodgson went quiet again. You haven't got him yet, Birch thought, you haven't quite convinced him. But the door in her mind was creaking open.

'Think about that guy,' she said, 'the one you mentioned earlier. The slaughterman who shot his colleague. He killed someone too, right? But there were all sorts of other factors. All sorts of things considered at the trial. And he was found not guilty.'

Hodgson snorted, and she thought he'd argue, but he didn't speak.

'This isn't over,' she said. 'Not yet.'

Hodgson still didn't answer, but he began to move. Birch squinted against the darkness to watch him unfold his arms, and push his knees away from his chest. He put out one hand and felt around on the stone wall behind him, finding a handhold and beginning to lever himself upright. Birch realised how much she'd relaxed since he'd curled up on the floor. As he lurched upright again, she braced herself, tightening her grip on Elise.

Hodgson straightened up, and patted himself down, as though trying to knock the dust and soot of the ruin off his clothes. He didn't reach down for the shotgun, like she'd expected him to do: instead, he turned his back on her, and inched towards the window. The outline of his head came into sharp relief as he peered out into the opening, looking up towards the bright eye of the floodlight and the perimeter beyond. Birch thought about the snipers posted around the cottage, wondered if any of them had a shot. His face must be at least partially visible, she thought – a small, pale moon in the window's black square. Hodgson stood there, looking out, for long enough that she began to wonder how she'd react if the shot came, if she had to watch him sprawl back from the hit. He'd die in front of her. She realised she didn't know how to feel about that. And yet she waited for it, the bright zipping sound of the bullet leaving its chamber. She realised she longed for it not because she wanted Hodgson dead, or even punished, but because she wanted an end to this miserable ordeal. She wanted an end to the helicopter's overhead battering. She wanted someone to reach out and lift Elise out of her arms, to safety. She wanted to walk out of this wretched pile of stones and fall down in the tousled grass outside and sleep, right there in the middle of the pasture.

'This poor kid,' she said, quietly, looking down at the shivery bundle in her arms. 'Both parents dead. So much to try and make sense of. You care about that, Gerry, I can tell. You don't want any more harm to come to her.'

Hodgson didn't turn around. They probably can't be sure it's him, Birch thought, the face in the window. They think it could be me, that's why they aren't taking the shot.

'You'll tell them that?' Hodgson asked.

'Sure. But if you let her go, they'll know. It'll be a powerful message.'

Hodgson stepped sideways, back into the shadows.

'All right,' he said. 'She can leave.'

The door in Birch's mind swung open, flooding her whole body with light. She tried to keep her body still, her face impassive, so he couldn't see the relief she felt.

'You're doing the right thing,' she said, evenly. 'I promise you.'

Hodgson didn't reply. He walked back to the spot where he'd fallen to the floor and retched. When he lifted the shotgun, Birch saw a seam of dim light run down the barrel, just for a moment. She waited until Hodgson had nestled the gun across his chest once more, until she was confident he wouldn't point it at her. Then she shifted Elise on her lap, and raised one hand.

'Okay,' she said, 'let's talk about what I'm going to do, so you know what to expect. In a minute, I'm going to stand up. I'm going to talk to Elise a little bit about what's happening. Then we can send her out of the door together, if you like. How does that sound?'

Hodgson was quiet for a moment. Then he said, 'What if they shoot her?'

Birch blinked.

'What do you mean?'

He let out a snort.

'You think I don't know how many guns are trained on the door of this house? You think I haven't heard how trigger-happy you people can be? The slightest movement outside that door, and they shoot. It's dark. How are they to know it's her?'

Birch glanced down at the flak jacket, still propped beside the chair. She realised she didn't know for sure if the microphone was still picking up. Her colleagues might not have heard a word of the deal she'd just negotiated. Hodgson had a point.

'The perimeter is close by,' she said. 'You talked to me by shouting over, remember? We'll shout to them. We'll make sure they know.'

Hodgson gestured towards the flak vest.

'You should put that on her,' he said. 'To be on the safe side.'

Birch froze. What Hodgson was proposing would send that microphone – the only connection she had to her team – back up to the perimeter. They'd be alone together, then.

'Problem is,' she said, 'it's very heavy. I'm not sure she could walk, wearing it.'

Hodgson shrugged.

'So try it out,' he said. He seemed almost amiable, his anguish gone now he'd made up his mind to let Elise go. Birch realised she'd really made him believe he could change things, doing this, and she felt a brief stab of guilt at manipulating a man whose mind was clearly not functioning as it should. But Hodgson was still speaking. 'Stand her up and put it on her, see if she can manage it.'

Elise had twisted her head round again to try and look at Hodgson as he spoke. Birch could feel that a hank of her blouse was balled hard in the little girl's fist. She didn't want to send the flak vest out of the door – didn't want to lose either the microphone or the protection it would offer if she put it back on. But she couldn't think of a way to keep hold of it without Hodgson becoming suspicious, and she didn't want to risk him changing his mind about the child.

'You hear that, Elise?' she said, wincing. 'You want to try on my police lady outfit?'

Elise turned her gaze and looked up at Birch. In the half-light, her little eyes were shiny.

'Come on,' Birch said, 'do you like dressing up? I bet you do. I bet you have all sorts of cool costumes at home.'

The little girl nodded.

'I have princess dresses,' she said.

'You do?' Birch hooked her hands into Elise's armpits, and very slowly, unfolded herself from the camping chair. She kept her eyes on Hodgson, but he didn't move. 'And which princess dress is your favourite?'

Elise tottered a little as Birch set her down on the floor, but she stayed upright.

'Elsa dress,' she said.

'Elsa dress,' Birch repeated, bending down so her face was near to Elise's. 'Elsa is from *Frozen*, right?'

'Yes,' Elise said. 'And Anna and Olaf and Sven.'

'Clever girl.' Birch began to disentangle the black sweatshirt from around Elise. The little girl yawned, swaying on her feet. 'What colour is Elsa's dress? I've forgotten.'

'Blue,' Elise said, moving her arms so the sweatshirt could be lifted away. 'And sparkles.'

'Blue and *sparkles*.' Birch tried to inject admiration into her voice. 'I bet you look super pretty in blue and sparkles.'

She glanced up again at Hodgson. He was sentry-like now, watching them, but not moving.

'So, I know it isn't a princess dress,' she said, reaching for the flak vest, 'but it is a police lady outfit. Can I try it on and see if it fits you?'

Elise turned her head, casting about the room until she identified where Hodgson was standing. She lowered her voice to a whisper, though it was the loud stage-whisper of a small child.

'Nasty man won't let me.'

Birch was holding the vest in both hands now. She imagined the officers on the perimeter, listening to Elise's spooky whisper through their radios. She waited to see if Hodgson would react. He saw the two of them watching him, but only shrugged.

'No, Elise,' Birch said, 'it's okay. See?' She lifted the vest. Elise's arms hung limp at her sides. Tiredness seemed to radiate from her little body.

'How about this?' Birch guided the vest down over Elise's head, over her smeared, dirty pyjamas. The edge of it reached almost to her ankles, and Birch nearly laughed. She looked like a kid inside a black cardboard box, her head sticking out of a hole cut in the top.

'Now . . .' She reached in through one of the armholes and felt around until she found Elise's wrist. Then she bent her tiny arm and guided it up and out of the vest. Elise didn't fight her, so she did the same with the other arm.

'There,' she said, straightening up. 'You're dressed like a police lady.'

Elise looked down at herself.

'This isn't a very pretty dress,' she said, solemnly.

'No,' Birch said, 'I agree. Can you walk in it, though?'

Elise was touching the vest now, tentative but curious.

'It's heavy,' she said.

'I know, honey,' Birch said. She looked up at Hodgson. 'I'm going to take a few steps, Gerry,' she said, noticing how her voice changed in register as she switched out of kid-talk. 'See if she'll follow me.'

Hodgson nodded. Birch nudged the camping chair out of the way, and backed up until she felt the stone wall of the ruin rise up behind her.

'Okay, come over to me, Elise,' she said, in the most encouraging voice she could manage. 'Let's see your best police-lady walk.'

Elise glanced at Hodgson once again, but turned back quickly, as though she didn't want to look at him too long, didn't want to think about him. She took a step, and then another.

'Is it too heavy for you?' Birch asked.

Elise teetered forward another couple of steps.

'No,' she said, and again Birch wanted to laugh. The kid was obviously lying.

'No,' she repeated, 'because you're a big strong girl, aren't you?'

Elise took the last couple of steps, then reached out and put her hands on Birch's thighs to steady herself.

'Yes,' she said, loudly. 'Elise Marianne Lowther is Mummy's big girl.'

Across the room, Hodgson made a sound. It was a sort of moan, like some kind of very old engine shutting down. Something in Elise's voice made it clear she was parroting a line she'd learned – she was repeating Sophie. Birch put both her hands on the child's head, a protective gesture, though had Hodgson chosen to raise the shotgun and fire right then, there would have been absolutely nothing she could have done.

Hodgson creaked out a word. It had been a long time since he'd spoken, and again, his voice sounded wet.

'Marianne,' he said. 'Marianne is Sophie's mother.'

Birch looked down at the little girl. She could feel her small palms as two warm, heavy spots through the fabric of her jeans.

'Is that right, Elise? Is your grandma named Marianne?'

'My Nana,' Elise replied, correcting her. 'My Nana's name.'

Birch reached down and scooped Elise up, propping her awkwardly on to one hip, the vest getting in the way. She could feel how much heavier it made her.

'How would you like,' she said, 'to go and see your Nana right now? I'm sure she'd really, really like to see you.'

Elise's face was level with Birch's now, close enough that she could feel the little girl's breath. Elise was studying her, her face tired but quizzical.

'Don't be silly,' she said, 'it's night-time. Nana asleep.'

Birch jostled Elise, putting on her best smile.

'No,' she said, 'I happen to know that your Nana is wide awake right now, and waiting to see you.' In her mind's eye, Birch saw an older woman, unkempt with grief, frantic and crying, watching the lurid ticker of a twenty-four-hour news station scroll by and by and by. How horrifying it must be, she realised, to lose your daughter and not be able to process it, not be able to sit with it at all, because your tiny granddaughter has also been taken away. Birch coughed back tears. 'She's waiting to give you a big, big cuddle.'

Elise was quiet. In the buzzy grey light, she peered at Birch, moving her face even closer. Then she lifted one small arm, and placed a hand flat on Birch's cheek.

'Why're you sad?' she asked.

Birch couldn't help it, then. The tears came up in her eyes, though she tried to keep smiling.

'I'm just sad,' she said, 'that we have to say goodbye now, Elise. It's time for you to go home.'

'Yes,' Elise replied, as though relieved someone had finally said something sensible. 'I go home and see Mummy and Daddy.'

Birch looked over at Hodgson, who was still standing sentry-like, watching them. She didn't have the energy to try and tell this child the truth. She wouldn't know how to start.

'Sure,' she said. Elise lifted her hand away as a tear rolled down Birch's face, wetting her little fingers. 'And Nana, and – and your grandad.'

'Gadda!' Elise bounced herself in Birch's arms. Gadda was clearly a favourite adult.

'Yes, and Gadda,' Birch said. She twisted her body so she was facing Hodgson fully, Elise now partly shielded by her body. 'Gerry,' she said, 'you're right, it looks like she's fine in this vest. If I walk her over to the door, can you shift it so she can get out?'

Hodgson didn't move. Birch hitched Elise higher up on to her hip, and pulled in a long breath through her nose.

'Gerry,' she said, 'I thought we agreed that this was the best thing?'

When Hodgson eventually responded, he moved like a man who'd just been freed from some kind of spell. His gestures were slow and jerky, mechanical somehow, as though he were forcing himself to make them. He crossed the floor of the ruin, and Birch met him beside the wrecked door. It was the closest they'd been to each other in three hours. She saw, as he passed in front of the window – not trying to duck this time – that his face shone with tears. Close up, his eyes were dark and sunken, his cheeks rough with stubble. Frail, she thought – he looked frail. Though the gun was still across his chest, she didn't fear it quite so much. Not now they were this close.

'The bad man,' Elise whispered, and she buried her face in Birch's shoulder.

'It's okay,' Birch said. She kept her gaze locked on Hodgson's face, watching for any warning sign, any flicker. 'Gerry here is going to say goodbye to you now, aren't you, Gerry?'

To her surprise, Hodgson leaned in close, bending over Elise. Birch wanted to leap back, but forced herself to stay still, her feet rooted in a wide V, bearing the kid's weight. When he spoke, his voice was soft and sad and tired.

'Bye bye, little one,' he murmured. 'I'm sorry. I wish I could tell you how sorry I am.'

The flak vest was twisted awkwardly around Elise's little frame, a big part of it wedged between their bodies – but Birch found herself hoping that the mic had picked that up.

'All right, Elise,' Birch said, as Hodgson stepped back. 'It's time to go now.'

She gave the little body in her arms a final squeeze, as though she thought she could bestow some extra luck or courage or protection over the poor kid. Then she lowered her to the ground, hands hovering around the child's shoulders until she was sure she wouldn't topple. Hodgson was scraping the door open, making a gap through which Elise could finally escape.

She was ready to go. The little girl toddled towards the opening doorway, awkward in the heavy vest, but determined. Birch put a hand on one of her shoulders, holding the kid still until Hodgson was done moving the door. She kept her eyes on the patch of darkness into which he'd laid the shotgun, even as she crouched down, into toddler eye-level.

'Elise, I need you to listen to me for a sec, okay? Do you see that bright light up there?'

The child nodded.

'Right. I need you to walk towards that light. That's where everybody is. Once you get to that light, you'll be safe.' Birch leaned in low so the microphone, if it was working, would hear her. 'Standing beside that light is a very nice lady called Rena. Rena will take care of you.'

Elise looked up at her.

'You come too?'

Birch shook her head.

'I'm going to stay here with Gerry for a bit longer,' she said. 'But I know you can manage on your own, because you're a brave girl, aren't you?'

'Yes.' Elise nodded emphatically. 'I'm a big girl.'

Hodgson had finished shunting the door around. He'd made a gap a couple of feet wide, and now he retrieved his gun and stepped back into the shadows at the far end of the ruin. Birch heard him knocking around against the masonry and old timber there.

'Time to go,' she said. 'Just walk straight towards that light. You understand, Elise?'

'Yes,' the child replied. After a pause, she added, 'I'm not scared.'

Birch smiled.

'Of course you're not.'

Elise clearly was. She moved into the gap Hodgson had made, but hesitated on the threshold.

'You have to shout.' Hodgson's whisper from beyond the door made Birch jump. 'You said you'd shout to them, so they won't shoot her.'

Shit, Birch thought. She'd forgotten. She stepped forward and leaned out of the doorway above Elise's little frame. It felt strange to have her head and torso outside the ruin, having been inside for so long. The air felt colder outside, and fresher. The desire to break free and run returned, though her limbs were so weary she wasn't sure she'd have been able to manage it. She thought of the sights of the various rifles around the pasture, all pointed at her. She wondered how distinct her face looked from Hodgson's. Probably not very, in the weird stretched light. The thought brought the call to her lips.

'Hold your fire!' she yelled. 'This is DI Birch. Hold your fire!'

She waited, listening to the echo bounce off the hills: *fire, fire, fire*. Then she heard the crackle of the loudhailer, and Rena's voice.

'DI Birch, what's happening down there?'

Birch felt her heart shudder. Was Rena playing along, or had they really had no way of listening up at the perimeter this whole time?

'Give the order to hold fire,' Birch shouted back. 'Elise is coming out.'

Elise was looking up at Birch now, her face puzzled. There was no time for Birch to speak to her, or explain: Rena was already calling back.

'Roger that, DI Birch. Send her up to us.'

'Did you hear that, Elise? That was Rena talking. That was the nice lady I told you about. She's standing by the bright light. You go on up to her now, okay?'

Elise looked down at her feet.

'Okay,' she said, quietly, and began to walk. Birch held her breath as a gap widened between them: a foot, then two, then three. Elise stepped sideways, a sleepy lurch into the beam the floodlight threw on the ground, and she was lit up, the curls on her head like the white down of a dandelion.

'Good girl!' Birch called. 'Keep on going!'

Ten feet now. Elise was slow, her knees knocking against the Kevlar, but she was going. She was getting away. Fifteen feet. Birch's heartbeat rattled in her ears. She'd done it, she'd really done it. She'd persuaded him to let the hostage go. She'd completed a successful negotiation.

Then she heard a noise behind her. A terrible, unmistakable noise: the metallic clack of the shotgun, as Hodgson levelled it, and took aim.

HOUR NINETEEN

irch spun around. Hodgson was standing back, still well inside the shadow of the ruin. He was aiming the shotgun directly at Elise. The lit-up, whitish puff of hair made the back of her head a perfect target.

'What are you *doing*?'

Hodgson didn't respond, didn't acknowledge that Birch was even still there. She saw him shift his aim a little, zeroing in.

It happened without her thinking. One minute, she was two feet away, watching him sight down the shotgun's length. The next moment, Birch had stepped in front of him, and the end of the barrel was poking into her breastbone.

'You will not shoot that child.' The voice that came out of her was low and icy, and she barely recognised it as her own. 'Not while I am alive to stop you.'

Hodgson lifted his head a little, but the gun stayed where it was.

'Move,' he said.

'No. I won't let you do this.' Birch planted her feet again, the way she had done when carrying Elise. 'Not to her, and not to yourself.'

The mouth of the gun felt hard and cold through the thin fabric of her blouse. Birch found herself wondering what the shot would feel like, there, in the centre of her. She imagined being blown open by it, her ribcage parting and the soft meat of her body spilling out.

'I don't think,' she said, slowly, 'that you know what you're doing. Not quite, not fully. Do you? Like this morning, with Sophie. I don't think you want to do this.'

She imagined Hodgson pulling the trigger, the way he had just hours ago – opening up her chest in the same way he had Sophie's. She imagined it would burn, like a brand, though right now, she was freezing cold. Her hands were numb and tingling, and her ears rang. Don't faint, she told herself. Don't you dare faint.

'If you shoot her,' she said, 'or me, for that matter, then that's it. *Then* it's over. You go away and you never, ever come out. And we're not talking about Low Moss this time. It'll be high security. It'll be so much worse.'

Hodgson was frowning, as though her voice were an annoying buzz at the edge of his hearing. He pushed against the butt of the gun, just slightly – a nudge, to try and shift her. The movement made her heart kick, and for a second she thought she might vomit. She squinted down at the spot where the gun made contact with her chest, and then it was as though she'd been lifted out of her own body, and into a memory. She was with her grandparents on Portobello Beach, watching Charlie – only a tiny boy around Elise's age – toddle into the waves. Then she was in the passenger seat of her mother's car, kicking her feet together, the sun glancing off her brand new, bright red patent Mary Janes. They were singing along to 'Do You Love Me?' by Brian Poole and the Tremeloes, a song Birch hadn't heard in maybe thirty years. She was lying on her stomach on her mother's living-room carpet, aged twelve or so, looking up through the doorway at the father she hadn't seen since she was small. She was out stapling up posters with her missing brother's face on them, smearing away tears with her sleeve. She was sitting her final police exam. She was standing outside her office, in the corridor, talking to Anjan and blushing. They say this happens, she thought. They say your life flashes before your eyes.

'You yelled at me,' she said, 'before, when I so much as *suggested* you might hurt that child. You yelled at me. So I *know* you don't want to do this.'

Hodgson nudged the gun again.

'*Move.*'

Though her legs were shaking now, too, Birch reached out and wrapped one hand around the barrel. She didn't try to move it, just held it, feeling its slippery coldness against her palm.

'Make me,' she hissed.

Behind her, there was a crackling sound.

'DI Birch?'

Hodgson flinched. She felt the gun judder in his grip. It was Rena, calling to her over the loudhailer.

'We have Elise here, she's safe and sound,' Rena said.

Hodgson lifted his head. Birch felt his hold on the gun go slack, so she unwrapped her own hand, and the barrel fell. She expected Hodgson to complete the movement by dropping the gun entirely, but instead it swung from his limp arm, the muzzle he'd pushed into her breastbone scraping the dirt floor.

'There,' Birch said, letting out a long exhale. 'She's safe.'

Hodgson didn't respond. He looked like a man who'd been overtaken by a passing wave: abject, letting the water run off him. Birch realised she was feet away from the door. The way was clear. If she could grab the shotgun, and run—

But no. Her legs were still shaking, threatening to give way. Her head buzzed, and she could see static in the corners of her vision. Don't faint, she told herself. Do. Not. Faint.

The light in the ruin was a little brighter now: more of the floodlight's glow was let in by the open door. Hodgson's eyes looked milky and dull. It was as though he'd gone into a trance.

'Gerry,' Birch said. 'Gerry, you did it. You let her go.'

It took a moment, but she watched his eyes refocus, and see her for perhaps the first time in several minutes.

'Yeah,' he said, barely louder than a whisper. Then, as though she'd spoken and he hadn't heard her correctly, he said, 'What?'

Birch shook herself. Her vision was still crackling. She wondered if she could leave the gun, but run anyway. Turn around and bolt, maybe along the side of the ruin. Would Hodgson follow her? She wasn't convinced he would – he seemed to be half in another world. She was eyeing the gun, its barrel now pointed downwards, and trying to think, when Rena called out again.

'DI Birch, are you both okay down there?'

The sound seemed to jolt Hodgson awake. He leaped behind the makeshift door, and without putting the gun down, began to shove it back into place with one shoulder. Birch watched as her window of opportunity closed, and the half-wrecked door blotted out the bright gaze of the floodlight like an eclipse. Hodgson breathed hard as he gave a final shove, and then straightened up. For the first time, they were truly alone.

'DI Birch?' Rena called again. Birch ignored it. The space between herself and Hodgson – still only the length of the shotgun's barrel – seemed to fizz. She worried that shouting back to Rena might disrupt something, might tear the thin membrane of understanding that had somehow prevented Hodgson from emptying the shotgun's chamber into her ribcage just now.

'You should sit down,' Birch said, after a moment. Her whole body pulsed with adrenalin. She could still feel the cold muzzle of the gun against her chest, the imprint it had left. 'Seriously. You haven't sat down in hours.'

She expected Hodgson to argue, but instead, he nodded. Hugging the gun to his chest, he trailed past her, his feet scuffing. He'd barely turned his back on her at all, the whole time she'd been in the ruin. Now she saw the nape of his neck as a white stripe above his collar, and the whorl on the back of his head where the hair was thinning and the scalp showed through. She realised she could, if she wanted, pick up a rock and hit him – put him down just long enough to grab the shotgun and bust out of the rotting door. Do it, she told herself. End this. But she'd made him a promise, hadn't she? *Whatever happens from now on, happens to both of us.*

Hodgson reached the camping chair and sank into it. He laid the shotgun across his knees, the barrel facing the wall.

Birch found she was following him: skirting her way back to the end of the ruin where the fireplace was. Her head felt like it was full of cotton wool, muffling her hearing – but she could also feel her body easing down out of fight-or-flight mode. She passed in front of the window and paused: there were blue flashes now, as well as the lone floodlight. An ambulance appeared at the top of the pasture. It must be for Elise, she thought – it must have been on standby, somewhere down the track. She prayed that she'd made the right call in keeping Elise still and quiet for so long in the ruin, and hadn't somehow failed to see that the kid was seriously injured. Hopefully it was just a precaution, there to check her over and get her warm and hydrated – but all the same, Birch felt that anxiety snake its way into the knot already writhing in her brain.

'What are you looking at?' Hodgson asked.

She jumped, and moved away from the window. She realised they'd switched places: she came to rest at the corner of the fireplace, where he'd taken up position when she first arrived. The blue flashing lights moved into the ruin, bouncing dimly around the walls.

'Ambulance,' she said. 'I was just watching it. Terrain like this is tricky to drive on.'

Hodgson shrugged.

'Not if you know what you're doing,' he said. 'Paramedics do.'

'True.'

Hodgson looked down at the gun on his lap, and then back up at Birch.

'Wait. Is the kid hurt?' He sounded genuinely worried.

'I don't think so.' She wanted it to be true, and she could hear that in the way she said the words. 'At least not seriously. It was hard to check her over properly, in this light. But I thought she seemed okay.'

'I don't want them thinking I'd hurt her.'

Birch frowned. She wanted to say, *but you just pointed a gun at her.* She wondered what it must feel like to be inside Hodgson's head. She thought of all the mental health training she'd ever done, all the CPD days and weekend courses in de-escalation and recognising trauma. Rena had told her to try and understand, but none of the things she thought she knew equipped her to understand this man. A real, flesh-and-blood person who was physically in the same room but who mentally seemed to be miles away at times, or present but shuttling wildly between states of exhaustion, recklessness, anger, despair and probably other emotions she couldn't parse. A yawn rose in her throat, and she pushed it down. She felt like she'd been awake and in this crumbling ruin for days.

'They'll check her over and find she's fine,' she said. Then added, 'I'm sure,' because she wanted to be.

Hodgson jostled the gun towards his belly, then rested his elbows on his knees, and put his head in his hands.

'You have to understand,' he said, his voice small. 'The things I did in 2001, they changed me. I feel like they changed me – well, profoundly. On a cellular level, you know what I mean? Is that possible? These twenty years, I've felt like a different person.'

Birch shifted her weight. She hadn't been standing long, but her legs ached.

'Twenty years is a long time,' she said. 'Anyone changes in that amount of time.'

'No,' Hodgson replied, 'I don't mean that. I mean that something started in 2001, some process. I stopped feeling like myself, when I was doing that work. When I was spending whole days killing animals. I thought I'd come back to myself – especially in prison. I thought, well, the silver lining is, I have lots of time to think, and get my head straight. But I never did. The process carried on.'

'What process?'

Hodgson rubbed his eyes.

'It felt like I stepped out of my body,' he said, 'and began walking away. With every year that's passed, I've walked further and further. Now I can't even see myself any more. I can't remember how to get back.'

He fell quiet.

'You feel lost?'

'I do. Yes, I do feel lost. And . . . helpless. Pathetic.'

Birch didn't know what to say. She wished Rena were here. She remembered that the microphone was gone, and no one was listening. That made her feel pretty helpless, too.

'Did you never . . . talk to anyone?'

Hodgson snorted.

'You mean doctors, therapy, that kind of thing? No way.'

Makes sense, Birch thought. Once someone's experienced prison, they tend to be leery of authority figures.

'But I should have,' Hodgson went on. 'I should have, because look where I am. Look what I've done.'

He began to cry again. Not the same violent, heaving sobs as before, but a quiet grief that Birch wasn't sure how to respond to. For several minutes she stood there, rocking slightly to ease the pain in her legs, and listened to his wet breaths. She found her thoughts drifting. She thought of Charlie, and what he might be like when he finally came out of prison. He'd never had much respect for authority, whereas she'd always sought it out – she blamed their absent father for those traits in both of them. Then she thought about Jamieson, a man who seemed almost allergic to responsibility, but who was trying it out anyway, forcing himself to live with it. For the first time, it struck her: how hard it must have been for her father to reach out again, after all those years. To have to contact his only daughter – a police officer – and tell her that he'd been a drunk and a gambler and a coward. To admit that he'd failed. To own the failings that began a chain of events that led to Charlie going missing. That led to Birch's mother wasting away with anxiety, and dying young. He must realise it now, she thought. Visiting Charlie in prison, Jamieson Birch had to see what his past actions had done. How must that feel? To see the black mark your presence has left on the lives of the only people who loved you, or once loved you? Suddenly, she understood. She knew why her father had broken down that day in Anjan's flat, and cried.

'You remind me of my dad,' she said. The words weren't planned, and she didn't realise how true they were until she said them. 'I'm not sure how, exactly. But you do. Something about you.'

Hodgson let out a spattering laugh.

'Your dad's a fuck-up too, then?'

Birch raised an eyebrow, though Hodgson couldn't see.

'I didn't mean it like that.'

'But he is?'

She shrugged.

'Kinda,' she said. 'Yeah.'

Hodgson lifted his sleeve and wiped the snot and salt from his face.

'In what way?' he asked.

Birch bit at the inside of her mouth. She realised she usually felt awkward whenever she had to answer questions about her father, but for once, the awkward feeling was absent.

'He just sort of . . . failed at fathering. Like, failed every possible test. He was drunk, he was violent, and then he walked out and never came back. Well, almost never. There was the odd disastrous visit. But he was never *around*, you know? Not until now, forty years too late.'

Hodgson snorted.

'And I remind you of him,' he said.

Birch frowned.

'It's your sadness,' she said, letting the words out, though she wasn't sure where they were coming from. 'You have the same sadness as him. My dad . . . I'm realising now that he's looked back at those things he did in the past, and he's seeing just how seismic they were. Like you, looking back at 2001 and everything you did then. They felt like small actions at the time, I'm sure – signing up for that freelance work, not quitting even though you wanted to, sitting down at that farmer's kitchen table that day. Just like I'm sure every time my dad had another drink or put his wages on a bad horse, it all felt like small potatoes. Like nothing at all – easy. But looking back at all of that in context, he must see patterns. See the consequences, the way I see them. My dad must see that the way he behaved moulded my brother into the man he is, and now my brother's doing a stretch for – well, everything. And Dad's cut up about it. He's got so much guilt and sadness.'

Hodgson wasn't crying any more. He was sitting with his chin propped up on both hands, listening. Birch spluttered, embarrassed that she'd said so much. But when he spoke, she heard a tone in Hodgson's voice that was new.

'You get it, then,' he said. Relief – that was what she was hearing. 'You get where I'm coming from. You understand.'

Not really, she thought. I don't even fully understand what I just said. But she nodded, hearing Rena's voice again: *try to understand where he's coming from, really try.*

'You look back,' Hodgson went on, 'and you think, how did I get here? How did I get this fucked up? You try to pinpoint the one thing that did it. I must have shot that bolt gun hundreds of thousands of times. Which was the shot that took me over the edge, that made me decide enough was enough? But then you think, was it something else? The morning I drove to that farm and took the cows, I'd had a fight with Sophie. I can't even remember what it was about, but she stormed out, got in the car and drove off. Normally I'd have driven that car to the farm. But because she was gone and she wouldn't pick up the phone, I had no choice. I had to walk down to the yard and take my truck.'

'Which meant you could load up all those cows,' Birch said, 'and drive away.'

'Exactly right. You can't help but think, was I on some sort of path to all of this, all along? Was it just inevitable?'

Birch put out an arm and leaned against the fireplace, realising as she did so that she was mimicking Hodgson's own pose from earlier. Her head buzzed with fatigue. She didn't like the question he'd just posed: it sounded an awful lot like he was saying *I couldn't help it*, and that annoyed the police officer in her. She didn't think she believed that people could steal things without being able to help it – and stealing was what Hodgson had done with the herd of cows, when it came down to it. She certainly didn't think it was possible to murder another person without being able to help it. She thought about Anjan, and how he might turn the question round in his quick lawyer brain. *But isn't it possible, Mr Hodgson, that you started the fight with Sophie on purpose, that morning? Perhaps you hoped she'd take the car, so you'd have an excuse to collect your lorry. Perhaps you'd planned the whole thing, and it went exactly as you wanted.* Hearing Anjan's voice in her head, Birch thought again of how inadequate she felt, standing in the ruin, playing the role of crisis negotiator. Anjan would have been better at it than her – perhaps just about anyone would. Her policewoman brain was getting in the way, and had been this whole time. It had sat better with her when Hodgson seemed remorseful, for example – when he was doubled over and sobbing. She'd liked him better then, she realised, and the realisation made her face turn hot. But something had changed in him: he felt that she understood. He trusted her now, she could feel it in her body. Somehow, without moving, he'd stepped away from her, and she didn't feel so threatened. But at the same time, she didn't like it. She didn't like him thinking they were on the same side.

'Can I ask you something?' she said, and Hodgson sat up a little straighter. 'It's something I've been wondering for – well, hours now.'

'What?'

Birch shifted her weight again. One ankle made a cracking sound, and then the other.

'Why me?' she asked. 'Why did you call me, this afternoon, when you got here? You told me you were scared. You could have called anyone, but you chose me – a complete stranger. Why?'

Hodgson looked down, and his face fell into shadow.

'It was another one of those things,' he said, 'that felt inevitable. Or – some sort of twist of fate, or something. I literally just heard of you – yesterday? I don't know what time it is, now. Was that just yesterday? Thursday. That was when I first heard your name.'

Birch gave her head a little shake.

'I don't understand.'

'There are these podcasts, right? True crime. You're police, you must know about them.'

Birch blinked. She knew what he was going to say, but she wasn't quite sure she believed it.

'I listen to some of them,' Hodgson went on. 'Not lots, just . . . a few. Ones about Scotland. I don't want you thinking that it means anything. That hearing about other people's crimes inspired me to . . . do what I did, or anything. I don't get a kick out of them or anything. I just listen to the odd one or two.'

'Let me guess,' Birch said, 'one of the *one or two* is the Scot Free podcast?'

He nodded.

'So you know about it?'

'I've heard of it, yeah.'

'Do you know they did an episode about you? It went online yesterday. Thursday, whatever.'

Birch sagged against the chimney breast.

'My understanding was,' she said, 'that the episode was about the Three Rivers case, not about me.'

'Oh, I mean, yeah – it was. It was. But . . . they talked about you quite a lot.'

She was exhausted, but still Birch made a mental note. Amy had said the episode was fine, but it might be a good idea to listen to it after all. Check for anything that might be defamatory. The idea of listening to the podcast had horrified her earlier, back when she was still preparing for a bright and breezy Friday. Back before she'd ever heard the name Gerald Hodgson. But now the idea of sitting at her desk at work, listening through her headphones as two overzealous twentysomethings gleefully rehashed the most traumatic case of her career – well, it sounded positively appealing. Just to sit down. Just to be in a room that wasn't this dim well of threat and anguish. Just to have slept . . .

Hodgson was speaking again.

'The way they talked about you,' he said, 'it caught my attention. They were criticising you, your approach – they said you'd got too close to the case, and you'd ended up on a disciplinary.'

Birch pressed her lips together. Hodgson was blowing on an old fire she'd thought had gone out. A curl of shame snaked out of it like smoke, filling her mind.

'Yeah,' she said, 'that happened.'

'They said,' Hodgson went on, 'that you had sympathy for the gunman's mother. That everyone was saying she had to have known, she had to have been involved. But you empathised with her.'

Birch pictured Moira Summers' face, as it had looked on the day of the shooting. She'd been brought into the station partly to be questioned, but partly to protect her from a growing mob of people posting credible death threats and publishing her address online. It had been only a few hours since she'd learned that her son had shot dead thirteen of his college classmates, and then shot himself. The first time Birch had looked into Moira's face, she'd seen a woman shattered into pieces. Moira had been broken apart by grief and guilt in such a way that the wreckage could never be recovered. Birch had known immediately, instinctively, that she was innocent – that she'd had no way of predicting what her son had planned to do and then done. And yes, that knowing had influenced her work. Influenced the case.

'I did.' There was no point lying: no one was listening, and yes, what the podcasters had said was true. 'It seemed like no one else felt for her, but I did. I couldn't help it, to be honest. And yeah, it got me into some hot water. I . . . didn't always follow the rule book, on that case.'

'You're saying that like it's a bad thing,' Hodgson said, 'but to me, it sounded admirable. You know I've had my share of encounters with the police. Not once in the entire process of being arrested, interviewed, charged or sent down did I experience anything that felt like empathy. I didn't believe police officers *felt* empathy. I assumed they trained it out of you.'

Birch shrugged.

'You were processed twenty years ago,' she said. 'I'd like to think we're better now than we used to be.'

Hodgson snorted. He didn't believe her.

'I think you're being modest,' he said. 'They put you on a disciplinary – they've made you believe that what you did was shameful. It isn't shameful. Earlier, when I needed to call someone, it meant I had someone to call. Empathy is a *good* thing, DI Birch.'

Birch realised she was biting the inside of her mouth again. She'd made a little cut, and she tasted the earthy tang of blood. She didn't know how to feel about Hodgson any more. He was flattering her – not just trying to, but succeeding. She *felt flattered*, and she hated it. *Remember this man is a murderer*, a voice in her head said. It sounded distant, muted.

'Not in this line of work,' she replied, trying to brush off his words. Then she realised how bad it sounded – how bad it made the police sound. *We don't see empathy as a good thing.* Would Rena ever have admitted to something like that? Then again, maybe Rena didn't care about making the police sound bad.

'Exactly,' Hodgson said. She hadn't succeeded in brushing him off at all. Again, she felt a crackle of understanding pass between them: he thought she was on his side, that she was agreeing. 'You're different to other police personnel, you do things differently. The episode got me interested, so I went away and Googled you. That was how I found out about your brother going to prison. I read a couple of articles about him.'

'Oh dear,' Birch said. She tried to push some levity into her voice.

'He sounds pretty hardcore,' Hodgson said, and Birch shook her head automatically. Her desire to protect Charlie – even after everything he'd done – always surprised her. It was an instinct she'd learned as a kid in the playground, and it burrowed deep, right into the heart of her.

'He isn't really,' she said. 'I mean, don't get me wrong, he definitely did all the things he went down for, and probably more besides. He deserves the sentence he got. But he was never a *bad person*, you know?' She felt instantly better talking about Charlie than she had talking about herself, so she went on. 'He got in with these guys who *are* bad people, and – he's easily led. That's his weakness. He's always been that way. Impulsive. A bit daft.'

'Not a bad person,' Hodgson said. His voice was an echo of her own: the same cadence.

'Not . . . no. Not deep down.'

Hodgson lifted his head, and let out a long yawn. As he tipped his head back, the pale stretch of his exposed throat glowed in the dim light.

'That's me, too,' he said, his vowels lengthened by the tail-end of the yawn. 'I hope you can see that. I hope you can see that I'm not a bad person, either. Not deep down.'

Birch squirmed. She wished she'd never led him down this particular road.

'I see that it's complicated,' she said, letting the words out slowly, giving herself more time to think. 'Things are often complicated. When it comes to good and bad, I mean. There are definitely people who are just bad, through and through . . .' She thought of Grant Lockley, his entire career of cut-throat behaviour, of devious acts accompanied by the constant refrain – *I'm just doing my job.* She thought of the mob boss Solomon Carradice, now rotting in a cell in Barlinnie but once counted among the most dangerous men in Scotland. '. . . and with those people,' she went on, 'you can tell pretty quickly that they're evil. But most people are more complicated than that. The vast majority of people.'

Hodgson let out a weary laugh.

'That's a politician's answer,' he said.

'It's what I really think,' Birch said. 'And besides, you never actually asked me a question.'

'Do you think I'm one of those bad people?' Hodgson asked, as she ought to have known he would. 'Do you think I'm evil?'

Birch looked at him, slumped in the camping chair. The godforsaken helicopter passed overhead for what had to be the thousandth time. She realised it was annoying her, too – she understood why Hodgson had complained about it earlier. It had to be the early hours of the morning now, she thought. Any real sense of time had faded away, but she knew she'd been in here a long time, talking. She realised she didn't know how she'd ever leave. Rena would doubtless have had a plan – an exit strategy to work towards – but she had no plan, and she felt too tired to think of one. Her own exhaustion was reflected in Hodgson's collapsed frame. He'd rested his head on his hands again, and in the half-light his eyes were sunken holes in his skull.

Birch was aware that she wasn't replying, that the lengthening pause behind his question seemed too long – but she couldn't help taking it. No one was listening: she could have said anything she needed to in order to keep Hodgson on side. But although she didn't know quite what this man was, she also didn't want to lie.

'No,' she said.

HOUR TWENTY

'That's it. I've had enough.'

McLeod uncoiled his large body without a great deal of grace. Someone had brought him a camping stool, and he'd been sitting folded down on to it for over half an hour, his eyes fixed on the ruin. Rena had taken to pacing a short length of the perimeter, counting the steps back and forth, thinking. McLeod lurched up just as she reached him.

'We have to go in,' he declared.

Rena glanced behind her. A few yards away, Leigh was standing beside the lit floodlight with a small group of armed officers. She saw its thrown gleam glancing off his face as he looked up. McLeod was speaking loudly.

'We've left it too long already,' he said.

Leigh began picking his way along the perimeter line, weaving around other officers who were sitting or standing in groups, talking quietly. Bottles of water were being passed around. Yawning was contagious: Rena had been distracting herself by watching one officer yawn and waiting to see which of her colleagues would be the first to catch the yawn and pass it on. It was two in the morning, and as dark as the night would get. The surrounding hills were thick black walls around them, though every so often one of the sniper teams would shine a torch or open up a phone screen, and wave a little flag of white light. The helicopter crew they'd grounded earlier were preparing to take off again, to relieve their colleagues in the single chopper still circling above. Rena thought she'd probably hear rotor blades in her dreams once this was over. If this was ever over.

'I mean it,' McLeod said, as Leigh reached his side. 'I think I've been pretty accommodating up to this point, but I'm putting my foot down now.'

Leigh's officers had followed him, and Rena stepped into their gaggle in order to join the small circle of the conversation. She didn't think Leigh looked tired at all: his eyes seemed every bit as sharp as they had hours ago, when he and his team had been scrambled to respond.

'Tell me what you're thinking, DCI McLeod,' Leigh said.

'I'm thinking,' McLeod replied, 'that we haven't heard a word of what's being said in there for over an hour. And the last thing we saw was Gerald Hodgson pointing a gun at my officer, right after she sent her flak vest out of the door on a three-year-old. Birch is unarmed, and unprotected. You can see why that makes me rather nervous.'

'We haven't heard any shots, though.' The voice belonged to one of Leigh's officers. McLeod whipped round to look at him.

'I'm aware of that,' he snapped, 'but I'm afraid it doesn't bring me a great deal of comfort. We haven't heard *anything*. We have no idea what's going on in there, and I've had enough.'

Rena was watching Leigh's face, trying to figure out what he was thinking, how he might respond.

'In fact,' McLeod went on, 'I don't know why no one's taken a shot at Hodgson yet. We've had eyes on him standing in front of that window enough times.' He gestured at the dark hills around them. 'I mean, someone out here must have had a clear line of sight, mustn't they? Explain this to me. Explain why we've done nothing.'

Leigh was shaking his head.

'Hodgson's been careful,' he said. 'Sure, we've seen him moving around in there. But if I'm going to give the order to one of my men to take someone down, I want a guaranteed hit, or as close as I can get. Imagine for a minute if we shot at Hodgson and missed. Imagine what he'd do.'

McLeod opened his mouth to interrupt, then seemed to change his mind.

'If your primary concern is DI Birch's safety,' Leigh went on, 'then trust me, you do not want us taking pot-shots at that building.'

'Besides,' Rena cut in, 'we already agreed. We want to avoid a fatality outcome at all costs. The chances of everyone getting out of this alive decrease massively as soon as a shot is fired.'

McLeod didn't look at Rena. He kept his gaze fixed on Leigh, his jaw working.

'We have to go in, then,' he said, after a moment. 'We have to storm the building. You're right, my primary concern is Birch. I want her out of there. I want this done.'

Leigh's eyes flickered. He's going to agree, Rena thought.

'We've been discussing next steps,' Leigh said, gesturing vaguely at his team. 'I was about to bring you in, to get your feedback.'

McLeod snorted.

'Generous of you,' he said. Rena continued to watch Leigh. He didn't register the comment.

'I wouldn't use the term *storm the building*,' he went on, 'but we came to a general agreement that we should progress things beyond negotiation. As you say, now that we've lost contact with DI Birch, we don't even know if negotiation is still ongoing. They may well have reached stalemate in there.'

'I doubt that.' Rena stepped forward, speaking up. 'DI Birch has done incredibly well thus far, especially for someone not trained in crisis situations. Getting Hodgson to release the little girl was a huge achievement. Her approach hasn't always been perfect, as we've heard, but she was moving in the right direction.'

Leigh turned away from McLeod, and Rena felt the eyes of the armed team follow his gaze. They were all looking at her.

'You want to give her more time?' Leigh asked.

'It's a difficult call,' Rena replied. 'I do worry that the last we heard, she still hadn't succeeded in building a rapport with Hodgson. He still didn't trust her.'

'*I* worry that we saw him pointing a gun at her,' McLeod said. 'If anything, it looked to me like things were deteriorating. She's in danger in there, and I'm responsible for—'

'I'm sorry, DCI McLeod,' Rena cut in. 'You must feel like I'm contradicting you an awful lot, but I have to draw your attention to the fact that we *also* saw Hodgson lower the gun and step away from DI Birch. I don't know what she said to him, but she managed to de-escalate a situation that for a few moments was looking very grave indeed. I'm sure I'm right in saying that, had any of the armed team had a clear shot at Hodgson, he'd have been taken down before that interaction was complete.'

She looked at Leigh, who nodded.

'DI Birch was able to prevent a fatality,' Rena went on. 'So as I said, she's done very, very well.'

McLeod straightened up.

'I would never suggest otherwise,' he replied, as though he hadn't just used the word *deteriorating*.

'The problem, for me,' Rena said, 'looks more logistical. I wonder, wouldn't it be better to wait until we had at least some daylight? There can only be another couple of hours until dawn.'

McLeod's face darkened.

'You can't be serious,' he said. 'Another *couple of hours?*'

Leigh held up a hand.

'Logistics is my area,' he said. 'I'll admit, working in daylight is easier. But we can work in the dark, too. We've got clear terrain here, and a clear target. We've trained for this. We can do it.'

The armed officers around him were nodding. Rena could see they were tired of standing around, ready to make themselves useful. She took a little step backward.

'I defer to your judgement,' she said. 'I just think DI Birch could definitely hold her own a little longer, if we needed her to.'

'And I say,' McLeod replied, 'that she shouldn't have to. I mean, Christ, how long has she been in there, now?'

Rena glanced at her watch, but Leigh was already speaking.

'Five hours,' he said, 'give or take. She went in a little before 9 p.m.'

Rena turned away from the group, and looked down the slope towards the ruin. It was dark here, on the perimeter, but there were spots of electric light and officers moved along the line wearing head torches, or carrying police-issue flashlights. Faces were lit up by the screens of phones and iPads. In the cottage, there was no source of light at all. It must be eerie in there, Rena thought. Frightening, sitting in the cold dark with an armed and agitated man.

Leigh was speaking again.

'As I said, DCI McLeod, I think we're in agreement.' He gestured to his team, more obviously this time, drawing them into the conversation. 'It's time for us to step in. Move things towards an outcome.'

Rena leaned into the circle again.

'Just to reiterate,' she said, glancing at McLeod, 'not a fatality outcome.'

Leigh nodded.

'That would always be my priority,' he said. 'As we've established.'

Rena gave a grim smile. She wanted to believe that Hodgson could be arrested, unharmed, but the idea was hard to hold on to when standing in near-darkness surrounded by carbine rifles.

'We'll need a little time,' Leigh said. 'I'll brief everyone in a short while, over by the vehicles. But I'd like to suggest that we move to positions around the pasture in small teams, so we avoid spooking Hodgson. If we all mobilise at once, it would only take a quick glance out of the window to see that there's movement, even in the dark. Last we heard, he was still very erratic, so we don't want to unsettle him. I propose that we circle the building, and then move in, gradually tightening the circle. Once all positions are secure, we'll let Hodgson know he's surrounded. It's my belief that at that point, he'll give himself up.'

McLeod made a face.

'And if he doesn't, and shoots my officer?'

Leigh looked at Rena. She thought she saw a look of exasperation on his face, for just a fraction of a second.

'It's a risk,' she said. 'As I mentioned before, I don't think DI Birch had quite succeeded in getting Hodgson on side, based on all we heard. There wasn't enough of a rapport for my liking. Once the person in crisis builds up a rapport, the chances of them hurting their negotiator become very slim indeed. But Hodgson hadn't reached that place.'

'I acknowledge that,' Leigh replied, 'but I also know he's tired. He's been awake a long time, hasn't eaten, hasn't moved from that ruin for hours. He has to be flagging, and I'm sure that whatever DI Birch is saying in there, she's working towards getting this resolved. It is a risk, you're right. But the more I consider the position Hodgson is in, the more I think he'll welcome the opportunity to end this.'

Rena closed her eyes. Something didn't feel right, but she couldn't quite tell what. The eyes of the armed team were on her once more. The decision had been made, she could feel it in the current of excitement that passed between the officers – finally, they were going to get to do their jobs. But something nagged at her.

'Ending this,' she replied, echoing Leigh, 'is pretty much the only thing Hodgson still gets to control. We have to remember that. When a person feels powerless – and now he's let Elise go, Hodgson must feel very powerless – they'll take any opportunity they can to grab at some control, however that manifests itself.'

Leigh frowned.

'What are you saying, Rena?'

Rena tested out her reply in her head. She knew it wasn't what anyone wanted to hear, but she said it anyway.

'I'm saying it's possible that Hodgson will shoot *himself*.'

McLeod made a noise of derision.

'That's still a fatality outcome,' Rena added, her voice cold. 'Which as we've just agreed, we do not want.'

Leigh leaned towards Rena a little, a gesture she recognised as placatory.

'I want you to know,' he said, 'that I hear your concerns. I acknowledge them. I do. But without any way of hearing what's happening in that building, we can't know what Hodgson's state of mind is. We can't know how things stand between him and DI Birch. We can only guess. And I think DCI McLeod is right in saying that we've been guessing long enough. It's time to move.'

Rena looked down.

'Then the decision's made,' she said.

Leigh straightened up again.

'It is,' he said. Beside him, McLeod was nodding.

'I know you said you needed time,' McLeod said, 'but let's get this done, yes? Quick as we can.'

For a moment, Leigh looked like he might argue. But then he made a swirling motion with one arm, and the team around him all seemed to stand up a little straighter.

'We're on it,' he said. 'Twenty minutes, and I'll brief everyone here. Then we go.'

He strode away, his officers following in a tight formation. Rena was left alone with McLeod.

'It matters,' she said, quietly, but not just to herself. 'It matters if Hodgson kills himself or not.'

McLeod sniffed.

'I know that,' he said. 'There'd be hell to pay if we let that happen.'

'No,' Rena replied, 'I don't just mean from a PR perspective. I don't just mean in terms of the internal investigation, or the inquiry that will almost certainly come. I mean it matters because it would be wrong for him to die here, now, like this, even by his own hand.'

'Ms Brooks,' McLeod said, 'you must know that I am every bit as keen to get this man into a jail cell as you are. He needs to pay for what he's done.'

Rena closed her eyes.

'No,' she said again. She was trying not to sound like an adult addressing a small child. 'I don't mean that, either. I agree with you that Hodgson did a terrible thing, and obviously we must make sure that justice is served for Sophie Lowther and her family. But there's more to it than that. It matters because *he* matters – Hodgson himself matters, even though he murdered somebody, and even though he rampaged around the Border Union Show with a gun. He's still a person, and a person in crisis at that. He's vulnerable, and he's in our care.'

She opened her eyes again. McLeod wasn't looking at her – he was looking over his shoulder, towards the great black wall of the hills.

'We should try to prevent his suicide,' she went on, 'not because the paperwork would be a headache, or because we want the chance to throw the book at him. We should try to prevent it because we don't want him to die. Because it would be a tragedy, and ultimately, a failing on our part.'

McLeod still didn't look at her.

'Is this how the training manual's written these days?' he asked, a nervous laugh in his voice. 'Seems exhausting. This is how you were trained?'

Rena felt a shiver run through her. She'd met plenty of men like McLeod, but she'd never learned to get used to them the way she'd seen other female officers do – never learned to just roll her eyes and rub along. DI Birch had learned: Rena had been able to tell from watching her and McLeod interact, before the negotiation began. She couldn't imagine working with someone like this all the time.

'It's how I was *raised*,' she replied, her voice icy.

McLeod didn't respond. Rena felt the hot prickle of annoyance.

'What are you looking at?' she asked.

McLeod held up a hand.

'I thought I heard a noise,' he said, 'back there, in those trees.'

Rena squinted into the darkness. A few metres back from the perimeter there was a line of scrubby hawthorns, old and twisty from years of bleak pasture weather. They were a barely visible blur until a torch beam shone their way – then they seemed to rear up, casting gnarled, horror-movie shadows on to the grass. Rena felt herself tense, listening, but she couldn't hear anything. She opened her mouth to say so, but then – wait. There was something.

'Hear it?' McLeod hissed.

'I do.'

'There's someone there.' McLeod fumbled around, looking for the torch he'd been given. 'Bastard press. This is a crime scene, they should be—'

Rena touched his arm, to quiet him.

'I can see movement,' she whispered. 'You're right, some-one's there.'

McLeod straightened up, the torch in his hand.

'Police,' he called out, 'who's over there?'

He flicked the torch on, and swung the beam. It lit up two faces, advancing towards them from the line of hawthorns.

'Oh Christ,' McLeod spat. His voice was still raised. 'What did I *say* to you, Chaudhry?'

Rena frowned. The two men were striding towards them now, one of them holding an arm over his face to shield his eyes against the light of the torch.

'Chaudhry?' Rena echoed.

'Birch's bloody boyfriend,' McLeod replied. 'I told him on the phone before, he cannot be here. *Fu*cking lawyers.'

Rena blinked. She really couldn't get used to men like McLeod.

Anjan Chaudhry was within ten feet of them now. He too lifted his hand to shade his eyes.

'Okay, James,' he said, 'you can lower that now, you've seen who we are.'

McLeod lowered his arm, and the torch's light pooled around their feet. Anjan came to a stop beside them.

'I *told* you,' McLeod hissed. 'I bloody *told* you on the phone. You can't be here; it's a crime scene, for Christ's sake!' He began to cast around him, looking for someone. 'I need a uniformed officer over here, someone with cuffs.'

Anjan snorted.

'You're going to arrest me?'

'Yes,' McLeod replied, still looking around, as though he thought he could summon a uniform to his side through sheer force of will. 'It'll give me great pleasure, in fact.'

'I'm sure. But . . . on what grounds, James?'

The other man reached their little circle of light. He was older, Rena observed, and panting slightly.

'DCI McLeod to you, Chaudhry,' McLeod snapped. 'On the grounds that I told you you weren't to come here, and you've come sticking your nose in anyway!'

Anjan was smiling.

'The problem with that,' he said, 'is that I don't work for you, do I? An order from you means precisely nothing to me.' He spread his arms out, gesturing to the hills around them. 'I'm just out taking a country walk. I'm sure you're aware of Scottish trespassing laws.'

McLeod stopped casting about, and leaned in close to Anjan.

'It's two o'clock in the morning and this is a *crime scene*,' he said, through clenched teeth. 'The normal rules do not apply.'

In the torchlight – which was wavering now with McLeod's shaking hand – Rena made eye contact with the older man.

'I'm Rena,' she said to him, trying to pretend McLeod and Anjan weren't there. 'Are you—?'

'Jamieson Birch,' the man replied, still out of breath. Rena heard in his voice the telltale crackle of a lifelong smoker. 'Helen's father.'

McLeod threw up his free hand.

'Great. Every word I said on the phone, ignored. It's like you *exist* to piss me off, Chaudhry.'

Anjan shrugged. Rena could see his mouth was still smiling, but his eyes were flinty.

'I assure you,' he replied, 'I don't. It's just a nice bonus.'

Jamieson Birch was still looking at Rena.

'Where's Helen?' he asked. 'I mean – DI Birch. Is she okay?'

Rena looked at McLeod, who looked away. A silence opened up between them.

'Well?' Anjan asked. '*Is* she?'

'She's in the house,' Rena replied, gesturing down the hill to the ruin. 'She's with Hodgson.'

Anjan folded his arms.

'We heard that,' he said, glaring at McLeod. 'We heard you'd sent her in there alone, unarmed, untrained, to—'

'Where did you hear it?' McLeod cut in. 'From whom? How the *hell* do the press know what's going on up here?'

'Not the press,' Anjan replied. 'One of your own officers. Down in the village.'

McLeod's eyes widened.

'Which officer?'

Anjan shrugged.

'I've no idea,' he said, 'I didn't note their badge number.'

'Liar. You note everything.'

'Maybe. But you know I'm not going to tell you, so why don't we talk about Helen?'

McLeod pushed his shoulders back. Rena heard them click.

'She's fine,' he said, coldly. 'Isn't she, Rena? Weren't we just talking about how well she's doing? The officer from the village, on the other hand, is going to get—'

Anjan held up a hand. To Rena's surprise, McLeod stopped talking.

'Tell me everything,' he said. He glanced at Birch's father, and corrected himself. 'Tell us.'

'I'll do no such thing,' McLeod retorted. 'You can't just barge into my crime scene, and demand—'

Rena took a step forward, towards Anjan.

'DCI McLeod is right,' she said. 'DI Birch – Helen – has done very well, thus far.'

She tried to ignore McLeod's glare, focusing instead on Anjan's face. It creased into a frown.

'I'm sorry, you're—?' Before she could answer, Anjan's eyes changed. There was recognition in them. 'Wait, you must be Rena Brooks, the negotiator.'

'I am.'

'Helen told me about you, on the phone.' To Rena's surprise, Anjan extended his hand, and she shook it. 'She told me to Google you, and I did. I was very impressed by what I read.'

'You'll know, then, that it ought to be me down there,' Rena said. 'It was meant to be me, going in to negotiate.'

'Yes.' Anjan's mouth turned downwards again, and he glanced at McLeod. 'What happened there, exactly?'

'There was no choice on our part,' Rena replied, before McLeod could jump in. 'I arrived before DCI McLeod's team, and attempted to start up a dialogue with Hodgson. I followed the usual protocols, but he wouldn't speak to me. He insisted that the only person he'd talk to was DI Birch.' She glanced at Jamieson, who was leaning forward slightly, seeming to watch her lips move as she spoke. She wondered if he was hard of hearing. 'He would only speak to Helen,' she added, a little louder.

'And she had to go into the house?' Anjan asked. 'Why isn't the negotiation being conducted over the phone?'

'Hodgson claimed his phone battery was dead,' Rena replied. 'But it's also true that negotiation can be more effective when you're in the same room as the person in crisis. That has always been my preferred way to communicate. When you're face to face with someone, you have more chance of building a real rapport with them.'

She closed her eyes for a moment. She felt like she'd said the word *rapport* too many times in one night. The word was starting to drift away from its meaning, becoming just a sound.

'But you're trained for that,' Anjan replied. 'Helen is not.'

McLeod looked like he might speak.

'We know,' Rena said, quickly. 'We do know that. It's by no means an ideal situation.'

'But we're going in shortly,' McLeod said, inserting himself into the conversation like a foot into a closing door. 'Give it half an hour, and this will be over.'

Anjan looked alarmed.

'Is that wise?' He was still looking at Rena. 'What about the little girl?'

McLeod let out a huffing sound, and muttered a curse.

'When this is over, Chaudhry,' he said, 'you and I are going to sit down in an interrogation room, and you're going to tell me exactly how you know so much about what's going on up here.'

Anjan let his gaze flicker over McLeod for a half-second.

'No, I don't think so,' he said, before turning back to look at Rena. 'I know I'm no expert in this field, but it seems incredibly unwise to send armed officers into that building when Hodgson has a hostage. When I think about how a court would—'

'You're right,' Rena cut in. 'But Hodgson freed the little girl, about an hour ago. She's no longer in the picture.'

'Ms Brooks,' McLeod hissed, 'you *really* need to stop talking.'

Rena ignored him. Beside her, Jamieson Birch made a wheezing sound.

'Och, that's—' The older man seemed to be struggling to speak. 'That's such good news, is it no?' Rena noted with some surprise that his eyes were wet.

'Yes,' she said, switching to a more soothing tone, 'yes, it's a very good outcome.'

'Sorry, hen,' Jamieson said, swiping at his eyes with the sleeve of his jacket, 'sorry. I jist – am so feart about Helen. Being in there wi a bampot like him, alone. Him armed, an aw that. But if – if he's let the wee one go, then he's more likely to let Helen go, too. Is he no?'

Rena nodded, and tried to smile.

'It was certainly a good sign,' she said. 'I was very relieved. And Helen was the one who made it happen. She negotiated the release.'

'Is the child all right?' Anjan asked.

Rena looked up towards the spot where the ambulance had parked, as though she expected it might still be there, throwing a stripe of yellow light out on to the grass through its open back doors. Elise's arrival at the perimeter had been met with a collective releasing of held breath: Rena had felt the same shudder of relief pass through every officer along the line. The little girl had toddled up to the base of the floodlight, stumbling under the heavy weight of Birch's flak vest, and lifted her face. In a voice thin with fatigue and uncertainty, she'd asked, 'Where the nice lady?' Rena had felt a surge of gratitude then, to be able to duck under the crossed tape and hold out her arms to this tiny child.

'Here I am, Elise,' she'd said, 'I'm Rena. I'm DI Birch's friend, Rena.'

She'd scooped the little girl up, and passed her over the tape to Jamal Leigh. Birch's loose flak jacket had clattered against Leigh's own: Rena had watched with admiration as he manoeuvred it off, carefully passing it over Elise's head and dropping it to the ground. Rena had lifted the loudhailer, stepping away so as not to frighten the poor shaking child with the sound, and called out to let Birch know that Elise was safe.

She shook her head a little now, dislodging the memory. Her eyes returned to Anjan's face. McLeod was speaking.

'We got an ambulance up here,' he said. 'She was checked over and found to be largely unscathed. No broken bones, at least.'

'They've taken her to Borders General,' Rena added, 'to be admitted for proper observation. We think it's highly unlikely that Hodgson had any sexual motive when he took her, but of course she will have to be checked out for sexual assault, just in case. We know she's dehydrated and hungry, at the very least. And of course, traumatised. Probably deeply traumatised. She'll need a lot of care, after this.'

Rena realised McLeod was scowling at her. She wasn't really speaking to Anjan any more, but thinking aloud, her mind troubled by what Elise had experienced, and must still be experiencing now. She pressed her lips together, realising how tired she felt.

'Poor wee scone,' Jamieson Birch whispered.

Rena nodded.

'You said you were going in,' Anjan said, after a moment. 'This decision was made because the child was released?'

'That,' McLeod said, 'and we've all just bloody well had enough of sitting up here in the dark having not a clue what's going on.'

Rena hadn't thought that Anjan's face could harden further, but now it did.

'What do you mean,' he asked, 'having not a clue what's going on?'

McLeod spluttered, realising his mistake, so Rena spoke again.

'DI Birch was wearing a wire,' she said, 'when she went into the building. It was fitted into the bulletproof vest she was wearing. But—'

'But?'

Rena bit her lip.

'She put the vest on Elise,' she said, 'to send her out of the cottage. Hodgson suggested it, and DI Birch seemingly had no way to prevent it. Indeed, it was a good job she did it, because we saw Hodgson train the gun on Elise as she walked away from the building. But thankfully, he didn't shoot.'

'So you're saying' – Anjan was speaking slowly, his teeth fixed – 'that Helen is in that house alone and unarmed, and that no one up here on the perimeter can either see or hear her?'

There was a pause in which Rena could have sworn she heard a crackle of static electricity.

'Yes,' she said, in a small voice. She found herself hoping, for a brief, strange second, that she never found herself in the witness box across from Anjan Chaudhry. It wasn't what he said, but the way he said it – his entire body seemed to radiate his displeasure at the situation. She was so focused on shifting her gaze away from Anjan's that when Jamieson Birch spoke, she jumped.

'Youse mean to tell me,' he said, 'that my wee girl is in that hoose and you've not a clue if she's even alive or deid?' He rounded on McLeod. 'Ah ken ye think that you're some big man, sunshine, but if anything's happened to Helen, I swear to ye, polis or no, I'll—'

Anjan reached out and wrapped his hand around Jamieson's arm.

'Come on, now,' he said. His voice was steady, though Rena could see how tight his grip was. 'This isn't how you do things, Jamieson. Not any more, remember?'

The old man struggled, trying to free himself. He was shouting now.

'That's my daughter in there! Wi a madman!'

Anjan twisted his torso, managing to pull Jamieson away from McLeod. Rena could see other officers moving towards them. She saw Anjan catch Jamieson by the shoulders, and lock eyes with him.

'Listen.' Anjan made his voice lower and quieter than it had been – a technique Rena used herself when a person in crisis was shouting. 'You're absolutely right to be worried about Helen. I'm worried about Helen. We just trekked across three fields because we're worried about her safety. And you're absolutely right to be angry at these people, too, because they seem to be badly mishandling this whole situation. But trust me when I tell you that if any harm comes to our girl, there will be *such* a reckoning for everyone involved, do you understand?'

On the word *such*, Anjan gave Jamieson a small but firm shake.

'If anything happens to her,' he went on, 'I will use all the means at my disposal to make sure they are punished. I give you my word.'

There were tears in the older man's eyes again now, Rena could see. She was aware of other officers clustered around them, shining torches at the interlopers and muttering among themselves. McLeod was speaking to some of them in a low voice, but she couldn't make out the words. Jamieson Birch made the same wheezing sound he'd made when she'd told him Elise had been freed.

'I jist,' he sputtered, 'cannae lose her now. Not after – aw that's happened. We jist started speaking again. She wis coming back tae me, after aw these years.'

'I know that,' Anjan said, his eyes still fixed on Jamieson's face. 'I know all about what's happened, Jamieson. Helen has told me everything.'

Rena looked around at her fellow officers, and then at McLeod. She wished someone would step in, say something, though she didn't know what could be said. She was aware of someone advancing through the small huddle, and then, as though she'd spoken her wish aloud, Jamal Leigh stepped into the small circle of torchlight. He placed a hand on Anjan's shoulder, and as though the gesture had broken some sort of spell, Anjan dropped his arms, letting Jamieson go. Both men looked at this new, unexpected person.

'Mr Birch?' Leigh said, and Jamieson nodded.

'Helen's father,' he said again, the same way he'd said it to Rena, earlier. 'This is Anjan. He's her, ah—'

'Partner,' Anjan said.

Leigh nodded.

'I don't know how you got up here,' he said, tilting his chin towards McLeod but not actually looking at him, 'but you're here now, and I'm glad of it, because when DI Birch comes out of that ruin, she's going to be mighty pleased to see you both.'

Rena watched the expression on Jamieson's face change. He still looked afraid, but the frustration in his eyes was replaced with relief. He didn't trust McLeod – or her, it seemed – but Rena could see he trusted Leigh. Anjan's face was harder to read, his mouth a wavering line.

'Now,' Leigh said, 'if you'll both come over to the vehicles with me, I'll brief everyone on our next moves. It's not an easy situation, but we're going to bring her out of there, gentlemen. We are. I can promise you that.'

HOUR TWENTY-ONE

Gerald Hodgson was fighting sleep. Slumped in his camping chair, his eyelids were fluttering. Every so often, he'd allow his head to fall forward on to his chest, and Birch would glance behind her at the ragged opening of the nearby window. The sill – or what remained of it – stood at waist height, and the window had no glass and the frame had long since rotted away. If Hodgson would just doze off, then she might be able to scramble through the opening without waking him. But he never closed his eyes for long: each time his head dropped, he'd snap it upright again almost immediately, his grip on the shotgun in his lap loosening and then tightening again in a slipshod rhythm.

'You're exhausted,' Birch said, watching him tip his head back in a luxuriant yawn. 'I am too, for that matter. Why not just end this? Walk out of here.'

Hodgson blinked, making his eyes focus on Birch for the first time in a good while. Neither of them had spoken for what she guessed was about half an hour, and her voice sounded over-loud after all that silence. She felt guilty for failing to keep Hodgson talking, as Rena had instructed her to, but she was focusing most of her energy on remaining upright. The ache in her legs had become so intense that she had taken to standing on one foot, counting to one hundred in her head, and then switching feet. Her throat and lips were dry and she felt light-headed, but she didn't dare make a move for the water. She imagined she'd probably be hungry if she weren't so tired. Her eyes itched, and she found herself forming two fists and rubbing them over and over again, in the manner of a sleepy child.

'I'll get my second wind,' Hodgson said. Though his voice was tired, there was a breeziness about this remark, as though they were running a race together, or pulling an all-nighter before an exam. 'It might help if we talk.'

Birch swallowed hard. Great, she thought – I'm such a failure as a negotiator that the perp has to prompt me to do my job. She heard Rena's voice in her head, then: *he's a person in crisis*, it said. *Not a perp.*

'I'm pretty sure he's both,' Birch muttered, realising too late she'd actually spoken.

'Pardon?'

She felt her face colour, and was grateful for the darkness.

'Nothing,' she replied. 'I'm just slowly going loopy over here. Hearing voices.'

'Then we should talk.'

Talk. The word from Rena's briefing that Birch had promised herself she wouldn't say.

'Okay,' she said. 'We'll talk.'

Another stretch of quiet opened up between them, and Birch almost laughed. The helicopter had disappeared: she hadn't heard it pass over in at least ten minutes. It left behind a blissful hush – in which Birch could hear the night breeze moving through the pasture – but she could also feel an anxiety growing somewhere in the centre of her body. What if the helicopter had gone because *everyone* had gone? What if her colleagues had decided none of this was worth it any more, so they'd packed up and left? The thought was irrational, but in her tired state Birch couldn't help thinking it. The glow of the floodlight persisted, throwing its jagged squares of light through the empty windows and on to the back wall. If she'd been abandoned, they had at least left her the light.

'Tell me about this morning, then,' Birch said at last. 'Or . . . yesterday morning. The showfield. Tell me how that came about.'

Hodgson didn't respond.

'Come on,' Birch said, 'you wanted to talk. Or . . . is this another memory thing? Can you not remember it all that well?' She hoped the needling scepticism she still felt didn't come through in her voice.

Hodgson seemed to be frowning, though it was hard to see. Birch had stopped counting, but she was still shifting from one leg to the other. When she moved, the bones in her feet clicked. She thought she could feel every single one: each of those fine little workings its own dull unit of pain.

'Sit down,' Hodgson barked, 'for goodness' sake.'

'I'm fine here.'

'You're not. You've been standing like a flamingo for God knows how long, and frankly, it's distracting. Sit down.'

Birch allowed herself to look over her shoulder, at the window. If I sit down, she thought, it'll be much harder to make a run for it, should the chance arise.

'If I sit down,' she said, 'I'm afraid I'll fall asleep.'

Hodgson shrugged.

'So fall asleep,' he said.

'I can't do that.'

He made a snorting sound.

'Why not?'

'Because I have a duty of care,' Birch replied. 'Towards you, I mean.'

'I can take care of myself.'

Birch paused. For a moment, she wondered if Hodgson might be sectioned upon his arrest. Something told her he ought to be. She realised she didn't like the idea of him being cuffed and bundled into the back of a secure van. She tried to imagine the conversation she'd have to have with McLeod in order to request an ambulance instead, and found her head was too fuzzy.

'I don't doubt it,' she said, 'but still. I don't want to go to sleep, thank you.'

'We'll talk, then,' Hodgson said again. 'We'll keep each other company. Sit.'

Birch did laugh then, an involuntary laugh that came out like a croak.

'I'm not a dog, you know,' she said.

Hodgson leaned forward in his camping chair. It creaked its one-note creak.

'Tell you what,' he said. 'If you sit down, I'll tell you what happened this morning, at the showfield.'

Birch felt the policewoman in her take over. He was offering a confession: you didn't refuse a confession. She put one arm out and placed a hand on the wall to steady herself, and then folded into a crouch on the ruin's dirty, uneven floor. She opted for a kind of rag doll position, her back against the stone wall and her legs stretched out in front of her in a wide V. It was darker down here, but she had to admit that sitting down felt incredible. Every muscle in her lower body sang with relief.

'Okay,' she said, 'tell me.'

Hodgson reached behind him with his free hand, the one not holding the gun. He rubbed his neck, and without the helicopter overhead, Birch could hear the small, scratchy sound of his skin.

'It sounds ridiculous,' he said, 'but I was in a kind of trance. I mean it: I felt like I was sleepwalking.'

He paused.

'This was after . . . after you left Sophie's house?'

'Yes. I don't remember walking out of there. I don't remember getting in the Land Rover or driving away. I know you won't believe me, but one minute I was sitting outside, parked up, trying to get the nerve to go and knock on Sophie's front door. The next minute, I was driving through the centre of Kelso, and . . . and the wee girl was in the back, crying.'

'I'm trying to believe you,' Birch said, 'though I can't visualise it. I can't imagine it.'

Hodgson returned his free hand to the gun: Birch heard the soft metallic sound as it shifted in his lap.

'The best way I can describe it,' he said, 'is like old-fashioned cine-film. Did you ever have a cine-camera? You're maybe too young.'

'Sure,' Birch said, feeling a distant memory unfurl in her mind like a leaf. 'I know the sort of thing you mean . . . like a camcorder, only out of the ark, right?'

'Right. They ran on reel-to-reel film, not video.'

'My dad had one,' Birch said, and she heard in her own voice a strange kind of wonder – how had she recalled this information, all of a sudden? How many other memories of her father were lying dormant like this? 'I remember watching some footage he must have shot before he left. It was one Christmas – I was only wee. He'd filmed me opening my presents.' She shook her head. 'I'd forgotten all about that, until right now.'

'The point is,' Hodgson said, making a slicing motion in the air with his hand, 'cine-film had those glitches in it, right? Where a frame hadn't developed, or something. It would be like, picture, picture, picture, blackness, and then picture again. There'd be a momentary gap. You know?'

'I do know,' Birch replied, 'I know exactly what you mean.'

'So that was what it was like. Sitting outside Sophie's house: picture, picture, picture. Then that gap. Then the picture came back, but it was a whole new scene. It was Kelso Square, everyone on their way to work. I got stuck behind a school bus. That was the first image I saw, after the blackness.'

Birch raised an eyebrow, but Hodgson couldn't possibly have seen – not now she was crouched on the floor, the darkest place in the ruin.

'I guess,' she said, 'that's what they call a blackout.'

'I guess it is,' he said. 'But I always thought – when I heard people talk about blacking out – I'd imagined it like a fainting fit. I thought you lost consciousness. I didn't realise you could still be awake. Still . . . do things.' There was a tremor in his voice.

Birch was trying to take mental notes. This was a confession, and no one was listening any more, except for her. She'd have to provide testimony, no doubt, for everything Hodgson had said since Elise walked out of the ruin wearing the microphone. But her brain felt like it was running on old batteries, its cogs and gears moving ever more slowly. *Blackout*, she thought. *He says he had a blackout. No, wait – I said that. I said the word first.*

'Okay, I understand a bit better now,' she said, trying to get back on track. 'So tell me what came next. You said you felt like you were in a trance.'

'Yes.'

'But the trance was a different feeling. Different to the blackout.'

'Yes. It was a sort of autopilot feeling. I was obviously functioning just fine: I was driving normally, doing all the things you do when you're driving. I stopped behind the school bus, and I remember putting my indicator on, pulling out, overtaking it – and thinking the whole time, how am I doing this? I could barely feel my hands or feet. Pins and needles, you know? But I was still driving.'

'That,' Birch said, 'sounds like a trauma response.' Stop it, she thought. Stop helping him. 'I've seen it a lot,' she went on, 'or used to, when I was still in uniform, attending call-outs.'

'Well, it was pretty freaky. I was trying to figure out what to do, trying to make a plan – any plan, anything beyond the next thirty seconds. But I couldn't. It was like all the energy I had was being used up, driving the Land Rover.'

'But something changed that,' Birch said, 'right? Something made you decide to drive to the showfield.'

Hodgson hung his head.

'Yes.'

'Okay. Tell me what that was.'

Hodgson let out a sigh, and it rattled in his throat.

'I'd come across the bridge,' he said, 'and I was driving past the road-end. The road that led to the showground. There were big signs for the event, but I didn't really register them.'

Birch was nodding. She could see that road-end clearly in her mind: it was the place where, hours earlier, she'd pulled over to ask the two Borders uniforms for directions.

'Why not?' she asked. Hodgson didn't answer. 'Something else took your attention, didn't it, Gerry?'

He dipped his head: *yes.*

'There was a man there,' he replied. 'I recognised his face.'

'What man? What was he doing?'

Hodgson had screwed his eyes closed: Birch could see his face was crumpled.

'He was in a big pickup,' he said, the words coming out slowly. 'He'd stopped at the road-end, and rolled down his window. There was a steward there, in a yellow vest, talking to him.'

'He was asking for directions, maybe?' *Stop helping him, Helen. You're leading him.*

'Maybe. I don't know. I just know that as I drove past, I saw his face through the open window of the pickup. And it was so familiar to me. *So* familiar, but for the life of me, I couldn't place it.'

'So what did you do?'

'I kept driving. I drove all the way to the edge of town, still feeling that trance feeling, but even more so now, because my whole mind was consumed with trying to figure out who the hell that guy *was*.'

Birch rubbed her eyes again, hard, leaving streaks on her vision that pulsed as they faded.

'And then I remembered.' His voice was cold.

'Who was it?'

'Veitch.' Hodgson practically spat the name out. 'I'd never met him, you understand, but I knew him all right. After I was arrested, he went to the papers with this ridiculous fake story about me. Something about me dumping dead animals in his farm track. I couldn't believe it. I didn't know the guy from Adam, had never been to his farm – never even heard of it. The story broke right as I was arrested, so it became part of my trial. The prosecution picked it up, and ran with it. I tried to argue it wasn't true, I didn't do it. But it didn't matter once they'd mentioned it in court. The jury would all have seen it in the papers anyway. There was this picture of Veitch that some photographer for one of the tabloids had taken: him standing at the bottom of his drive with this sheep carcass. He'd *kept* the carcass there, rotting away on the track, all for a photo opportunity. And people said *I* was sick.'

'You recognised him,' Birch said, 'from a photo in the paper, what – twenty years ago?'

Hodgson had hung his head now, so his face was entirely in shadow. She could see the spot on the top of his head where his hair was thin, glowing slightly in the eerie light.

'I'll admit,' he said, 'that I got a bit fixated on Veitch for a while, once I was sent down. I had this idea that, had his story not come out when it did, I might have been cleared. Or been given a lighter sentence, at least. I tore that photo of him out of the paper, and kept it pinned to the wall in my cell. Just for a while. I took it down after a few months, when I felt like I ought to try and get my head in a better place.' He made a sound that Birch didn't initially realise was a laugh. 'Didn't do a very good job of that, did I? But yeah, I recognised him. I'd looked at his photo every day for months. It was Veitch all right. Older, but the same man.'

'So you turned around.'

Hodgson looked up at her again.

'Not immediately,' he said. 'I turned off the road, into an industrial estate. Then I pulled over, to try and think. I wanted so badly to shake off that trance feeling, and be able to hear my own thoughts. But I couldn't. And then the wee one ... she'd been grizzling the whole time, but she started really howling then, maybe because we'd stopped moving. And I couldn't think. This whole time, I've felt like I just can't *think*.'

Birch could feel something rising in Hodgson: the pitch of his voice was ticking up.

'What made you go back, Gerry?'

He was shaking his head again now, rhythmically, as though trying to dislodge something. For a moment, he didn't speak.

'I think,' he said, 'it was despair. I couldn't remember what I'd just done, at Sophie's house, but I knew what it was. I couldn't make a picture of it in my mind, but I knew, somewhere deep down, what I'd done. And I wasn't in a place to *reason*, exactly, but with hindsight, I guess my thinking was: I've done that terrible thing, so now my life is over. And if my life is over, I may as well go and deal with Veitch, while I have the chance.'

Birch didn't reply – she'd asked enough leading questions already. But she knew what he was talking about, had seen it in perps before. Realising the gravity of their actions, they think *fuck it, what else can I do?* She'd seen it in her own brother. Once Charlie had become invisible – a man outside of the law, outside of society – he'd decided to find their father and settle an old score. He'd done all sorts of things that she wouldn't have thought the boy she'd grown up with was capable of.

'And I had that same feeling,' Hodgson was saying, 'from years ago. Remember when I said that it felt like fate, everything that happened back in 2001? Sophie taking my car that day, and me driving to the farm in my truck. I had the same feeling, driving back along the road towards town, turning off at that road-end and following the signs for the show. The feeling that fate had done this. Fate had put Veitch right there, right then, *right* when I had absolutely nothing in the world to lose. I felt like a wind-up toy, like I had no control at all.'

'But,' Birch replied, her voice quiet, 'you didn't only shoot at Veitch, did you?'

Hodgson didn't speak.

'Did you, Gerry?'

'No.'

'No. And that can't be blamed on a trauma response, or a trance, or a vendetta, or on fate, can it?'

He hung his head again.

'No.'

'You know what I think?' Birch could feel herself getting angry again, in spite of her weariness. It was the same annoyance as before: it nettled her that Hodgson thought he could claim that this was all down to fate, and he couldn't help it. He couldn't help spending years obsessing about his ex-partner – obsessing to the point where, when he finally found himself standing on her doorstep, he couldn't control his own actions. He couldn't help abducting her tiny daughter, couldn't help rampaging through a crowded place, firing a shotgun indiscriminately. He thought fate had somehow arranged for him to commit his bizarre act in 2001. Yet he didn't seem to see the prison sentence that followed as a part of this pre-ordained destiny. Birch prickled. She'd done what Rena asked – she'd tried to understand – but this *fate* excuse just pissed her off.

'I think,' she went on, 'that you drove into that showfield and saw what you thought was an embodiment of the world that turned its back on you. You said to me earlier, the farmers blamed you for what happened in 2001. They didn't want you on their properties. They saw you as a kind of angel of death, coming to lay waste to their flocks.'

Hodgson was staring at her. She could see his eyes shining in the floodlight's smudgy glow.

'They blamed you,' she said again. 'They decided you were guilty before the courts did. And then twenty years later, you found yourself in a position to settle some scores.'

'No.' Hodgson's voice was a hoarse whisper.

'I think,' Birch went on, rolling with the rising cadence of her own voice, 'that when you drove into that showfield, just for a minute, you were back in 2001. You were that slaughter-man all over again, your hand on the trigger, shooting and shooting like a mindless machine.'

Hodgson opened his mouth to speak, but no sound came out. After a moment, he closed it again.

'I'm right,' Birch said, 'aren't I? You felt that old muscle memory kick in, didn't you?'

There was silence. Birch held her breath, imagining she could hear the echoes of all those words she'd just said bouncing off the sooty, decrepit walls. She wondered if her colleagues had heard her raised voice – were they even still there? The strange, irrational thought came back to her, and she imagined that, were she to haul herself upright now and look through the ruin's ragged window, she'd see nothing but a line of trampled grass where the perimeter had been. Hodgson sagged in the camping chair, his face turned down. In the silence, a bird began to sing, and Birch looked up, towards the sound. The sky above had turned from almost black to a dark, dark blue. The voice of the bird faded out, but was answered by another, further off. The night was ending. It would be dawn soon.

'I can't say,' Hodgson replied at last, 'that it wasn't like that.'

His voice was so quiet she could barely hear him, and he couldn't look at her. He looked down at the gun across his lap, as though it were a cat he was petting.

'What's going to happen to me?' he whispered.

'Honestly? I don't know. There are too many variables, at this point. If your lawyer—'

'No, I don't mean hypothetically, in court or whatever. I mean next – what's going to happen to me *next*? I mean . . . if I walk out of here, are they going to shoot me?'

'They?'

'Your colleagues. This place is surrounded by men with guns. Are they going to shoot me? Is that the order?'

'Never,' Birch spluttered. She tried not to think of McLeod, how frustrated he must be by now. 'That would never be the order.'

'But it happens. It happens all the time, we both know that. People get shot by the police.'

'They do. But only if they themselves are threatening to use lethal force. Only if there's a real danger to people's lives.'

Hodgson sighed through his nose. He was arguing with her, but still he was quiet, downcast.

'There's no one up here, though,' he said. 'No one but you lot. No one who isn't police. No witnesses. They could shoot me and say I threatened you. This sort of thing happens, I'm sure it does.'

Birch closed her eyes. She wanted to argue with him, but something stopped her. Could she guarantee that what he was suggesting *wouldn't* happen? She thought of Jamal Leigh, the man whose job it was to give the order. She could trust him, she was sure. But McLeod was up there too, on the perimeter – though he was not a firearms specialist, he was technically the superior officer. Birch knew herself how tempting it was to do as he asked, if only to get him to stop badgering.

'Rena's here,' she said, the words coming out of her mouth automatically, as the thought struck her. 'Rena is a witness.'

'Rena?'

'The woman you spoke to, before I got here. The woman with the loudhailer.'

Hodgson shrugged.

'Isn't she just a policewoman, too?'

'Technically. But if you were to talk to her, you'd find she's not like most of us. She briefed me on . . . your situation, earlier, before I came in here. I think she feels a lot of compassion for you.'

Hodgson didn't speak. He seemed to be grappling with this information, trying to decide whether or not he ought to believe it.

'She's trained,' Birch went on, 'to get the best outcome for the person who's in crisis. Not the best outcome for the police. I'll admit, I do have colleagues whose priorities aren't quite in the right place. But I believe Rena's are.'

Hodgson snorted.

'And what's she going to do? Stand in front of the barrel of a sniper rifle?'

Birch felt herself jerked backward through time. Shivering, she saw herself standing in the doorway of the ruin, the muzzle of Hodgson's own shotgun poking into her breastbone. The image made her feel momentarily sick.

'You know,' she said, her voice colder now, 'I wouldn't put it past her.'

Hodgson was looking down at the shotgun again. Birch heard a slippery, shiny sound as he tightened his grip around it: his palms were sweaty. To her surprise, he began to rock back and forth in the camping chair, making its bearings squeak.

'I don't buy it,' he said, the whisper gone now, his voice more commanding. 'I don't buy it. I don't buy it at all.'

'Okay, Gerry.' Birch shifted on the ground, bending her knees so her feet could be flat on the floor, ready to stand. 'It's all right, don't get agitated.'

'Don't get agitated,' he mimicked. 'Don't get agitated, she says. I'm a sitting duck in here. I'm surrounded by armed bastards. I've killed two people, DI Birch. Just because I don't remember it, it doesn't mean I don't know. I killed two people. Maybe I killed more; I didn't stick around to find out. Did I?

Are people dead, from the showfield? I'm a murderer, I'm a maniac. I'm a headcase. Aren't I? Isn't that what you think?' He was shouting now. Birch glanced towards the window – could they hear him, at the perimeter?

'And the police are famous for their sensitive treatment of headcases,' Hodgson spat. 'Famously gentle and caring towards murderers. Towards *mass* murderers. Isn't that right? Kill more than two people, and that's what you are. That's what I am. Mass murderers don't walk free. They get shot by the police and everyone sleeps a little bit better at night knowing they're dead.'

Birch held up a hand, palm out: *stop*. Her blood pressure was rising – her temples began to pulse, her eyes. The sudden shouting was scaring her.

'Calm down, Gerry,' she said, 'you're getting ahead of yourself.'

'Getting *ahead* of myself?' Hodgson jumped to his feet, and Birch flinched. She watched as he flipped the shotgun from horizontal to vertical. The long barrel swept through the air, almost in slow motion, though the movement was deft. For the first time, Birch saw how well Hodgson knew his gun, how accustomed he was to handling it. But she barely had time to register this, because now he'd jammed the muzzle of the gun under his chin.

'How's this?' he taunted, arranging his hands around the trigger guard. 'How's this for getting ahead of myself?'

Birch wasn't aware of having the thought that she ought to stand up. She simply found herself there, on her feet, closing the gap between Hodgson and herself.

'Don't,' she said, stepping towards him with one hand out, carefully, as though he were a spooked horse. 'Don't do that. I know you don't want to do that.'

'Don't come any closer.'

She stopped, standing in the middle of the room now. Hodgson was about four feet away, and once again she could see the stubble on his chin, the deep purple circles under his eyes.

'You don't think I'll do it?'

'I don't know, Gerry. But I don't think you really want to, and I certainly don't want you to.'

'Oh no? And why's that, then?'

He bared his teeth as he spoke. The grey light gleamed off his incisors.

'Because,' she said, slowly, her hand still raised towards him, 'you're saying things that aren't true. There are things you obviously don't know, and if you shoot yourself now, you'll never know them.'

Hodgson looked at her. His face was snarling, but in his eyes she could see a pure, deep terror. She wondered if it was the same fear she'd felt, when he'd pointed the gun at Elise and she'd stepped into its path. It must be similar, she thought. The way she'd reasoned with him then, while imagining her own body being split apart by the fatal, any-second blast – he was doing that now, too, except he was silent, reasoning with himself. That silence seemed to stretch and drift, crackling like a storm cloud before the lightning strike. Into it, a new bird sang its near-dawn song. From somewhere, Birch heard the distant throb of rotor blades.

Hodgson's eyes widened.

'I thought that thing was gone,' he said.

Birch didn't dare look up, didn't dare look away from Hodgson's pale face, the gun still pointed up at it, the mouth of it leaning against his throat.

'I did, too,' she said.

'Bastards,' he hissed.

Birch swallowed. There was a lump in her throat.

'I don't want you to do it,' she said again. 'Please don't. Not after all this.'

'All what?'

She brought up her other hand now – what had been a *calm down* gesture became a beseeching one, a plea.

'All our talking,' she said. 'All this back and forth. Why do all that? Why tell me all that? Why even come out here, only to end up shooting yourself?'

'Because,' Hodgson said, his voice cold, 'it's made me realise some things. There's no future for me, there's no life after this. Even if they don't shoot me as soon as I step out of that door, they'll throw me in jail for the rest of my life. And like you said, it won't be Low Moss this time. It'll be the big hoose. And I can't do it, DI Birch. I just can't face it.'

His hands moved. In spite of herself, Birch took another step towards him.

'But,' she said, 'remember what I said before. About Elise. About letting her go. You've done some things here that you didn't have to do. Things that might redeem you, in the eyes of a jury. Things that might . . .'

She trailed off, feeling the futility of what she was saying. Hodgson was looking at her outstretched hands, hovering in the air only a foot or so from his chest.

'What don't I know?' he said, slowly.

'Sorry?'

'A minute ago, you said . . .' She saw his eyes refocus, moving his gaze from her hands to her face. It was their first proper eye contact in over an hour, and Birch could barely stand it – Hodgson's fear was almost too painful to look at. 'You said there were things I didn't know.'

She couldn't help it, she had to look away. She found herself looking at the gun – its action shining with his wet fingerprints – and that was almost worse.

'There are,' she said. 'For example, you didn't kill anyone at the showfield.'

A flicker of something crossed his face. She looked up too late to see for sure what it was. Annoyance? Relief?

'No?'

'No. A few people are in hospital, but no one has injuries they'll die of.' She tried to arrange her face into a kind of coaxing smile. 'In fact, my DCI made a comment about not being able to hit a barn door.'

Hodgson blinked at her.

'But,' she went on, 'I know that you know your way around a shotgun. You said that to me, earlier, on the phone – do you remember? Having spent all these hours with you, watching you handle that thing' – she gestured at the gun, but didn't look at it again – 'I know it's true. I'd testify to it. It's my belief that you could have done a lot more damage at the showfield, had you wanted to. You *could* have killed people. But you didn't.'

Hodgson's eyes were wide. He didn't reply.

'You felt that muscle memory,' she went on – worried she was babbling but not wanting to stop, because every second he was listening to her talk was a second he wasn't pulling the trigger – 'and it overtook you for a little while, but I think you fought against it. Made sure you aimed too high, or something. You tried to stop the worst from happening.'

The helicopter was getting closer. Birch could no longer hear the birds, or the rustle of the grass outside in the pasture. Only those rotor blades, a sound she hoped she'd never hear again in all her life.

'Veitch?'

Birch replayed the smile, or tried to.

'Seen by a medic at the scene,' she said, 'and patched up. He's probably back on his farm right now. He was the person you wanted to hurt, and you didn't. Not really. Not badly.'

Hodgson's face twisted. She couldn't figure out what he made of this new information.

'What's more,' she said, 'you didn't kill two people. I'm afraid that . . . yes, Sophie. Sophie is dead. But her partner . . .'

She couldn't finish the sentence. The information she had was hours old, and she didn't know if she could say, truthfully, that Elise's father was alive.

'Her partner?'

Hodgson's face became suddenly hopeful, and the hopeful-ness was almost as unbearable as his naked fear had been. But it gave her hope, too: he was listening. This was working.

'I've been in here for . . .' Birch tried to count, but realised she couldn't. She'd lost all track of time in the ruin – it felt as though she'd been awake in the dark well of this falling-down room for days. 'Well, several hours. But when I came down here, the husband was alive, and being treated in hospital. As far as I know, little Elise still has a father.'

The helicopter was almost overhead now, and it seemed louder than before, almost unbearably loud. Birch couldn't figure out if it was because of the spell of silence they'd had, or because she was tired, or – no, it was flying lower, surely? She still couldn't look up, but she felt like the helicopter was literally on top of them, as though it were about to land in the ruin. She imagined it as a huge vulture, perching on the crum-bling gable end, and peering down at them.

Hodgson's eyes had gone dull. Black. Birch barely had a chance to register the change, before she found herself staggering backward, tasting vomit in her mouth. Hodgson had raised the shotgun, and levelled it squarely at her chest.

'You told me he was dead.'

Birch still had one hand out, her palm pointed towards the gun, as though she thought that flimsy star of bones and skin could stop the fired shell in its tracks. With her other hand, she felt around for the wall she'd been leaning against just a few minutes ago.

'Gerry, please.'

The last time he'd pointed the gun at her, she'd felt time slow down. She'd thought of what the blast might do to her, how it might feel. Though her legs had threatened to give way, she'd been able to think, able to speak. Now, her mind was blank. Her vision twinged and swam. Something in Hodgson's face was different now, and it frightened her. She felt the wall at her back and pressed herself up against it.

'You told me that,' Hodgson spat, 'though you knew it wasn't true. You told me that so I'd send the kid out of here.'

'I did,' Birch stuttered, 'I did. But Gerry, that was the right thing to do! The fact that you let her go, it'll help you—'

'Nothing can help me now.' His voice was cold. 'I'm fucked, DI Birch, like I said before. And so are you.'

Birch inched towards the window, flattened to the wall behind her. Her arms were by her sides now; she could feel herself trying to become smaller, trying to disappear.

'I'm sorry,' she said, but Hodgson didn't seem to hear her.

'Before,' he spat, 'you told me whatever happened would happen to both of us.' He rolled his shoulders back, bringing his elbows up, ready to fire. 'And here we are.'

The *whack-whack-whack* of the rotor blades overhead vibrated through the ruin, and on the edge of her vision, Birch could see the helicopter hovering above them, a gigantic, predatory insect.

'Please don't.' She was having to shout, now. 'Please, please don't.'

'I trusted you!' Hodgson yelled. Then he closed one eye, and sighted down the barrel. Birch pushed herself away from the wall, and ran.

HOUR TWENTY-TWO

Time seemed to harden then, and crack into jagged pieces like a shattered mirror. One of the shards was Birch, bolting to the far end of the ruin. Her legs felt sluggish, heavy, as though she were running through water. There was fallen masonry here, thick timbers slanting down from what had once been the roof. Why had she come over here? What was her plan? Running was useless in such a small space. She was trapped, she was penned in. She was one of Hodgson's cows, retrieved from the pulled-over lorry and destined for the bolt gun, no matter what she did.

Another of the shards was a beam of bright light, which crashed into the ruin like a pillar, dropped from the sky. For a second, Birch was blinded, having spent so many hours in the almost-dark, and then she was amazed, seeing the building around her redrawn in fine detail. But it was only a second, because now she could also see Hodgson striding towards her, adjusting his aim with the benefit of this new flood of light. Under the helicopter's searchlight, the shotgun gleamed, and Birch could see that his hands were steady, his resolve fixed. She raised her own hands, the instinctive *don't shoot* gesture, and took a long step back.

In a third broken shard, the cottage's rotting door seemed to detonate, sending a thousand chips and splinters blowing into the room. Someone shouted *POLICE! DROP YOUR WEAPON*, and then Birch was picked up and carried backward, lifted clean off her feet by some unseen force. She moved through the air on her back, as though swept up by an invisible wave, and she looked up at the dark underside of the helicopter, the white light pouring down out of it almost painful, almost—

Another shard, and Birch was falling, and someone was screaming a ragged scream that frightened her. She could hear gunshots being fired, but couldn't twist her body round to see where they came from, or who was making the terrible, animal sound. Her body felt as though it had been hewn roughly in half, like the magic trick with the lady in the box and the comically overlarge saw. What was left of her was falling, falling, and the belly of the helicopter was criss-crossed now with the long ribs of fallen timbers. The ground rose up to meet her, and then—

Flashes of things. Jamal Leigh's eyes, looking into hers. His big, gloved hands moving over her body, looking for where the hurt place was. Rotor blades, impossibly loud and then distant, then loud again, the sound of them crashing in and out like the sea at night. Rocks like crap statuary, ragged cornerstones, chunks of a fallen-down house. The smell of blood and something oily: some strange machine. Shouting. So many people shouting. McLeod, as Birch had never seen him before: kneeling in the thrown stairwell of light, a picture of anguish, his hands in his hair. And then her father's voice, somewhere far off. Her father, crying, saying her name again and again and again, like the toll of a bell. Her father, doing what he'd never done: opening the back door of his house at teatime, lifting up his face in the purple dusk light, and calling his little girl home.

HOUR TWENTY-THREE

Birch's first thought was to check that her legs were still there, because she couldn't feel them. Couldn't feel anything, except the dry, frazzled heat of the vehicle – heat that dried out her eyes, made the air feel thick in her lungs. She looked down. Yes, she still had legs. She was wearing her favourite jeans, in fact: the acid-wash pair with the embroidered cuffs. She placed a grateful hand on her own thigh, and saw her fingernails were bitten down, the cuticles sore. A patch of black glitter polish clung to the thumbnail. Unhygienic, her mother always said. Germs get trapped in the lacquer, and *that's why you always get colds, Helen*. Her usual reaction was to yawn as a sign of dismissal, and thinking about it made her yawn now, her eyelids heavy in the muggy warmth.

'It's hot as baws back here,' Charlie said. She twisted her head, and smirked at him. He'd leaned his right temple against the car window, and she could see a greasy spot being made there by the residue of his super-hold hair wax.

'You watch your language, Charles Arthur Birch.' Their mother glared at him in the rear-view. 'You can open a window in a minute, all right? Let's just get beyond it all, first.'

Charlie rolled his eyes, a theatrical gesture, designed to be seen.

'Listen,' his mother said, 'it's a bad smell. I mean a *really* bad smell. I don't want it in this car.'

Charlie snorted.

'Come on, Maw,' he said. 'Isn't it just like barbecue?' He stuck his tongue out and licked his lips.

Birch reached back to swat at him. Two wooden bangles clattered on her wrist.

'Don't be evil, Charlie. It's serious.'

'Whatever. It's cows, Nella. Cows die all the time, and get turned into tasty burgers. We're not all pious veggies like you.'

'That's enough,' their mother snapped. 'Let's just have peace for a minute, can we?'

Birch swivelled back round in her seat, and looked out through the windscreen. They were driving under trees whose leaves were a brand-new green, almost neon against the glowering sky. They'd been driving for hours now, but had been rerouted off the M6 – something about a police incident.

'Great,' her mother had said, setting her teeth as she peeled off at the diversion sign. 'We'll have to pass by it all, then.'

Outside it was suddenly and unusually dark, as though they were driving into a storm. They passed a sign that read *Welcome to Longtown, Historic Market Town and Ancient Parish of Arthuret*. Birch looked out along the wide main road with its low, terraced buildings, and thought how apt a name it was: Longtown seemed to be a single, straight street that stretched on for ever.

'Whoa.' Charlie shuffled upright in the back seat. 'This is some post-apocalyptic shit.'

Their mother smacked the steering wheel with her palm.

'*Char*lie. What did I just say? Language.'

'I'm eighteen now, Maw. An adult. I can say whatever the f—'

'Do *not* back-chat me, Charles. It was me who brought you into this world eighteen years and eleven days ago, don't you forget that.'

Birch might have laughed, but for the landscape they were driving towards. Charlie was right. A pall hung over Longtown: a thick, grey-black cloud that poured and roiled. On its underside, a red glow. The few pedestrians they passed wore face masks, or scarves wrapped tightly over their noses and mouths.

'Just typical,' Charlie sulked from the back. 'We go away for my birthday, and there's a plague.'

'*You're* a plague,' Birch snapped.

'Your face is a plague,' Charlie snapped back.

Their mother was doing The Face.

'*Peace*, I said.'

They could both hear Charlie's jaw working, as he decided whether or not to make a retort. But then the buildings ran out, and they were in it. The killing fields stretched out before them, and Birch's mother flicked the front fog lights on. Although the windows were wound tightly shut, the car began to fill with the pyres' smell.

Birch watched Longtown shrink in the wing mirror. The road curved, and they passed a barred gate. Through it she saw a new-built track, the humped roofs of army trucks, men in visors and white boiler suits clustered around. A pyre that looked half a football pitch long: a thick black line raised up above the churned grass around it. And sticking up out of it, legs. Knuckled cows' legs stoppered by hooves. The smell not like barbecue at all but more like singe and shit and fear. The smoke pure black where it churned up out of the terrible heap.

This is it, she thought. Black smoke. Red sky. 2001. This is the memory.

And then she wanted to look at her mother, to study her hands white and shaking on the wheel, her profile, the ragged overhang of her frown. She wanted to turn around, reach back and put a hand on Charlie's knee, touch his skin through the hole he'd artfully ripped in his jeans and say *don't leave us this time, don't go*. But she couldn't, because she hadn't: her eyes had stayed fixed on the tower of smoke as it twisted and hung. And then she blinked, and the scene was gone, and there was only a blind numbness, like sleep devoid of dreams.

HOUR TWENTY-FOUR

Her father was chiming her name again, over and over, though his voice was softer now. He was close by. The stifling heat of her mother's car was gone, but so too was the numbness. Her body was built entirely out of pain: a deep, dull pain that seemed to have a pulse. A pain that was alive.

'Helen. Helen. Come on, lassie.'

She opened her eyes. The fingers of her right hand were pressed between her father's two palms. Just the fingers, because out of the thick vein on the back of that same hand, a cannula with a pink fixing jutted up. Birch blinked, trying to make her eyes adjust. Blinking hurt. Her father was smiling, his eyes damp.

'You're awake,' he said.

Birch swallowed. Her mouth felt slimy and disgusting. Above her, the panel lighting buzzed. She closed her eyes again for a moment, and it hurt. Having them open hurt, too.

'Dad? What happened?'

'They sedated ye, hen. Gave ye something strong, fer the pain.'

Birch shifted her weight. She wanted to sit up, but found that as soon as she began to try, that same pain knocked the air from her lungs.

'No,' she whispered, 'I mean – what happened? Why am I in the hospital?'

Her father cocked his head at her. The whites of his eyes were bloodshot. She wondered how long it had been since he'd had a cigarette.

'You dinnae remember?'

She frowned.

'I was dreaming,' she said. 'I saw Mum. And Charlie.'

Her father's face darkened.

'He shot ye, Helen,' he said. 'That fucking lunatic. That man.'

Birch craned her neck, though it hurt, and looked down the bed at her own body. Her hospital gown made a soft crunching sound as she moved. There were no blankets, and now she saw the bed was not a bed at all but a gurney, its plastic surface clammy beneath her. Tubes snaked under the hem of the gown and went somewhere – presumably into her body – but her eyes wouldn't focus on them properly, so she couldn't tell where.

Her father had slid his phone out of his pocket: she saw the movement out of the corner of her eye.

'Put that away,' she said. 'This is a hospital.'

Jamieson grinned at her.

'Once a polis,' he said, 'always a polis.' But he threw a furtive glance over his shoulder nevertheless, before swiping open the screen and thumbing out a text.

'We dinnae have very long,' he said, 'before they take ye. I'm telling Anjan you've woken up.'

'Take me where, Dad?'

He nodded towards the door.

'Surgery,' he said. 'They said I could have a wee minute wi ye, before.'

'Surgery for *what*?'

He shook his head, then looked over at the door. Though her brain seemed able to do little beyond registering *this hurts, this hurts, this hurts*, she felt a spike of frustration at her father.

Why could he never just *communicate*? But then, he was here. He'd heard she was hurt, and he'd cared. That felt new.

'Here's Anjan,' he said, 'he'll tell ye better than I can.'

Birch twisted her neck again, so she could follow her father's gaze. It hurt, as she now knew it would, but she couldn't help it. She couldn't help but look at Anjan whenever he stepped into a room.

'Helen.'

She'd never seen him like this. Anjan's face was almost grey, his eyes red-ringed, the same as her father's. It took her a moment to realise that it wasn't nicotine withdrawal she'd seen in Jamieson's eyes, as she'd first suspected – they'd been crying, the two of them. For a moment, she recalled her father's outburst in Anjan's flat, the one that had taken her so much by surprise. That was the first time she'd ever seen him cry, and she certainly hadn't ever seen Anjan in tears until now – he was much too measured for that.

'Hello, gorgeous,' she said. She smiled, and found that even smiling seemed to hurt.

Anjan crossed the room, and her father stood, scraping back his chair against a floor she couldn't see. They didn't speak, but Jamieson laid a hand on Anjan's arm, and they shared a look that Birch struggled to parse. If she didn't know any better, she'd think they'd been friends for years, these two men who had absolutely nothing in common except for her.

'I'll jist be oot there,' her father said. 'Call me in again when it's time.'

Anjan nodded. Her father looked down at her, and smiled a tearful smile.

'Dad,' she croaked. She was beginning to feel a soft fizz of panic, like static in her blood. It felt important to say the words. 'Don't leave.'

Jamieson's mouth sagged a little, but he kept his smile on.

'I'm no leaving ye, lassie,' he said. 'Jist stepping oot fer a minute, so youse two can . . .'

He looked at Anjan again, and Anjan matched his sad, wet smile. Then her father did something else Birch had never seen before: he lifted his hand to his mouth, and blew her a kiss. It made her want to sob.

'Anjan will tell ye everything,' he said.

Anjan waited until Jamieson had left the room, then sank into the chair her father had just vacated. He pressed her fingers between his palms, just as Jamieson had done. Anjan's hands were bigger, his grip firmer.

'I can't tell you,' he said, 'how good it is to see you awake.'

For a moment, Birch couldn't speak. She was replaying her father's blown-kiss gesture in her mind, strangely fascinated to have seen it.

'I feel like I've been sawn in half,' she said. Her voice sounded too serious, so she tried to laugh, then regretted it. 'What the hell happened?'

'Well.' Anjan's eyes flitted down her body, towards the tubes. 'To be honest with you, chaos happened. But the main event was Gerald Hodgson shooting you, twice, at close range.'

'Dad said – surgery? Where was I hit?'

'In your left side, your abdomen.' There was a thin strain of something in Anjan's voice that Birch couldn't identify. He sounded tired, but there was something else, too. 'Initial X-rays have shown that your pelvic bone is shattered, all down the left-hand side.'

She realised her heart was hammering. Sure, everything hurt, but she hadn't expected *that*.

'Fuck,' she said. Her mouth was open, but she couldn't make any other words come out.

'I know.' He squeezed her fingers tighter. 'But you were lucky. Jamal Leigh gave the order to breach the building just as Hodgson was about to shoot. It seems that in all the noise and confusion, and with the searchlight being lit, Hodgson's aim was off. It could have been a lot worse.'

Birch could feel her head beginning to swim. She remembered, as if through a fog, telling Hodgson that no one had died at the showfield. Telling him she believed he'd deliberately aimed high, *or something*. He hadn't been able to stop himself firing the shots, but he'd tried to minimise the damage. Was it really good luck that she was awake, and talking? Was it really the noise and confusion, or was it Hodgson himself? She tried to feel grateful to him, but found she couldn't. She hurt too much.

'The head injury,' Anjan was saying, 'is unrelated. When you fell, you hit your head on a piece of masonry, in the ruin.'

'Head injury?'

Birch lifted her left hand. It was the one without the cannula, and felt lighter, the more obvious choice of the two. But as soon as she did it, a new, hot streak of pain ran up the left-hand side of her body. She cried out, and dropped her arm again. Anjan's face twisted.

'I'm sorry,' he said, 'I didn't realise you couldn't feel it.'

'I can't feel anything specific,' she said, clenching her teeth until the new pain quietened down. 'I just *hurt*.'

'It isn't too serious, your head.' Anjan was mimicking her father now, taking out his phone and opening up the screen. She watched him swipe to the camera app. 'Though it knocked you out. You've got a temporary dressing on at the moment, so you still need some patching up. You'll have a pretty severe concussion, the doctor told me.'

It was still there, that edge in Anjan's voice. Before she could arrange her face into any kind of real expression, he held up the phone and snapped a photo of her. Then he turned the screen round, so she could see. She gasped, and her breath was ragged.

'Jesus,' she whispered.

Around her head ran a strip of thick bandage, with a chunky bulge on one side where gauze had been packed against a wound. Someone had obviously tried to clean her up, but the effort had been slap-dash: there was dried blood caked into her hair, and streaks on the side of her face and neck where more blood had been wiped away. Her face looked blueish, the whites of her eyes grey, and her skin dirty, presumably from lying on the floor of the ruin. She couldn't look at the image for long, and flinched the phone away.

'I look like death.'

Anjan shook his head, and said in that same strange, spiky voice, 'Nonsense.' Something clicked, and she realised what it was she could hear in him – anger.

'I'm sorry,' she said, a lump forming in her throat. 'I'm so sorry.'

Don't cry, she thought. It'll only hurt. Anjan tilted his head.

'What for? You have absolutely nothing at all to be sorry for.'

Yes, it was going to hurt – but trying to stop herself crying *also* hurt, so she let the tears come.

'I messed up,' she said, 'back there. In the house, with Hodgson. I totally, utterly fucked it up.'

'No, Helen.'

'I did. I promised Rena I'd try to understand him, but I didn't try hard enough. I didn't care enough about him.' She thought of Hodgson's face, the great unscalable wall of fear she'd seen behind his eyes. 'I behaved like a policewoman, rather than a human being. Although . . . towards the end there I think I just behaved like an idiot. I did this to myself. And don't pretend you're not mad about it, Anjan, I can tell from your voice that—'

'Stop.' Anjan was crying now, too, and Birch quietened down partly because she wanted to stay still and watch this thing she'd never seen happen before. 'You have to stop talking like that. None of what you're saying is even remotely true. You did the best that you could, in circumstances which were . . .' He tailed off, and wiped a hand across his face, smearing the tears. 'You're right, I'm angry. But of course I'm not angry at *you*. You were failed at a fundamental level by your commanding officer. James McLeod sent you in there without so much as—'

Birch held up her free hand to stop him. A bolt of new pain came with the gesture, as she realised – a fraction of a second too late – that it would.

'Wait,' she said. Anjan using the words *commanding officer* made her picture Jamal Leigh. A memory flashed behind her eyes: Leigh's face above hers, his hands on her abdomen, pressing, pinning her to the ground. His voice cracking as he said her name, the sound of him yelling, *she's hit!* Something wet on her face, her neck. And in the midst of it all, the knowledge that Gerald Hodgson was gone: the shotgun was no longer pointing at her. She'd escaped.

'What happened to Gerry, Anjan?'

Something rippled across Anjan's face. Was it pity?

'Gerry?' he echoed.

Birch blinked.

'Hodgson,' she said, realising she'd surprised him. 'Hodgson, I mean. Where is he? Where have they taken him?'

Anjan lowered his eyes. He fixed them on his own hands. She followed his gaze, knowing what he was going to say before he said it. A little chequerboard reflection of the ceiling's strip lights danced on the face of his watch.

'He was shot too, Helen. By one of the firearms officers.'

'He's dead.' It wasn't a question, nor was it a shock. As soon as she said the words, it felt like a fact she'd always known: Hodgson's death at the business end of a police-issue rifle a fait accompli he'd been walking towards since the day he was born.

'Yes.' He paused for what seemed like a long time before adding, 'I'm sorry.'

They were quiet for a moment, and Birch thought about the feeling Hodgson had described to her – the feeling of stepping out of his body, and beginning to walk away. Walking so far that when he turned round, he couldn't even see himself any more.

'It's okay.' Was it okay, though? She was frowning, though it made her skull feel like it was on fire. What had been the point of all those hours in the ruin? All that talking. She heard Rena's voice: *speaking, not talking.* She felt a flicker in her chest and realised that she, too, was angry.

'Helen?' Anjan was regarding her with a look of concern. 'What is it? What are you thinking?'

A million things, she wanted to say. All of Hodgson's words, everything he'd said to her in the past few hours, rushing back like a fast tide.

'That I should have stopped it,' she said, eventually. 'It was my job to keep him alive. To keep everyone in that building alive, and unscathed. And I failed.'

Anjan sat still at first, not replying. Then he leaned forward, stretched out his arm, and placed the palm of his hand gently against her face.

'That doesn't hurt, does it?'

It did, a little. But Birch gave her head a tiny shake.

'You did so well,' Anjan said, his voice gentle now. 'You got the little girl out of the equation. She's fine, by the way – she's here, somewhere, in this hospital, but only for overnight observation. There's barely a scratch on her, and that's thanks to you.'

Birch hadn't entirely stopped crying, but there were new tears in her eyes as she remembered the warm weight of little Elise curled up in her lap. Heard again the child's frightened whisper as Hodgson came close to her – *the bad man*.

'What about her father?' she asked. 'Sophie's husband. No one told me – did he die?'

Anjan shook his head.

'No. And they don't think he will. McLeod tells me his condition was grave, and is now critical. So he's not out of the woods, but he's going in the right direction.'

Birch closed her eyes. She felt as though she'd been holding her breath just a little, all this time, and now she could exhale.

'That's good,' she said, and then again, 'that's good.'

'Yes. And thanks to your actions, that man still has a daughter. That's not nothing, Helen. You did incredibly well. Not just given the circumstances, but in spite of them. In spite of the way they failed you – McLeod, and all the Specialist Crime lot.'

Another flash of memory: McLeod on his knees, his head in his hands. A picture of despair so far from her DCI's usual demeanour that she couldn't quite believe she hadn't dreamed it.

'Please,' she said, 'try to understand. It was such a weird situation, up there. Such a delicate situation. And yes, maybe a case of too many cooks, with Specialist Crime being deployed. But that wasn't McLeod's fault. You don't know what he was up against.'

'Actually, I do know. I was there.'

Instinctively, Birch jerked her head towards him, as though she hadn't heard properly. For the first time, she *felt* the head injury – the slash and ooze of it – and let out a yelp.

'Stay still,' Anjan said, 'it's okay.'

Birch closed her eyes. Red and orange patterns flashed across her retina: throbbing squares, shadows of the ceiling lights.

'What do you mean,' she said, 'you were there?'

'I drove to the village,' Anjan said. 'Town Yetholm. You'd told me, on the phone, that you'd let me know when you got there, but you didn't.'

Birch opened her eyes again.

'Shit,' she said. 'I'm sorry. I arrived, and just got immediately swept up in everything.'

'It's all right.' She heard him moderate his tone, so she'd know he meant it. 'I understand that. But nevertheless, I was worried, and there was no new information on the news. So after about an hour of slowly going out of my mind, I phoned Amy.'

Birch smiled.

'Going out of your mind? That doesn't sound like the Anjan Chaudhry I know.'

Anjan smiled back.

'To be perfectly honest,' he said, 'I've never been so panicked before in my life as I have over the past few hours. It's rather a new feeling for me.'

In spite of the endless drone of pain, Birch felt her heart flutter, just a little.

'And,' Anjan went on, 'it was Amy who told me what they were doing out there. That they'd be sending you in to negotiate with Hodgson. You can imagine my reaction.'

She nodded.

'Poor old Amy,' she said.

He raised an eyebrow.

'Maybe you can't imagine, then,' he said. 'Because I didn't take it out on her. I got as much information as she was willing to give me – which was probably more than she ought to have given, but still wasn't much – and then I walked out of the office, and went to find your father.'

Birch could feel her eyes boggling. She couldn't decide what was more surprising.

'Wait,' she said, 'you just . . . up and left the office? Right then?'

'Of course I did.'

'But . . . you must have had clients, who—'

Anjan looked stung.

'Helen. Have I really given you the impression that, in an emergency, I'd care more about my clients than I would about you?'

She opened her mouth to reply, but then closed it again.

'Of course I haven't,' he said.

'And . . . my father?'

'Yes – I'll admit, I thought it over for a bit before I did it. But I reasoned, if I was worried enough about your safety to drive all the way to the Borders, then I ought to give him the option of coming with me.'

Birch snorted. Predictably, it hurt.

'Like my dad would ever.'

Anjan fixed her with a look, but his eyes were smiling.

'This is why you're not a lawyer,' he said, 'but a policewoman. You think you've got everyone figured out, but sometimes, you're way off the mark.'

'Wait, he went with you? *My father?*'

Anjan nodded.

'Once I told him what Amy had told me,' he said, 'he was every bit as worried as I was. We set off there and then. He didn't even go back into the house for a coat.'

Birch glanced over at the door, imagined her father standing just outside it, leaning against the wall of the ward as though it were a bar. Itching to smoke a cigarette. Rubbing his pink-ringed eyes. She wondered if he'd heard her just then, being flippant about his worry.

'I can't—' she spluttered. 'I don't—'

Anjan was still smiling.

'Once this is over with,' he said, 'once you're out of surgery and we start to put all this behind us, I want you to do me a favour.'

'Anything.'

'I want you to start cutting your father a little more slack. I know I wasn't party to everything that went on between you. I know he treated your mother terribly. I know you struggle to trust him, and you have good reason. But over these past few hours, I've learned a lot about him. I've learned just how much he loves you, Helen.'

Birch was quiet for a moment. If she listened, she could hear the muffled sounds of a hospital operating at night: the distant roll of a trolley, the repeated *swick, swick* of shoes across a waxed floor. Anjan was watching her.

'You say you were there,' she said, 'but you can't mean *at the scene*, surely? McLeod would never have allowed it – I'd have seen the mushroom cloud go up from in that ruin.'

Anjan laughed.

'It did go a little something like that,' he said. 'I sweet-talked my way as far as the outer perimeter, but they wouldn't let me drive the car off the road and up the track. I stood and argued with the scene guards there for – well, I don't know how long. But it was Jamieson who came up with the alternative. After a while he told me to get back in the car, and we drove off. A little way along the valley, we found a gateway where I could park up, and he suggested we make the rest of the way on foot. He reasoned – correctly, as it turned out – that they'd only have scene guards posted at the access points. And it was so dark and quiet up there, we'd be able to find the main perimeter by following any light or noise. He was right, of course.'

Birch's mouth had fallen open.

'Wait,' she said. 'My dad suggested that you – Anjan Chaudhry – tramp across an open field . . . and you *did it*?'

'I did. Though it turned out to be several fields, one of which had livestock in it.' He glanced down at his feet. 'I wore my Armani brogues today, too.'

This time, Birch was prepared. She knew it would make her head throb with pain, but still, she allowed herself to laugh. It was worth it.

'Incredible,' she said. 'We'll make an outdoorsman of you yet.'

There was a noise, over by the door. Birch looked up, and saw a nurse standing there – a petite fiftyish woman, in a blue tunic. Beside her, she could see Jamieson's right shoulder and most of his face – he looked strangely childlike, peeping around the door frame.

'Helen,' the nurse said, 'I'm Ruth. I've been keeping an eye on you the past little while. I just wanted to let you know we'll be collecting you for surgery in just a minute, so if you want to say anything to your family, now's the time.'

Birch felt frozen then, lying on the tacky plastic surface of the gurney. She was gripped by a strange, cold fear, and could only nod back.

'Thank you,' Anjan said, and Ruth made a funny little bob, almost a curtsey, as she backed out of the doorway. Jamieson took her place, standing on the threshold, but not stepping in. He seemed to be watching Anjan, waiting for a sign.

'Wait.' She wanted very much to sit up, then – to stand, to walk around, to do something that felt normal. She tried to shift her weight so she could turn a little, look at Anjan more directly, but the movement sent hot forked lightning through her abdomen. 'This isn't going to . . . I'm going to be okay, aren't I?'

Anjan opened his mouth to reply, but it was Jamieson who spoke, from the threshold of the little room.

'Of course ye are, hen,' he said. 'They've tellt us whit the surgery involves, and it's tae make sure there isnae ony internal damage. They'll check ye oot, patch ye up, and it'll aw be fine.'

Birch looked at Anjan. She wanted to trust her father, but she hadn't had enough practice yet.

'Is that true?'

Anjan's face twisted a little.

'It's not a life-or-death surgery,' he said, 'if that's what you're asking.'

Birch frowned.

'That's a lawyer's answer,' she said.

She watched as Anjan tried for a smile.

'You know me too well,' he said. 'But really, Helen – they seem pretty confident that you'll come through and be fine. Like your dad says, they need to check for internal injuries that they might initially have missed. Then they're going to try and reset your pelvic bone as best they can. That sounds like a daunting task to me, but then, I'm not a medical professional. They know what they're doing. They'll look after you.'

'And . . .' Birch didn't want to know the answer, but she had to ask the question. 'I'll still be able to walk after this, right?'

Anjan and Jamieson exchanged a look.

'Honestly,' Anjan said, 'they didn't tell me that. But they did say the surgery is absolutely vital. Whatever comes after it, we'll deal with on the other side, okay?'

'But Anjan . . . my work. I have to be able to walk out of here – I have to be able to drive! What if I can't—'

Jamieson had stepped into the room, now. He rounded the end of the gurney with some urgency, coming to a stop just behind Anjan's chair.

'That's enough now, hen,' he said. 'That's enough getting yersel intae a mither. Ye cannae get oot o here until they've fixed ye, can ye? So it's best tae let them dae the work they're trained for. They'll no mess it up. They want the patient tae be able tae walk oot intae the world after as much as anyone does.'

Birch spluttered. She remembered how she'd felt, standing in the doorway of the ruin, the muzzle of Hodgson's shotgun pressed into her breastbone. Watching memories stream across her vision like a film montage. The same thing was happening now, only with the immediate future: she saw herself unconscious on the gurney, cut open, bright lights glinting off sharp-edged instruments. She saw her own blood, coating a pair of gloved hands.

'I'm sorry, hen,' her father was saying, 'I ken whit ye're like. But fer once you'll jist have tae *trust*, all right? Trust these people tae make ye better.'

Birch couldn't seem to close her mouth. She stared at her father, feeling just about every emotion available to her, one after the other. She wanted to ask who the hell he thought he was, walking in here and telling her what she was like, when she was little more than a stranger to him. She wanted to tell him she trusted people just fine, thank you. But she also knew her brain was protesting precisely because he'd nailed it, in twenty seconds: he knew the story of her life. He knew it because he'd written it: she struggled to trust anyone, because she'd never been able to trust *him*. He'd never been there to build any kind of trust *in* – never cared enough about her to show up. Until now.

Jamieson Birch shuffled on his feet, reading her face.

'I ken it's awfy late fer me tae be here dispensing fatherly wisdom,' he said, 'but there's a time fer everything.'

Birch felt her face crease into tears once again. Her eyes blurred, but at the edge of her vision, she could see other people moving into the room, the blue cotton figure of Ruth leading the way. It was time to go.

'Thanks, Dad.' She remembered her promise to Anjan, only a couple of minutes before. 'We'll speak more, when I get out.'

Rena Brooks' voice appeared like an echo in her head. Ruth was at the foot of the gurney now, waiting for her attention. Birch made a mental note of her father's face, a kind of screen-cap of reality, to carry with her into the dark. He was smiling.

'In fact,' she said, 'we'll talk.'

Acknowledgements

I am forever grateful to be surrounded by a dream team of incredible women, without whom my books simply would not exist. Chief among them are Cath Summerhayes, my superb agent, and editor of the century Jo Dickinson. Jenny Platt, special thanks to you, for all the times you cajoled and consoled me through this strange year: you're a star. I'm grateful to everyone at Curtis Brown and Hodder & Stoughton who has worked on this book.

This novel is set in the Bowmont Valley, where I grew up, and I have to give a special mention to Lesley Janaway, who first took me to the pasture at Seefew when I was thirteen years old. Lesley, getting to work with you on the farm shaped my life in ways I'm still coming to understand – thank you.

One of the characters in this book was named as part of a charity auction in aid of the Anthony Nolan Trust and Blood Cancer UK. The name was chosen by Claire Stanley, in memory of her mum, Rena Brooks.

Also deserving of special thanks is the utterly brilliant Stella Hervey Birrell. Stella, your regular check-ins and endless kindness and encouragement got me through this novel, and through the plague times of 2020. You also did the best sensitivity read I could have asked for. You really are my writing rock.

2020 was the hardest year many of us have ever known, and I feel truly indebted to the people who helped me survive it.

Alice Tarbuck, Leon Crosby, Natalie Fergie, Jane Bradley, Kerry Ryan, Sasha de Buyl, Dean Rhetoric – I love you all dearly. Special thanks to Dominic Stevenson, who helped me become the woman I am. And I can't not mention Al Smith, whose steady refrain of *it's fine, it'll be fine* was like the beam of a lighthouse in the dark.

Last but not least, I have to thank Team Askew.

Nick, I hated how 2020 kept us apart, but I thought of you every single day.

I wrote a lot of this book under COVID lockdown in my parents' spare bedroom and they did the absolute most to support me: they were the manuscript's first readers and they proofed the very last draft. In between, they provided endless cups of tea and a lot of laughs. Mam and Fath, I love you. This one's for you.

A Matter of Time **Book Club Questions**

1. What did you expect the book to be from the cover and copy? Did your reading experience match that?

2. What three words would you use to describe this story?

3. What was the most gripping section of the book?

4. What was the most moving section of the book?

5. How do you feel the author used landscape in the story?

6. What did you think of the book's structure?

7. What are your thoughts on Gerald Hodgson and his back-story? Did you feel sympathy for him?

8. How did you relate to Helen? How did you feel her relationship with her father and brother was explored alongside the hostage situation?

9. Did your opinion of the book change as you read it?

10. What emotion did you feel when you finished the last chapter?

Q&A with Claire Askew

Where do you write? Do you have a strict routine or can you write anywhere?

Unlike many writers, I don't have a dedicated writing space, or even a desk: I usually write on my sofa, with my laptop on my knee. I can write in most places, as long as I have a decent stretch of time, and my headphones. I have an app that plays an endless loop of rain noise: it blots out any distractions and helps me think.

How did you first create your lead character DI Helen Birch? Does she share any characteristics with you?

When I created Birch, I wasn't entirely sure what I wanted her to be, but I knew what I *didn't* want her to be. I wanted desperately to avoid the trope of the Strong Female Character: a woman so smart and capable she's almost a superhero. Birch is clever, she's brave, and she's doing a very hard job – but she's also flawed, and sometimes messy. She spills coffee down herself, orders too many takeaways, and though she's passed the police driving certificate she sometimes screws up her parallel parking. As for the characteristics she shares with me, I was also keen to make sure she wasn't just a self-insert fantasy – but I can't deny I do have some of those same failings!

Edinburgh is a character in its own right through the series; why did you set the books there?

Edinburgh has inspired a fair bit of crime fiction over the years, and I knew I'd be walking in the footsteps of giants like Ian Rankin and Ambrose Parry by setting my books in Edinburgh, too. But I've lived in the city for seventeen years, and to me it's like a very brilliant jewel: there are so many facets to look at, and so many ways of appreciating it. I felt hopeful that, though I was working in familiar territory, I could find ways through it that hadn't yet been mapped. And I just love the place: its history, its weather, its architecture, its street names. Edinburgh is endlessly fascinating to me.

How do you research your novels?

I'm quite old fashioned, in that I get most of the information I need from books. When I was writing *What You Pay For*, the second book in the DI Birch series, for example, I read a lot of non-fiction books about organised crime, and a lot of gangster memoir. There's a book called *The Crime Writer's Guide to Police Practice and Procedure* by Michael O'Byrne, which is basically my bible. But I occasionally turn to Twitter, too: sometimes I have a burning question that I need to have answered fast before I can keep writing, and Twitter's hivemind is absolutely brilliant for that.

Have you enjoyed writing any one of them more than the others? Or do you love them all equally?

I was very worried about *What You Pay For* before I started it, because a lot of people had made ominous noises at me about the so-called 'difficult second novel,' but I found that once I got going, I really enjoyed writing that book. I loved the challenge of fitting Charlie's story – which needed to span more than fourteen years – into the book's seven-day timeline. And ever since I started the series, I've wanted to write a book that took place over a single twenty-four-hour period. I finally got to do that with *A Matter of Time* and really liked getting to cross it off the writing bucket list.

Your fourth novel, *A Matter of Time*, tackles the effects of the foot and mouth crisis on the farming community. Why did you choose this topic?

I grew up in the Bowmont Valley, in the rural Scottish Borders. As a teenager, I did casual work on a local sheep farm – many of our neighbours were farmers, and farming is a huge part of the Borders identity. I was fifteen when the foot and mouth crisis arrived in our valley, and remember only too well how frightening and devastating it was. When the COVID pandemic hit, the anxiety I felt about this invisible pathogen seemed familiar. I saw a lot of parallels between COVID and the foot and mouth crisis, and as I wrote my way through 2020, the two things converged to inform the novel that became *A Matter of Time*.

***A Matter of Time* has a very tight, structured timeframe which delivers terrific pace to the plot. How hard was that to write?**

If anything, I find it easier to write if I have a very clear structure. *A Matter of Time* is twenty four hours long – each chapter is one hour. There's only so much plot you can realistically fit into an hour, so that prevented me from going on tangents or adding too many superfluous details. There's also only so much the characters can know and understand in such a tight timeframe. They're given no time to reflect or analyse – everyone in this book is just reacting to what's in front of them. That felt like a gift while I was writing: I was able to think, 'okay, if Birch were faced with this situation, what would she do? What would any of us do?' I was able to just write what was obvious and immediate, which was a joy.

***A Matter of Time* also ends on a cliffhanger; please tell us there's a book five?!**

There is! But it would spoil the cliffhanger if I told you anything about it…

You also write poetry and non-fiction; do your various strands of writing feed off each other?

I wrote poetry for ten years before I ever wrote a word of fiction, and my Masters degree and PhD both had a poetry focus. Learning the craft of poetry helped give me an ear for prose, I think – I listen carefully when I'm writing, and try to pay attention to the rhythm of my sentences. The flip side of that is, my poet-brain wants to spend a lot of time on details: what the light is doing in any given scene, for example. There are times I really have to rein in that desire to stop and gaze at things!

What advice would you give any aspiring writers?

The same advice I'd give to students about to sit an exam: eyes down, and get on with it. Resist the temptation to sneak a look at what your neighbour is doing. Comparing yourself to other writers, or trying to shape yourself into another writer's mould, is always going to be a bad idea. Focus on writing your own book as well as you possibly can: that's it. That's your whole job.

Who do you like to read for pleasure?

Poetry. My all-time favourite poets are Mary Oliver, Kim Addonizio and Dorianne Laux.

What do you do when you're not writing?

I run a little online shop for vintage jewellery and collectables, which keeps me busy and happy – it gives me an excuse to indulge my love of rummaging through charity shops and eBay! Like most writers I read a lot of books, drink a lot of tea, and go on walks to think. I also knit rather badly, but it helps keep me sane.

Read on for an extract of Book 1 in the DI Birch series . . .

All The Hidden Truths

Winner of the McIlvanney Prize for Scottish Crime Debut of the Year

The day before

13 May, 12.30 p.m.

Moira Summers was on the top deck of the number 23 bus, her face turned up to the sun like a cat – it was the first day that year that could really have been called *hot*. She felt the bus pitch and begin to chug up the Mound. She'd always loved this view from the 23: on the right, the Castle, black and hewn, seeming to rise up out of Princes Street Gardens' seething trees. On the left, the whole of the New Town laid out in its smart grid. In the sunshine, Jenners department store and the Balmoral Hotel looked like gilded chocolate boxes, and the Scott Monument was Meccano-model-like, unreal.

She forced herself to press the bell and shuffle out of her seat, down the aisle and then the stairs of the swaying bus. She alighted outside the National Library of Scotland, whose double doors were mobbed by a gang of school kids. Moira felt herself tense. She'd come to sit in peace and do some studying for her OU degree, but the thought of being holed up in the dark, oppressive reading room on a day like this had already put a sullen feeling in her chest. A school-trip group clattering about the place practically guaranteed that she'd get nothing done.

'I want you in pairs!' A young, blonde woman was standing at the top of the steps inside the library entrance. 'In *pairs*, in *pairs*,' she chimed at the teens, but they paid no attention. Moira guessed they were maybe thirteen or so, but she'd become increasingly bad at guessing the ages of children. She always guessed too young – her own son, Ryan, was twenty, and although he looked like a man, she felt sure he could really only be ten at the most. Surely. Had time gone by so fast?

'*Pairs*,' the teacher said again. She looked young, too. Out of nowhere, Moira thought of her husband, Jackie: he'd been a teacher when she first met him. He'd taught PE to kids this age for decades, and she could imagine him making the same sing-song chant as this young woman. She tried to picture him: the young, lean man he'd been when they met, and found that she couldn't. *It hasn't even been that long*, she thought. *I can't lose him yet.*

As Moira blinked away her tears' warning sting, she realised the young, blonde teacher was speaking about her. She pointed down the steps at Moira – the pointing hand weighed down by a massive, turquoise-coloured ring. 'Kids, this lady wants to come in.'

Moira flinched.

'Oh no, I don't,' she sang over the heads of the children. Then she laughed, because it was true. But the mob did begin to trickle over to one side of the steps, and form a vague line.

Moira dithered. The ring on the teacher's hand looked like the lurid, sugary gobstoppers Ryan used to whine for in the corner shop, back when he really *was* ten years old. The children in front of her seemed to bear no resemblance to him, though – to the kids he'd been in school with. Children – and especially older children – seemed so much tougher, more streetwise, these days. The girls lounging on the steps before her all wore the same black, elasticated leggings, tiny skirts stretched over them so tight that Moira could see which girl was wearing lacy lingerie, and which was wearing piped cotton. She blinked and blushed, feeling like a pervert and a pearl-clutching granny all at once.

'Come on in,' the teacher called, over the heads of the chattering line.

But the boys at the top of the mock-marble steps were shoving and elbowing. Moira watched one of them take a slow, calculated look over his shoulder, and then swing out backwards, slamming his weight into a smaller boy on the step below. The big kid kept his hand firmly on the banister, making sure that he didn't fall – but his victim careened sideways into empty space, landing with a clatter and smack on the hard staircase.

'Jason!' The young teacher barked out the name in a way that sounded well practised. Moira winced, looking at the young man now sprawled on the steps. *Another Jason*, she thought. *The bad ones are always called Jason* – something Jackie used to say.

She turned away from the steps and the library, walking quickly until she had left behind the snickers of the tight-skirted girls. Moira thought of that boy's mother – how later, her kid would likely come slamming home morose, silent, and pound up the stairs without looking at her. Had that mother also given up asking what happened? Had she too begun to assume that this was just the man her son was growing into? And did she also, in moments of barefaced honesty, suspect that her own behaviour might be to blame?

Again, Moira blinked the sting from her eyes: *stop it*. She'd essentially just bunked off school, and it was a beautiful day. *Don't waste this*.

Across the street was an orange-fronted sandwich shop, not much more than a fridge and a space where two or three people could stand. Moira ordered a BLT with mayo – old-fashioned, she thought, scanning the fridge's display of quinoa, hummus and pomegranate seeds – and swung the meal in its brown paper bag as she paced up the ramp into Greyfriars Kirkyard.

This was a popular picnic spot: office workers in smart clothes sat in ones and twos on the grass, some with their shoes kicked off. A knot of people took it in turns to snap photos at the grave of Greyfriars Bobby, and to add to the pile of sticks left as presents for his canine ghost. Moira veered away from the kirk itself, heading downhill along the pea-gravel path. Her breath caught in her chest. A slim, vigorous laburnum tree blazed over the path in front of her: its vivid yellow blooms hung so thick that they bent the branches groundward in graceful arcs. She couldn't believe no one was down here, photographing *this*. She fished out her mobile, and thumbed a couple of photos of her own. They didn't do it justice.

Clutching her lunch, Moira ducked under the laburnum's branches and settled herself on the grass at its foot, leaning back against the trunk. It wasn't a comfortable seat, but the sunlight filtering through the tree's canary-coloured blooms made her feel warm and safe. Like sitting in her own miniature cathedral, or – Moira smiled – one of those plastic snow globes filled with glitter instead of snow. She chewed on her sandwich and looked out across the kirkyard. Many of the headstones were disintegrating now, having borne centuries of Edinburgh's famous sideways rain. Some had fallen face down on top of their graves. But in sheltered spots, there were still a few intricately carved gargoyles, winged and grinning skulls, hourglasses . . . even the occasional angel. The fancier Edinburgh families had crypts, sunk into the grass – ironwork grilles protecting underground rooms where no one living had set foot in years.

A peal of laughter clattered across the kirkyard, and Moira looked up. A boy of about Ryan's age was sitting on the roof of one of the crypts, swinging his legs off the lip of the doorway. Across from him, a girl with pale-coloured hair balanced atop a headstone, her back turned to Moira. She'd stretched over the pathway to pass the boy something, and it had dropped onto the gravel below. The graveyard rang with their laughter: the laughter of two people who were very drunk, or perhaps high on some substance or other. Moira watched as the boy climbed gingerly down from his vantage point – his tender dance on the gravel below made her realise he wasn't wearing shoes. The thing he retrieved was white, and he cradled it in both hands like a kitten. It was, Moira realised, a half-wrapped fish supper. He picked his way across the path, and handed it up to his girlfriend, waving away what seemed to be an offer to share. They looked radiant, the two of them: lit up in the sunshine, framed by shifting yellow blossoms, and young, so impossibly young. The boy stood at the base of the headstone, rubbing his girlfriend's feet as she ate – even at this distance, Moira could see that apart from his bare feet, the boy was well dressed, smart. Sunlight flashed off his glasses. The girl's kicked-off flip-flops were splayed on the grass below, near where the meal had fallen. Moira quietly gave thanks for her steady hands, holding the sandwich in its clean, brown paper.

She wandered out of the kirkyard dazed, everything a little too bright outside the laburnum's golden cocoon. She turned right, passing shop-fronts with their windows dressed for summer: sunhats, gauze scarves, sandals with rainbow-jewelled T-bars. *I'm walking to work*, Moira thought. But it was nearly a year since she had taken early retirement – two years since Jackie had died and his life insurance had allowed her to – and far longer since she'd worked *here*. And of course, when she turned the corner, the old Royal Infirmary looked nothing like it had when she'd walked here every day as a young staff nurse. Behind the original sandstone hospital buildings, the developers had stacked up blocks of flats that looked to be made entirely from glass. On the lower floors, twenty-foot blinds hung from the ceilings to keep out prying eyes. But the topmost floors seemed to have no curtains or blinds at all: they were transparent boxes, open to the sky. Moira sighed. She was glad that her old workplace was being put to good use, now that the new, state-of-the-art hospital had become established in the suburbs of Little France. She just wished it had been turned into something more accessible: a brief internet search had told her a while back that even a studio in the development would cost nearly a quarter of a million.

Moira crossed the street, and stepped into the patched shade of the sycamores at the entrance to the Meadows. There were no gates here, but there was a sandstone monument built to mark the entrance: tall as a bungalow, a stone unicorn carved at the top. Moira gave the unicorn a very slight nod, as she always had, walking to and from the Infirmary each day. She remembered Jackie again – little scraps of him seemed to be everywhere today – standing in the shadow of that monument, waiting for her to come out of work so they could go to the pictures, or walk through the park to the ice-cream parlour. She could pick out his tall, wiry figure a mile off, even in the dark, with the orange streetlight slanting over his shoulder and hiding his face in shadow. That was the way she saw him now: half obscured by time's fallen curtain. She thought she'd been so careful, too – trying to preserve every memory.

She idled down the hill a little troubled, passing through the park, along the east side of the old Infirmary site. She stepped into a little flagged courtyard, with saplings planted in square beds, and angular, dark-coloured marble benches. This both was and was not a place Moira recognised. A lot of the so-called modern buildings that had made up the hospital had been torn down: only the listed sandstone remained. She sank onto one of the hard benches, tipping her face upwards as though trying to *hear* the memory that was forming. She thought about the night shifts she used to do in summer, coming on in the evening – finding herself climbing the stairs yet again because the lift was full or broken or just too slow – and stopping for a moment on a high landing. Those long summer evenings, the last of the light would stream in off the park, slightly green, and dust from the hospital's bodies and blankets would swim in shimmering eddies up and down the stairs. She'd treasured those small, still moments in the midst of a chaotic shift. She wondered now if she'd lost the ability to feel things as keenly as she used to as a young woman: that perhaps it was age that kept her from properly remembering Jackie, from properly committing to her OU course, or from talking to Ryan about why he was so moody these days. Even now, lounging on a bench in a pretty courtyard, on a beautiful late spring day with absolutely nothing in the world that she needed to do, Moira still didn't feel as calm and whole as she once had, pausing mid-shift in that stairwell.

She could hear an ambulance somewhere. At first, she wondered if the sound was inside the memory; ambulance sirens had been a big part of the general background noise in this place. Perhaps it was a ghost ambulance, hanging around the old building where it had drawn up so often. But no – Moira's more logical mind kicked back in. It was somewhere behind her, held up at the Tollcross junction, perhaps, and moving closer.

The siren grew louder until it felt like the vehicle must be almost on top of her. Moira half expected it to screech round the corner and into the little sheltered square. She could hear the engine now, as well as the siren – it could be only metres away. She'd learned as a nurse that there was nothing quite like the sound of a siren to grab the attention of passers-by – that there's something in human beings that is drawn to screams and spatter and tragedy. People *want* to see what will be wheeled out of the back of an ambulance. They want to see it happen to someone else, because if it's happening to someone else, it isn't happening to them. But even as she had this thought, Moira found herself rising, and walking towards the sound.

As she rounded the corner, the siren was shut off, and the back doors of the vehicle were being banged open. Three young men in fluoro vests and hard hats were shouting at the paramedics, telling them to hurry, gesticulating with wide-open arms. They all looked very young, Moira thought. She loitered at the corner of a building, trusting that her middle-aged-woman status would keep her from being seen. The workmen all had tool-belts strapped to their waists, and as they hustled the paramedics and stretcher into the building site, the D-rings and instruments jingled like chunky chatelaines.

I should leave, Moira thought. A couple of other people had stopped to gawk, and she realised how distasteful it looked. But she didn't move. She looked up, past the hoarding, at the visible bits of the building site sticking up above. There was a huge pile-driver, bright yellow and oddly gallows-like with its supporting struts. A massive crane swung in the air, visible only in bits between the buildings. She could see part of its latticed central mast, and the ladder inside, which a man was now slowly climbing down. Clearly, all work had stopped. This crane operator looked tiny – the drop, if he fell, was massive. Moira felt a prickle of fear: there were so many horrible ways to be hurt in a place like this. Did she really want to see what might be brought out to this ambulance?

It was too late to move. The paramedics came rattling back into view, trailing their patient on a stretcher. For a moment, she forgot how to breathe. On the stretcher was a dark-haired young man – same fluoro vest, same tool-belt – the upper right corner of his body impaled by an iron-coloured rod.

'Ryan,' she heard herself say. It wasn't – the boy didn't even look that much like her son. But he was about the same age, the same build, and just for a second her imagination superimposed her son's face over the face of this stranger. His teeth were gritted hard, she could see. Even with a starter bar jammed through his shoulder, he was determined not to cry out. To be brave.

'Wait, you know that kid?' Another of the rubberneckers – a young woman with blonde hair, young enough to be a student nurse – appeared at Moira's elbow.

'No,' Moira said, unable to pull her eyes from the stretcher, 'no, I just—'

But the girl had already started towards the ambulance, waving an arm to get the paramedics' attention.

'Hey!' she was shouting. 'Hey! There's a woman here who knows this guy!'

The two men were bumping the stretcher into the ambulance. The one at the back, still out in the open air of the site, poked his head round the vehicle's open door. Moira flinched. She ran after the girl, the two of them arriving by the ambulance at the same time.

'Listen,' Moira said, 'I'm sorry.'

'You know this man?' The paramedic looked exhausted, but then, she thought, they always did.

'No,' Moira replied, unable to meet his eye. She made the mistake of looking into the ambulance instead, where the young man – now sheltered from the collective gaze of his workmates – had begun to hiss in pain, pulling quick, ragged breaths through his teeth.

'She's mistaken,' Moira said. She looked hard at the girl – perhaps too hard, because she shrank away behind the open door of the ambulance, and out of sight.

'I – I'm a nurse.' Moira's face burned. As if this information could do anything to explain the last thirty seconds.

The paramedic raised his eyes heavenwards. She wanted to apologise to him – she wanted to apologise over and over, to grovel – but she couldn't form the words.

'Sorry, love,' he said, 'but I think we've got this covered. I need you to stand clear *right now.*'

He swung himself up into the ambulance, and slammed the door. Moira leapt back as the siren started up again, clanging in her ears. The driver turned the vehicle neatly around and then it sped off, kicking up a brown haze of building-site dust.

Moira stood listening to the siren as it moved off through the city. To stave off the crushing embarrassment she felt, she tried to imagine the route it might be taking to get the boy to Little France. She listened as it looped round the far end of the Quartermile, and then onto the long drag of Lauriston Place, where it could pick up speed. But beyond that, she lost the thread of the journey, and could only listen as the wah-wah-wah got slowly quieter, swallowed by traffic noise.

Looking up, she saw that the trio of workmen had returned, and were doing the same as she was – standing still and quiet with their heads cocked, listening. She tried to imagine what she must look like to them, with her mousy wash-and-go hair and the same faded jeans she'd worn while she'd been pregnant with Ryan. *They'll just think I look like someone's mum*, she thought. *Someone's mum, someone's wife*: nothing to identify her but the wedding ring her dead husband had given her. Moira cursed herself for having said her son's name at that crucial moment, for pulling the attention of the paramedic towards her, and away from the suffering boy. She imagined *his* mother, probably hard at work somewhere right now – tapping away at a laptop, or chairing a meeting. That woman had no idea, but she was about to get a terrible phone call. Then Moira remembered the boy from earlier – the little boy, who'd been pushed down onto those hard stone steps. She straightened, giving her head a shake to dislodge the last of her embarrassment. She turned to walk back the way she had come, now with a purpose for the rest of the day: whether he liked it or not, it was time. She'd left it too long, but no longer. She was going home to talk to her son.

Have you read all of Claire Askew's acclaimed crime novels?

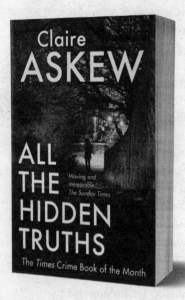

Winner of the McIlvanney Prize for Scottish Crime Debut of the Year

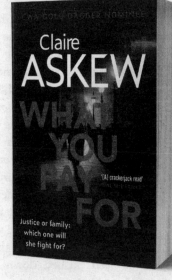

Shortlisted for the CWA Golden Dagger

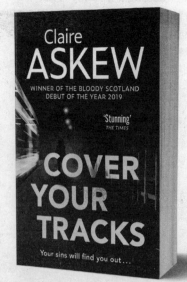

'It's as good as Rankin!'
The Peterborough Telegraph